CARRY ON S

Chris Lo

aided by many o

Charitable Intent

At least 30% of the profit, after publication costs, from the sale of this book will be donated to Blind Veterans UK, of which I am a member and supporter, Blind Veterans UK provides free support to vision-impaired ex-service men and women throughout the United Kingdom.

Donations can be made to Blind Veterans UK at:
www.blindveterans.org.uk/smiling

At least 30% of the profits, after publication costs, from the sale of this book will be donated to the First Note Music Trust.

The First Note Music Trust's prime objective is to encourage vocal and instrumental creativity for young people in schools and other organisations.

Donations can be made to The First Note Music Trust at:
www.firstnotemusic.com

CARRY ON SMILING

366 Quips and Quiddities to brighten each day

Cover illustration by Abigail Terry
(**http://sustainabilityexposed.com/**)

ISBN: 9798858852926
Paperback

Black Castle

Publishing

ABOUT THE AUTHOR

Chris Lowe CBE, TD, D.Ed. MA, LL.B was a teacher and head teacher for 40 years in Croydon, Leicester and Oundle, Northamptonshire. He was president of the Secondary Heads Association (SHA) (now the Association of School and College Leaders) in 1990-91 and of the European School Heads Association (ESHA) between 1992 and 1997.

Born and educated in Newcastle-under- Lyme, Staffordshire he went on to Downing College, Cambridge after his national service in The North Staffordshire Regiment. He graduated in English, followed by a law degree from London University. He never practised law professionally but served the SHA for many years as the Honorary Legal Secretary.

He served in the Territorial Army for 14 years, in The North Staffordshire Regiment and The Royal Anglian Regiment and was awarded the Territorial Decoration in 1972. He was made a Commander of the British Empire (CBE) in 1992 for services to education.

He has also received an honorary doctorate from the De Montfort University and been elected to honorary Fellowships of both the University of Wolverhampton and University of Northampton. For three years he was Visiting Professor of Education Law at Edith Cowan University, Perth, Western Australia.

For five years, he was chair of the Education Council of the Royal Opera House, Covent Garden and a member of the Board of the Royal Opera House from 1993 to 1998.

Since retirement Chris has collaborated with the former pupil, Colin Sell, the renowned pianist of the radio panel show *I'm Sorry I Haven't A Clue* to write light-hearted works for choirs.

Chris lives in Shropshire with his wife Mary.

CARRY ON SMILING
366 Quips and Quiddities to brighten each day

INTRODUCTION

A 'quip' is a short witty remark; a 'quiddity' is an essential peculiarity of some thing or someone.,,, and they are what *'Carry on Smiling'* contains in abundance – 366 one-liners, jokes, witty observations, anecdotes and short stories that will make you smile every day of the year. They have been written or collected by me, over a lifetime of being interested in people's love of good humour, even when it is 'black humour', and the relish of anything that takes away the sameness, sometimes amounting to drudgery, of everyday living.

The work contains many funny pieces from education, unsurprisingly since I was a teacher for forty years and teachers and pupils and students are inherently hilarious people. But there is humour and wit from many other sources. Even in wartime human beings can be funny, as witness the radio programmes in the World War II and the uproariously funny *'Wipers Times'* produced by soldiers in the First World War trenches.

Some of the funnies come from professional raconteurs like the late, great Barry Cryer, whose mantra was that all jokes and funny stories belong to the world, and that comedians only add their style and nuances to the humour. That seems a fair point of view. But where I have knowingly repeated a direct quotation whose source I know, I have acknowledged it.

Not all the entries are funny ha-ha. Sometimes we smile when we recognise something funny-peculiar, a job well done, a problem averted or justice fairly meted out. There are a few of these smiles, too.

JANUARY

Rustic Ruminations: The New Year

Christmas festivities have been given the push,
Picture card snow transmogrified to slush,
Last year, with baubles, now shoved in the attic;
A New Year beckons; nothing is static.

2nd *What else could be more apt to ease in the New Year than reflecting on the inalienable rights of Man, the central concepts of the United States Declaration of Independence in 1776 -'Life, Liberty and the Pursuit of Happiness? 2,000 years beforehand the Greek philosopher Aristotle had declared the pursuit of happiness to be a central goal for mankind, but he was unsure what happiness was. Countless philosophers since then have been equally puzzled. It was with some relief that while at university- many years ago - I came across a student who exuded certainty.*

It was the practice of the university Science faculty at that time to set a general paper for first-year students, to ensure, vainly, that they read and thought about issues beyond their main studies. One year the candidates were faced with this compulsory question.

'Can a man be happy on the rack?'

In the twinkling of an examination room eye one student wrote,   'Yes, if it is a very bad rack…… and he is a very happy man.'

The undergraduate then ruled a line under his work, folded his paper, walked out and went for a beer and an afternoon on the river.

When confronted by his tutor he was unrepentant. ''I look at it like this. My fellow students spent an anxious, frustrating three hours struggling to remember what Aristotle and the great philosophers had written. They wrote about happiness; I found it.'

3rd **Maths Teacher:** If the shopkeeper sells you a bag of sweets for 10p   how much would he charge for ten bags?
Maddy (aged 8): Nothing…. My mother doesn't let me buy sweets.
Teacher: But what if she did…..
Maddy: If I tell my mum that you are forcing me to buy sweets she'll send my dad down 'ere…. And then you'll be for it…

4th *Across the world there is concern about climate change. It seems to be a very modern alarm   – but it has hovered around for ages.*

This poem was written by a 16 year old in 1955 just before the Clean Air Act 1956 was enacted. It wasn't written to celebrate the Act. He hadn't even heard of it.

During an A Level English lesson, where his teacher was extolling the virtues of the pastoral poetry of poets like Grey, Wordsworth, Keats and Yeats, he noticed through the window the daily cloud of black smoke spreading over the 1,400 factory chimneys of the Potteries. He spent the rest of the lesson writing it.

The title is from Wordsworth's sonnet 'Composed Upon Westminster Bridge'.

A Sight Touching In Its Majesty

Clouds don't wander lonely where I come from;
They don't fly high over hills at all;
They scowl down in wadges like washing-day scum,
Then opening their jaws, letting the contents fall.

Nor do you see hosts of kaleidoscopic flowers,
Fluttering in our council vegetable plot;
Golden daffodils don't bedeck inner city bowers,
Because dog-walkers have trampled the lot.

Sunflowers stretch up without seeing the sun
Like miners in elastic waist-bands;
Vines and roses round thatched eves don't run,
Only strident weeds surprise the wastelands.

No curfew tolls the knell of parting day,
Bellringers are out scavenging for coke,
There are not enough vicars around to pray,
And plowmen plodding home are rare in Stoke.

I can't afford to arise and go to Innisfree,
And I don't have any spare wattle to hand;
Even though local mud and straw are free,
You can't get the bricks nor the sand.

And unlike for Chaucer's medieval pilgrims
Our current April showers are not very 'soote',
But soot they do indeed hoard and carry;

For our comfort they care not a hoot.

Our city's seasonal mists aren't mellow,
The close-bosom'd sun is not really mature;
Smog envelops all in a jaundiced yellow,
Carrying a poisonous whiff, much like manure.

No prancing nymphs, nor woodland sprites.
The canals don't meander, lambs don't gambol,
Yet city folk find other simple delights,
Old men may fish; besotted lovers ramble.

So, before you drop into deep depression,
Let me tell you more about our ordinary folk;
Let me leave you with a last ceramic impression;
Daffodils do wave and do flutter in Stoke.

They dance round the rims of saucers and dishes,
While yeomen strut across the edges of plates;
Painted forget-me-nots send ladies best wishes
Nature is forwarded daily, in crates.

Laud expert saggar-maker's bottom-knockers,
Our spinners of jiggers and jolleys and pugs,
The factory equivalent of mods and rockers,
All deserve our kisses and admiring hugs.

Whether a dappled hillside or Van Gogh tree,
A steep Alpine meadow or Vermeer flat polder
Beauty is truth and truth is beauty -
Which really does lie in the eye of the beholder.

5th   The company CEO kept on insisting that he only wanted men and women with 'get up and go', and after a year that is precisely what they did.

6th   *A university lecturer, musing on management styles, remarked to students:* In modern companies the CEO and management team resemble a coxed eight rowing boat - eight people who know what they are doing are rowing backwards, steered by the only person looking forward…. who cannot row.

7th   It is a sobering thought that Noah's ark was built by amateurs and the Titanic by professionals.

8th

Top Tips For Train Trips

When travelling from home with the family
And arriving at the station,
Be sure to check you've got all the kids,
And tickets to the right destination.

Missing either of those is a nuisance,
Lost tickets can cause some remorse;
But losing a son or a daughter
Is grounds for a quickie divorce.

When using the stairs or escalators
Don't think of running, either up or down
Stand on the right and pass on the left,
Unless, that is, it is the other way round.

Stand back, please, from Number One platform
Stand well behind the bright yellow line.
An express train is passing through,
Stand right there and you ought to be fine.

If you want to cross to another platform,
Remember the red signal means 'STOP;
Don't try to nip over before it's green,
Or assuredly you will be for the chop.

Do not lean out of the carriage window,
When the train is moving ahead;
At first it may seem quite exciting,
But you could end up losing your head.

And please give up your seat to disabled,
Or an oldie who looks in a daze;
You know you should, you ought to do it,
Because it will be you one of these days.

And if you get to the end all in one piece,
Successfully completing the cyclic loop,
Thank the train company and your lucky stars,
Having avoided being plunged in the soup.

Dylan and his DNA

An old schoolfriend Dylan - Welsh….very <u>South</u> Welsh actually – the ones more desperate to demonstrate their Brythonic roots because they don't actually speak the language of their forefathers…. a rugby player…. of course…. and avid male voice chorister…. but no less a friend for all that…. telephoned me a couple of days before Christmas……. in what I call these days 'the early hours'….i.e. around 8.30am. Full of languid good cheer he was…. high on that post-80th birthday ennui of chocolates, eaten…. single malt, sipped…. and twelve more pairs of black socks safely, packed away.

He was jubilant… unusually so. I could sense it, even over the airwaves…. I was intrigued, but at that hour I was not predisposed to a prolonged conversation, so gave him half-hearted encouragement.

'Go on,' I said. I felt that was quite enough…. at half past eight. At the rate his heartbeat was going the explanation did not take long.

'Guess what,' he yelled down the phone…. I did not have time to guess. He was off galloping down the airwaves.

'On the breakfast table this morning I found the most wonderful present imaginable….. 'from Megan, would you believe it,…..

'Really up with the technological mainstream is Megan,' he enthused. 'I can scarce believe it….. She's bought me a Family Tree Maker…. from Ancestry.com…. . great…. very easy to use… it says.' He added this last bit of information without a full-stop…. 'and what's more, an Ancestry DNA package as well. How about that!..... How many wives would have thought of that, eh? And at a cut-price, too.'

I could not bring myself to deflate his unbridled enthusiasm by remarking that I was not into internecine 'go-compares' nor in the frame of mind to care tuppence about uxorious price-cutting sprees, so I simply went along with his joyful encounter with the past by muttering, 'How nice.'..... and after a pause, to let him know how pleased I was for him…. 'you must let me know how you get on with it…. in due course…' And there we left it.

Today, being now some weeks later and well into the first week of the New Year…. and not having heard a peep out of him, not even on New Year's day, I decided to give him a ring…. if only to make sure he had not succumbed to any pandemic, Covid19, 'flu…. or any other lurgi. I was also, I have to admit, curious as to what had transpired with the Family Tree Maker.

Gone was his previous excitement. 'Hello, Dylan *yer*.'

' So, Dylan old pal….. what goes with the jolly Tree Maker then, eh? Kept you busy? No time for old friends with your new toys?'
There was a rather ominous pause.
'CJ, I hope you are not being facetious….. Do not speak about Tree Makers….. or DNA Ancestry, if you don't mind.'

'Come on, Dee, spill it out. Whatever is bugging you, it will be a sort of therapy to share it with an old mucker.'

Another pause.

'Well, I suppose it will have to come out sometime… it's been all too much for a delicate soul like me………'

'What on earth are you talking about?' I had never considered 6 foot 3, 15 stone Dylan a delicate daffodil.. and I was actually getting more and more intrigued… so I deferred making a cutting point about the false self-analysis.
Third…. and final…. pause.
'I will tell you this only once, CJ…. and I want no discussion…. Just leave me to cope, right….'

'Well, yes, right…. if you say so…. let's hear it….'
'I decided to make the Ancestry website a Christmas gift as well as birthday …..as Christmas Day was only two days after my birthday….We…. or rather I… woke up early on Christmas morning…

'Before eight then?'

'Er not exactly…. Before 5 actually…'

'Five! Blimey!..... serious stuff then.'

'Well, it was at that point, CJ…. anticipation got the better of good sense….I couldn't wait to get started. … Just as excited as I was when I was eleven…. when at 4 o'clock I leaped out of bed and found my first pair of football boots in my Santa stocking…. I put them on an went back to bed in them…. next morning I couldn't walk, or even stand up for two hours…… never forgotten it….it was just the same excitement this year. I had wanted for years to find out all I could about my Welsh heritage…. so I could pass it on to our grandchildren, you know…now it was going to come about…..well Megan joined me around seven o'clock….. by which time I had got nowhere…. Comes of not taking much interest in all this new-fangled stuff. but Megan soon got us started….'

'Seems ideal, I added encouragingly.

'Yes, it was…. at eight o'clock….. Megan was well away…. It wasn't long before she had confirmed…. for herself full Nye Bevan, Dylan Thomas, Owen Glendower Welshness…. And then from 1925 rebellious, red-blooded, red-flagged Welsh Labour Party thrown in….PROPER Welsh like …. in all its power and glory. Not far off proving a link with Saint David himself by now, I shouldn't wonder.'

'Great stuff…. Well done, Megan…you must be so proud of her….' I was determined to be in at least one of my old friends' good books.
'Yes, well done, Megan indeed….. but what about me, CJ?…. Me…. called 'Dylan' after the greatest national poet, 'Lloyd' after Prime Minster Lloyd George, and 'Llywelyn ap Iorwerth' after the great king of Wales….

'Albeit only north Wales….' I couldn't help adding.

'Now look yer, butty that's really below the belt. Let's have a bit of wara teg …. Just 'yer me out…. and be sympathetic like… I could 'ardly contain myself as I settled down with Ancestry and AncestryDNA.. What greatness was I going to discover for David Lloyd Llywelyn ap Iofweth Jones, eh?'

I was about to cut in again, but he got in first…

'Tragedy, CJ…. oh, the deflation… the consternation… the humiliation…bashin' my breast'

'Give over, Dylan…. It's me you are talking to, your old pal…not a Radio Wales chat show…. just get on with it.'

There came a big sigh from the other end.

'Far from finding I was five-star, full-blooded Welsh, CJ…. my DNA makes me 40% Scottish…. and….. I will only whisper this….30% bloody English…..'

'O my Lor' !' I really did feel for him at this point. 'So,….er…. how much Welshness then?' I hesitated to ask this but felt he was waiting for it.

There was silence …….DYLAN?…..DYLAN?…Dylaaaan?

'Eight percent ……. EIGHT PERCENT Welsh… just bloody 8 ! -- and a bit other rubbish - who cares

Silence again. I didn't know what to say…. Best say… nothing! Let him pour out his heart.

'The worst of it was,' - voice now breaking - 'when the letter with the DNA results arrived I was sat down in the kitchen having a cup of tea with Megan and our mam.'

'Forty percent Scots" shrieked our Mam 'You'll have to buy one of those kilt things and nothing to wear underneath !'

'Well our mam laughed so much at 'er own joke I thought we'd have to get her over to the Royal Gwent,. and her the wife of a Deacon at Horeb Baptist an'all! But before I could do anything, Megan leaned forward.

'Don't you worry, love,' she said patting my hand… 'It'll never happen….They'll never make one long enough for you!'

10th **History Teacher:** How did Roman legionaries fight off their enemies?
Jimmy (after a bit of thought) : They stood back to back, pushed swords up the front, shoved spears up the rear, and. held their scrotums above their heads.

11th A local newspaper reported that at the town choral society's concert on Saturday Mr. Jacques sang '*I shall pass this way no more,* which was greeted with prolonged applause.

12th **Henry:** The mass of a body is measured in killer grams.
Henry – again: There are two forms of sugar – granulated and castrated.

13th *Politicians often strive for grandiose metaphors to enliven their speeches. Here is one brave, but ultimately bizarre, Ministerial attempt at impressiveness, reported in a housing charity magazine.*
'The immediate priority is to switch the system round from top-down sticks to bottom-up carrots.'
The charity was impressed by the intentions but doubted whether it could be turned into a campaign slogan – *'Minister calls for bottom-up carrots.'*

An Old Alliance

Britain and France in 1904
Came to a good understanding;
They agreed not to fight any more,
Over land or goods or anything.

So, in nineteen hundred and fourteen,
And nineteen thirty nine,
They stood steadfast together,
In one unbroken line,

In ten hundred and sixty six
Duke William invaded Hastings;
With Norman Conquest's clever tricks,
He gave Harold's army a pasting;

William was crowned top of the bunch,
And founded a royal dynasty;
Well-satisfied, pleased as punch,
He knitted the Bayeux tapestry.

For the next 800 and something years,
Les Boeufs returned the compliment,
Fighting the Frogs, and anyone else,
All over the European continent.

The final battle between these two,
Rocked up and down at Waterloo;
Result uncertain until the Dutch turned up,
And the Prussians weighed in, too.

Wellington in his water-proof boots,
Turned out to be smarter and keener;
He got the better of Bonaparte,
Who was banished to Saint Helena.

After two world wars, settling many scores,
Europe formed a Union ;

Then the UK left, went its own way,
Causing some mutual confusion ;

So, instead of shooting, the usual looting,
And a spot of deft sword-swishing,
The old amis now spend hours and hours…
On the problems of North Sea fishing!

15th *This from a Year 7 pupil…. who had obviously taken in the broad picture but
not grasped the detail:*
King Harold was shot in the eye by an arrow fired by William, a henchman of
King Norman the Conquest. William is depicted doing Harold in, when his
wife knitted the Bayeux tapestry.

16th Now that male hair-styling has become mainstream, and not the five minute
'short back and sides' that it was, mostly, in my teenage days, it is worth
preserving for posterity the priceless observations of generations of army,
navy and air force Non-Commissioned Officers, NCOs, kept ready in their
linguistic lockers for the opportunity to unleash their wit on rookie soldiers. It
was a baptism I underwent with millions of others from the Boer War to the
end of National Service, and even before and after, for all I know.
Remember, soldiers' hair had to be of the Number 1 variety, that is, nearly
bald. But hair has a tendency to grow and sometimes not evenly; there can
be short tufts appearing here and there. Any decent NCO would spot these
aberrations immediately.
        You would feel hot breath on your neck and a fearsome voice would
mutter or shout loudly,
        'Soldier, next time you go to the barbers, stand nearer the razor!'
Or, as I remember when I was an Officer Cadet, undergoing officer training,
a red-faced, gnarled and very awe-inspiring Guards Regiment sergeant
whispered into my ear,
        'Sir, am I hurting you?'
        'No, sergeant,' I replied.
    'Well I should be. I'm standing on your hair!'
    The officer cadet in the next row, whose blond hair, cut down to almost
non-existence, but who sported at least a vestige of locks round his ears,
was asked.
        'Are you trying to be a Teddy Boy or Fancy Boy …. because you are
neither, you are a soldier of the Queen! Now, quick march to the barber and
get to look like one!'

Another one with a short tuft in his ear-hole was asked,
'Are you trying to create your own camouflage sir.

17th   *A government inspector once said to a Conference:*
'Do you know, if you stretch out all the sociology university graduates head to-toe across the Sahara desert…….. it would be a jolly good thing……'

18th

A local guide was showing a tour party round the French town where the group was based…. high up in a narrow valley in the Cevennes, She had told them what a wonderful place it was to spend your life in and then gone through all the usual guff about the long history, the religious wars, the architecture, the geography, the economy. Eventually she stopped and asked if there were any questions.
'Yes, I've got one that has been bugging me,' said the group swot, Ferdinand. 'Where's the sewage works?'
There was a long silence while the poor guide blinked, gulped and racked her brains before finally confessing she had no idea.
A voice piped op. It was an old gentleman sitting on a nearby bench. 'I'm an ex-pat, from the UK, and have lived here for twenty years…. and that's the canniest question I've ever heard… very perspicacious of you, sir….. more important than all the rest of the information you have been given. It is the one I asked twenty years ago when I came here. I'll give you the same information I was given then… go down the steps to the river…. and then follow your nose….. that's all.'

19th   *A Notice in a rural churchyard.*

> **PRAISE THE LORD**
> **Please Note:**
> **The Archdeacon has had to postpone his**
> **sermon next Sunday.**

20th   A Head who prided himself on his modern, progressive approach to education said, in a kindly way, to Miss Leadbetter, who had just accused Johnny Pettifer of being a 'thief':
'Miss Leadbetter, we don't use such pejorative descriptions about our little charges. Johnny is simply the current custodian of missing articles.'

21st Little James in Year 1 put his hand up: I've got a penny to spend, miss.
Teacher: That's nice James…. isn't it, children?
(Chorus of, Yes, miss/dunno, miss/)…. But I don't know what you could get for a penny, James…. What are you going to spend it on?
Little James: I've already spent it, miss, (peering down at a pool under his chair)

22nd <h2 align="center">Intimations of Salvation</h2>

Today is the anniversary f the Allied landings on Anzio beach in Italy 1944. The assault led ultimately to the fall of Rome. This story was told to me by one of the soldiers who fought in that colossal struggle, a major and company commander in 1958 but an infantry platoon sergeant in 1944..
It is not a funny tale; it is not light-hearted but like so many tales told by soldiers it has its humour. It is fascinating how soldiers can see a comic side in the direst of situations. However, I am not going to dwell on details of the awfulness of what transpired and the tragedy and futility of war that Anzio along with so many other battles exemplifies.
The main reason I feel impelled to share Harry's story with you is the light it throws on real leadership as opposed to the make-believe sort. It is worth a smile of appreciation.

Harry explained to me that after the initial landings and the struggle to gain a foothold beyond the port of Anzio, his infantry battalion was held up outside a ruined town of Buonriposa. Harry was the Platoon Sergeant, the second-in-command of a group of some forty men, led by a young lieutenant, who very soon became a casualty, leaving Harry to lead the platoon. The twenty or so soldiers who were now left, out of the initial forty, were crouching in the bed of a tiny stream, one of many that criss-crossed the plain. Bullets pinged all around them; they did not dare raise their heads above the parapet. His wireless operator a couple of yards from him could hear no messages on the frequency he had been given. 'But I can get an Eyetie bloke singing about a girl called Rosa,' he added. 'Not bad either….'
Harry's orders were that his platoon and the rest of the company of a nominal 120 men were to attack a German machine gun in the middle of the German line some 50 yards in front of them, behind a railway embankment they could make out even through all the smoke and mayhem. The start-time for the attack was in ten minutes time.

'It's utter madness,' he thought. They had neither the manpower nor apparently the artillery support they had been promised for the past two days. He decided he had a duty to make this plain 'higher up'. So he crawled down a ditch to get closer to his company commander, a major, and held a shouted conversation.

'I understand your concerns, sergeant,' shouted the major. 'But orders are orders and we have been promised artillery support. The general has told the colonel who has told the company commanders…. that he is fully aware that massive artillery support is the key to breaking through.'

'I know that,' replied Harry with growing frustration. 'but where is it?

'That is not for you to worry about,' said the company commander. 'That's the job of them back there, the General Staff. The General assures me they are doing all they can to arrange for two full Field Artillery regiments to be in support at the earliest opportunity. That is a massive increase in fire power. The General says he is sure it will turn the tide. You never know, sergeant, it may be in place now….or perhaps a bit later. Just get back and prepare to lead your thirty men to take that German post in front of you….'

'Sir, begging your pardon. I don't have thirty today. That was yesterday.

'There are only twenty of us left.'

'Oh….well, just lead twenty, then. Get on with it!'

So they did.

And three hours later the platoon lay in another ditch just ten yards in front of their previous one….exhausted and battered….and by now just ten of them, and three of those, including Harry had wounds. By some good fortune his wireless operator was still by his side. Both were panting hard and stemming blood from each other's wounds.

'Can you raise anything on that thing?' Harry asked his W/Op.

'Still no luck, Sarge. But the Eyetie bloke is now a woman….or it's a bloke with very tight trousers singing very high notes.'

Harry patted him on the back. 'Great stuff, Wood. You're a b…inspiration …..even if you are no good as a wireless op!'

'I can't help having manky equipment, Sarge,' said the hapless Wood. 'I can shout further than this effing machine will transmit!'

The company commander eventually made his way down various ditches and culverts to find out what was happening to Harry's platoon and issue further orders.

'The last thing we wanted,' Harry told me twelve years later in the officers mess in Minden, where we were part of the British Army of the Rhine, 'was any more orders. We were just intent on survival. That would be a victory as far as we were concerned.'

But, at last, someone was about to talk honestly and openly, and that would buck them all up. The major got to a few yards behind Harry. 'Sergeant, some good news.'

'Oh no, sir! Not more of the bullshit. We haven't been trained for it! ….Just give the orders, sir!'

Harry could not contain his anger.

'No, Sergeant. It really is good. It seems that the General has seen the light. He is at last levelling with us. The artillery he has promised….and which he keeps saying is the key to our breaking through…has arrived in the port and will be in place during tonight. Guaranteed! Not wishful thinking. Even better, a Guards battalion will also relieve us during the night…. I repeat, these are not hopes and expectations. These will happen. But if we are to withdraw in an orderly fashion you will have to hold this ditch for the next five hours……'

Silence.

'Do you understand what I am saying, sergeant? You and your ten men are the only group between here and the only route left to take the battalion back through…. If we are to save the majority. Do you understand?'

'You' are asking us to stay here and fight to the last man, is that it?'

'I'm afraid I am not asking you, sergeant ….I am ordering you to. It doesn't make much difference, but at least the men will know it's not your decision….But I will make sure that the six mortars that the battalion has left will spend the next five hours pounding the German line in front of you, before the battalion withdraws. Just keep any stray enemy away until then, and then…..well, then get out.'

'Oh, is that all, sir….I thought you might ask for something really difficult….it's a piece of cake…!' The company commander smiled though Harry could not see it. 'Sarge, I have a sneaking feeling that you and I will be meeting again. Good luck!' With that he was gone. Harry then told me he knew exactly what he could do with ten men and the might of the German army facing them…. who they could actually see scurrying back and forth preparing to make a counter-attack. 'My favourite book at school was 'Beau Geste',' he told me. 'I had a battered copy in my belongings back on the ship in the bay. Great adventure stuff. I really loved the scene where Beau, who was in the French Foreign Legion, finds himself defending a fort in the desert - alone with a load of dead men on the parapet. He kneels each body against a firing hole, shoves a rifle through the hole and runs up and down firing each rifle in turn, giving the impression that the fort was defended by a hundred men. Just the inspiration I needed. I got my ten men to line up all the rifles they could gather – and there were plenty of them lying around – We got about twenty five in place plus two Bren guns in the centre. Our mortars started bombarding the Germans, and they started shelling us. When they left their cover we darted from gun to gun and eventually stopped them in their tracks. We did this for over four hours…..and do you know what?.....we never thought for a moment that we would be over-run. We just felt on top of things….we were in charge…confident in ourselves….believing in what had been promised….sure of the support. When the artillery barrage began in the dark we sort of knew it would…so we left…. all ten of us. Not a single one had either been killed or wounded for five hours.

I have never felt on such a high…. My ten great men would follow me anywhere after that…they thought I was a veteran…. who knew it all. It was actually my first taste of active service. I never told my soldiers that. But neither then nor ever after did I treat them as cannon-fodder. I always made sure they knew the score…the reality….no mist and mirrors for me or them.' And then at the bottom of my page of notes from the past that I had found in a folder in my file last night I read a final little scribbled entry: *Harry says, 'if you consider yourself a leader never pull the wool over the eyes over those who rely on you…..or one day they will pull a blanket over your head…. And pull it tight.'*
It was, perhaps, not very sophisticated management advice…… but, my goodness, it isn't half relevant to the crises the world is facing nowadays..

The Catch In It

Will you have this man or woman
To be your wedded husband/wife?
Will you love and honour him or her,
And hold them dear for life?

I will, I will, I really will.
I really will be true.

And me, too.

And will you cherish this paragon partner,
And enjoy their cheerful banter?
Spreading good cheer wherever you go,,
Take life at a rollicking canter.

I will, I will, I really will.
I really will so do.

And me, too.

Will you spend his/her money wisely,
Playing always the fifty-fifty game?
And will you promise to do your best,
So long as they do the same.

I will, I will, I really will,
I really, really will.

And I really will, too.

And will you this person you are
Promise at once to honour and then… obey?

Not on your flippin Nellie, not for a single day.
No way, no way, no flippin' or way,
Not for a single day.
And me, too, I say.

> **Please note:**
> **In July the local Automobile Association will be holding crash courses for students who have completed their examinations.**

25th Eric was a lovely six-year-old pupil, bright and enthusiastic. His one drawback was that he habitually came to school unwashed and with dirty clothes, which never varied. Neither staff nor fellow pupils could avoid the malodorous effect. And neither the Head nor staff wanted to refer the issue to the local authority. They considered that a polite note to parents expressing their delight with Eric's progress but suggesting the occasional change of clothes might do the trick. The Head wrote what she thought was one of her best, most subtle letters home.
The next day she received a curt reply.
'Mind your own business. Eric comes to school to be teached not smelled. He's not a ruddy daffodil.'

26th A retail store manager who had just returned from a Head Office conference, fired up with zeal for the Chief Executive's call for more staff participation in management decisions, put up a notice in the staff rest room. It read: *'There's a Problem needs Fixing. What is It?'*. The next morning there was another notice next to it….. *'Don't know….but we've fixed it, what was it?'*

27th *After both the First and Second world wars jokes would often be made about circumstances that were anything but funny in themselves. They were eras of Black Humour. My mother, whose husband, my father, had served in the RAF in Burma had a favourite story she liked to tell.*
One January day a few years after the war three bricklayers, Peter, Paul and Phil were sitting high up on the 5th storey of a block of flats they were building, having their lunch break and chatting about their wartime experiences. Suddenly Phil stood up and threw himself off the ledge. Pete looked at Paul in astonishment.
'What on earth made him do that? He seemed happy enough to me.'
'I've no idea,' said Paul ….. 'I was just telling him that I flew in Wellingtons in the war and how reliable they were…..'

High Hopes

For young Fred Jones his parents had great schemes,
he'd realise their ambitions, all their dreams,
the heights they'd never reached; that far-off goal
he'd claim by climbing up life's greasy pole;
the world his oyster, pushed by mum and dad,
achieving fortune they had never had.

He'd be so famous, clever, high of rank;
a High Court judge, a statesman – head a bank.
A Method actor, athlete, polyglot;
success assured, they smiled into his cot.
Admiringly the neighbours would all say,
"We know that boy will reach the top one day."

So sadly they received his school reports,
each full of 'failed', of minuses and noughts.
No Einstein he, Fred couldn't do the sums,
(not much to boast to other dads and mums.)
Writing no better, their son just couldn't spell.
How might he earn his living? Hard to tell.

Intensive coaching failed, for no tuition
could bring his brain to Mensa-like fruition.
In spite of all encouragement and threats,
promises of dogs, stick insects and other pets,
he fell far short of heights his parents planned,
and obstinately, his head stuck in the sand,

condemned them to embarrassment, despair
so disappointed at their son and heir.
Bad at all sports, he couldn't hit a ball,
athletics had no use for him at all.
The Joneses could do nothing more for him -
but glory be, he flourished in the gym!

Discovered horizontal bars, and ropes
and on them built up all his hopes -
realised his dreams, became a steeple jack,

balanced on roof tops, scaled a chimney stack.
And neighbours, craning necks, were heard to say,
"We knew he'd reach the very top one day."
Jill Rhodes

29th *Everyone know 'Ring-a-ring 'o' roses'. It is an old 'action' or 'game' rhyme. All the singers dance around and then fall down at the end, amid great hilarity. But there are perhaps dark hints of children falling down dead very quickly after they had caught 'The Great Plague' in the 17th century...... and the earlier 'Black Death' of the 14th century.*

Ring-a-ring o' roses,
*A pocket full of **posies.***
A-tishoo! A-tishoo!
We all fall down!
A modern rendering has to be linked with the 21st century killer...... Coronavirus (Covid-19)

Ring- a- ring 'o' daffodils.
A pocket of anti- Covid pills.
Atishoo, atishoo,
You've forgotten to wear a mask.

Will it ever catch on?

30th **History Teacher** to a Year 7 class: What was one of the greatest achievements of the Romans?
Miriam: Learning Latin.

31st *International conferences are serious affairs but there is usually time for relaxation. A friend of mine attended an international conference in steamy North Carolina. On the rest day at the weekend he and five of his fellow delegates decided to visit Washington D.C.*

We were returning on the Sunday afternoon - - in our hire car – a Pontiac. After stopping for lunch in a diner in Roanoak Rapids NC, we were looking to get back onto Route 95. It was 90deg. F and 90% humidity. We were not in agreement as to the actual direction. That, it seems to me, is a common status with academics.

The occupants of the blood-red Pontiac at this point were:
Front: Dr. Alein Santos, Manila Philippines 5ft 2in (driver) short and bespectacled

Prof Y. Takimhome, Tokyo 5ft.1in, shorter and also bespectacled
Prof I Joginder Singh, India 5ft 5in, elegant, blue turban
Backseat: Me in corner 6ft 3in, pale and sallow, not thin
Sri U. Kantha, Sri Lanka 5ft 1in, thin
F.T. Chalady, Thailand, , very thin
Prof Suwardi Prabowo, Indonesia 5ft 1in, even thinner
Conversation was subdued at this stage. Each had made his point about direction of travel – from due east to due west. We were taking the middle road, due south, which had been the driver's preferred compass point, when…..

Flashing blue lights, wailing siren….colourfully striped Chev Corvette shoots across our front. We pull up…hard.
A 6ft 5in, 18stone town cop in khaki and Stetson easies himself out of the passenger seat, approaches casually and puts his foot on our bumper bar…..fender, I believe in the USA. We bounced up and down, increasing the tension. Cop pushes back Stetson and stands in front of our vehicle, legs slightly apart, thumbs in belt. Classic John Wayne. Tension increases.
Cop indicates our driver, diminutive, bespectacled Dr. Santos, to open the side window. Cop leans in and addresses us all. Shake of head….and a pointed finger at Doctor S.

'You have shot a red light.' Another shake of head….'My, my, yes, sir, you sure have….Get out of the car, sir.'

An ashen Santos is ordered out and begins immediately and flatly to deny the charge…No, no, never shot lights…

Now this was not a brilliant idea…..because in fact we had.
The Officer peers into the darkened automobile, and his eyes widen….'Uh, uh…' He has spotted six gentlemen of various hues ranging from sallow white to dark black…. this is clearly beyond his pay grade. 'Uh…uh..' he growls again, and with no suggestion of racial profiling, he picks me, cowering in the rear, as the obvious leader and orders me out of the car.
'Driving Licence!'
I produce my definitely legal New South Wales licence.
'Dis may be OK in China,' he remarks, waving my own piece of paper at me, 'but it's no good here. Follow me!'

Discretion being the better part of valour I get into the driving seat and drive anyway. I follow the police car to the local lockup where there is another very large and bored looking copper. He sees the six of us. He is no longer bored.

Without a great deal of ceremony, we are locked up in a large cell with benches - like the pews from a Baptist church.

We remonstrate with colleague Santos
'Just admit guilt and we'll pay the fine!'

No way! Dr. Santos knows what the Manila police are like. He says all police the same. He is petrified and point blank refuses. Neither cajoling nor the offer of a hundred dollar 'incentive' will shift him. We are desperate.

We can hear the second cop talking on the phone to someone he addresses as 'Judge'. The judge appears to be half way through a golf round. Nothing happens. Presumably the golf round would take time. After a couple of hours cooling our heels the cop unlocks the cell door. A very unhappy looking Senior Cop accompanied by an even unhappier, sweating older gentleman arrives - the Judge, dressed in checkered plus-fours, green polo shirt and large white flat cap. This array made him incongruous, but did not stop him 'judging'.

The judge is carrying a large tome, which he flips over from page to page until his eyes alight on one that attracts him.

He surveys all six of them, but again addresses me, 'the leader' - me.

I haaaave to in…form you, sir, that there is noooo Extradition Treaty between the Phillaepaaines and the State of North Carolina".

Colleague Professor Khan Singh whispers to colleague Dr. Santos
'Look, we'll be here till Christmas! Just admit guilt!'

No luck.   No answer.

Getting nowhere Judge and Senior Cop, go into a huddle.

Judge comes to his decision. 'I am going to judge… I am going to take statements from each of you.'

Judge turns abruptly to a very nervous and diminutive Professor Takamine. 'You, sir, What exactly happened… in your own words?' -
The good Japanese professor, remembering that we had all been arguing in the car, beamed.

'Honoured Judge…. as we say in my country, 'too many captains send ship to mountain.''

Judge looks wildly from one to another. He gets no help.

'WHO ARE THESE GUYS??'…..Fine $55…. and just get the hell out of here…. AND North Carolina!

FEBRUARY

1st   **Teacher:** Who was the first person to sail around the world?
       Henrietta: I think it was Leonardo da Vinci in the good ship *Mona Lisa*.

2nd   *Simple Simon' is a 'round song' first published in the 18th century but may well go back much further. 'Simon' might refer to a real person but there is no conclusive evidence of that. Simon meets a sad end as the rhyme follows the tradition of containing dark scenarios in what are otherwise light and jaunty verses.*

> *Simple Simon met a pieman,*
> *Going to the fair;*
> *Says Simple Simon to the pieman,*
> *Let me taste your ware.*
> *Said the pieman unto Simon,*

> *My modern re-make reflects the times we live in..*
> Simple Sara met a farmer,
> At a country fair.
> Said simple Sara to the farmer,
> 'Let me taste your ware.'
> Said the farmer to simple Sara,
> 'Show me first your money.'
> Said simple Sara to the farmer,'
> Sir, that's not fair nor funny;
> You know I don't have any!'

> 'Then go to the food bank ,' said the farmer.
> 'There you will find good and plenty.'
> Said Sara, 'I've already been over there,
> And now all the shelves are empty.

3rd   One of the tasks of the diligent manager is to comfort the afflicted… but another is to afflict the comfortable.

4th   Maths exam question: 'Explain 'probability'.
     Henry: 'Maybe'.. or 'maybe not'…..as in $2x + 3x = 15$, or probably not if $x =$ something else….

5th   *A note in a school log book for a date in the late 19th century said::*
Mrs X is dismissed from her position as head teacher by the school managers who considered her drinking habits set a bad example, and because she was aged,

6th   In 1903 the Western Australia examiners reported that 'in the History paper for the 'C' Teaching Certificate, teachers showed an ignorance which was perfectly appalling, seeing that they were actually teaching children in this subject.'

7th   An elderly lady advertised for a handy man. A young chap turned up.
'Can you do gardening?' she asked.
'Well, sorry, no, I'm no gardener,' he replied.
'The bathroom basin needs attention. Can you do plumbing?'
'No, sorry, not plumbing.'
"How about fixing the lighting?"
"No, sorry, I'm no electrician."
'So, what makes you think you're a handyman?'
'I only live round the corner.'

8th   The essential ingredient for being a successful management trainer capacity for ingenuity and stealth plus the gift to talk nonsense convincingly. Once acquired the knack never goes away.

9th   *A school magazine's spoof gossip column 'The Listening Ear' …. before it was banned….reported the following:*
The headmaster denied that he had fallen asleep at morning Assembly during the address by Councillor Boggle. He emphasised to Listening Ear that he always closed his eyes when thinking deeply. When asked what the audible yawns signified, he became quite agitated…and demanded that our Ear be silenced.

10th   Listening Ear also heard in the School Office a distraught Year 7 pupil on the phone to the local bus company's Lost Property office:
'I've left my sandwiches on a seat on a red bus in north London . Can you trace them for me?'

The Toilet Roll Of Time

We are just microdots, microdots, microdots,
Standing small and in our prime;
We are just microdots, microdots, microdots,
Stuck in the corner of sheet number one....
Of the toilet roll of time.

Just rip off. rip off, just a few flimsy sheets,
Of the toilet roll of time.
That's two million years bashing stones on rocks;
Humans ground out hammers, axes and knives,
For cracking open eggs and knocking off blocks.
Trying to keep themselves alive..

Finally fed up with bruising thumbs and fingers,
Stone-Ager mixed copper with zinc instead;
Then added arsenic to suit their taste,
Plus a smidgen of silicon and a choice bit of lead;

How on earth did they think of that!
Where did the idea come from?
And who was the first to try it out?
There's no-one left to tell;
There's no-one left to tell.

Then the iron man arrived, rather late in the day,
Ready to make things for cutting and thrusting,
Useful items for slicing your beefsteak, or for
Bashing and cracking, crashing and brushing,
If you've nothing to do on a rainy day....

Then onwards and upwards we get to sheet one,
And this is where we stop,
Where Ancient History starts at the bottom,
And we stand small at the top.
With aeroplanes, computers and central heating,
With extraordinary utensils for gourmet eating;
And families with two or more gas-guzzling cars;
With spacecraft to take us whirling round stars;

Telephones and gadgets, replacing meeting and reading.

So much we've achieved in half a sheet
Of the toilet roll of time;
There are no sheets left;
We've reached the end of this toilet roll;
We have to open another new box!

12th

Son: Mum, the headmistress says we are going to see an opera called 'Carmen'.
Mum: That's nice. What's it about?
Son: Some garage mechanics, I suppose.

13th *A memorial inscription in Selby Abbey to a highwayman who fell off his horse, and broke his neck:*
Twixt the stirrup and the ground,
He mercy sought, He mercy found.

14th *What could be more fitting for Valentine's Day than a romantic poem. It can be sung to the tune of 'Lili Marleen'.*

Romance of the Teacher

Underneath the Maths Block, by the cycle shed,
That was where I met him, some years before we wed.
Then in the school hall's disco light,
He held me tight,
And said that night,
I'd always be his true love
My ever faithful, Shane.

We built a great department, best in all the school,

We lived the teacher's dream, and made the pupils cool.
Then one night at last he saw
I bulged some more,
My tum was sore
And soon little Duane had joined us
Me and my faithful Shane.

Rolls then started falling; they had to cut the staff.
The building was neglected, the Hall became a caff;
One of us had to leave the school.
Life was cruel
In the redundancy pool
The pupils were all crying,
They always count the cost.

Then the place was shut down, weeds were growing high.,
The nearest school was miles away, enough to make you cry;
Then along comes a very rich man,
A man with a tan'
A man who can;
The Maths block's gone, the cycle rack, too.
A new glass palace has appeared.

We are both employed again; I got my old job back,
We're with the academy, and no longer face the sack;
Duane is now in Year Seven,
And in seventh heaven,
In the cricket eleven,
And his dad is still my true love,
My Executive Principal Shane.

15th *A 'story' about military experience was told to me by a very proud Sikh
soldier who had served in the Far East and ended up at the end of the war in
Malaya.*

    One day he was feeling the effects of an old injury and joined the
daily sick parade. The British army doctor examined him and pronounced
that the injury was not serious but needed attention. He said, 'I'll just give you
a local anaesthetic and patch you up.'

The soldier looked aghast, rose from the couch, drew himself up to his very impressive height and said in clear but pained voice, 'Sir, I will not have a local anaesthetic…. I demand a British anaesthetic.'

16th A Chair of a company board of directors told a conference that he was rung one day by the CEO (now former) who said, 'I have an opportunity to go on a decision-making course, but I can't make up my mind. What do you think?'

17th *This story was told to me by a Probation Officer who worked mainly in the juvenile realm.*
A new juvenile court judge found a young boy guilty of breaking and entering. He was not used to dealing with juveniles. He pronounced the boy's guilt and felt he should add a suitable explanation and appropriate admonition. He wagged his finger at the boy in the dock.
'You are clearly guilty of this crime. You need to be taught a lesson. Your despicable deed means that for the sake of the safety of the general public, you must be properly castigated,….and…'
He got no further. The boy's mouth gaped…he uttered a guttural gurgle and fainted in the dock.
The judge's own mouth now opened and shut like a floundering trout. He turned in astonishment to the boy's father sitting nearby, who was himself now looking bewildered.
He chose his words carefully.
'I was only going to tell your son that he would have to be incarcerated,….
The boy's father clapped both hands on his head….and he, too, fainted.
The judge appealed to the social worker.
'What on earth is going on, Ms Jolly?…. It's perfectly obvious we have no alternative but to circumscribe him.'
The social worker gave a little cry and she, too fainted.

18th *Some testimonials for employees are clearly two-edged.*
`   Mr. X arrives at 9.00am and leaves at 4.00pm. What he does in between I have not yet discovered. Yours sincerely.

19th *The next testimonial is more enigmatic. Perhaps a 'not' has been missed out along the way!*
I have been a friend of Mr X for 15 years and am sure you are likely to have many better candidates than him.'

20th Maud approached her teacher, demanding, 'My mother says I must not do sex today.'
Teacher, with a sigh. 'It's not 'Sex', Maud. It's *'Sex Education .... and Personal Relationships'.* And in any case this is a music lesson.

21st A report to the General Manager by Fred Jolly (Mr)

    Dear Mr. Entwhistle,

    I beg to report a curious incident. I was taken short, while walking through the production lines. I rushed to the staff toilets, but found the male cubicles were all taken. So, I nipped into the ladies toilet next door. Unfortunately I slipped down on the tiled floor and found myself.... inadvertently.... looking up through the gap between floor and toilet door and straight at Ms Ida Mann seated... quite properly I might add... on the loo. She screamed and threw a toilet roll at my face. I was unhurt but quite shaken by the experience.

I am reporting it, just in case Ms Mann submits a terribly misleading version of her own.

22nd In industry today', said an aspiring middle manager, ''we managers are always being faced by our directors with insurmountable opportunities'.

23rd   It was coming up to one of my wife's 'significant' birthdays, and in an act of bravado and self-sacrifice (hers not mine) she agreed that I should cook a spicy Thai dish with a salad, something I had never cooked before.

    I had no trouble with the cooking… it was the shopping that blew my head!;;;;

    It was during my headlong dash p and down the aisles to d that I discovered (what my wife, of course, had known for ages) that mango chutney was not in 'Pickles and Sauces' but in 'World Foods', and that gluten-free flour is not on the flour shelves but the 'Free From' section and that a Cornish Savoy is not an Anglo-French pastie nor a species of lettuce. My final realization of the technical nature of shopping came when I tried to source a Seville orange (which my dessert recipe specified). I picked up a large one and asked the assistant at the 'Customer Care' desk whether it was indeed an orange from Seville.

    She looked at the orange and then at me. Then deciding perhaps that I was probably more gullible than the orange, said sweetly,

'Near Seville, sir.'

I expect she will be running the store before long.

24th *Even English teachers can be caught in the snares of too much explanation for their good.*
English Teacher: Claud, why did you write on both sides of the paper when I distinctly told you not to when you asked?
Claud (in high dudgeon): No, you didn't, miss…. you said 'No, definitely not…' and that's two negatives, and you taught us only yesterday that a double negative makes a positive. I think you should stick to the rules, miss, and not confuse us children.'

25th *An unfortunate incident that a friend had to report to his insurers*
I hired a mountain-bike at a French Alpine resort and while descending a steep slope at a reasonable but impressive speed I pulled on what in the UK is the rear brake but which in France is not…. It is the front brake. The front wheel of the bicycle inevitably came to an abrupt halt, but I did not. I sailed over the handlebars, severely scraping my nose and cheeks.
Then the bike rolled over the top of me causing a deep furrow in my brow and substantial damage to my ears and much astonishment to a passing group of Belgian school pupils. I might have laughed the whole thing off, but for my friends and the passing pupils breaking into uncontrollable laughter and cries of 'Encore!'. I consider that to be unreasonable behaviour.
I believe I qualify for a payment for cuts and bruises, psychological injury and irreversible damage to ripped shorts, expensive cycling ones, of course..

26th   **From a newly qualified PE Teacher**

I opened the Head of PE's locker and was showered upon by a rain of cricket balls, tennis rackets, football pads, and, finally, jock-straps… recently used….
. from the sight of which I have not yet fully recovered. It was not part of my Post Graduate Certificate of Education course.

27th *Two more examples from exam papers Illustrating the comic possibilities of the English language,*
The spending of all revenue was decided in the governing chamber, which was directly under the king.
which is matched by:
The king did his business while sitting on the throne.

Lament of the Project Manager

This little rhyme will self-destruct
In twenty seconds flat.
But then I'm very, very sure
You're quite immune to that.

We built a block back in '61;
Well, it wasn't what purists call 'built',
But we laughed, we joked, we carried on,
Weighed down just occasionally by guilt.

Never quite forgot all the things we clad,
Thinnest this, cheapest that, giving profits a timely boost;
The good out in front, dodgy at the back;,
Kept chickens and inspectors away from the roost.

The years went by; we cavaliered on;
The dream was almost real –
People moved in, and deals were done;
The penthouse suite was the ultimate steal.

Then men from the ministry, wise in their job,
Moved in to prod and to pry and to poke';
Guessed instantly what we had tried to fob,
Saw through every flaw we had tried to cloak.

So now they're pulling it all down, you know,
Not a bit, not a morsel, not a teeny jot;
With their nostrils were flaring, their eyes aglow;
For them it had to be the whole ruddy lot.

29th   *A little extra for leap year.*
Teacher of French: 'Stop day-dreaming and get back to your translation, Edith.'
Edith (indignantly): I was not day-dreaming, miss, I was working out the meaning and having a jolly good thunk.'
Teacher: And what did you conclude from this jolly good thunk?
Edith (with a sigh): How very much cleverer French children are than us. They understand French so easily.

MARCH

1st *Overheard in a Conference bar:*
My CEO is so middle of the road that he is in danger of being hit by cars in both directions.'
And a piece of advice from the Conference stage..'. advice that should be noted and followed by more people than do at present.
'Smart managers speak from experience. Even smarter managers, from experience, do not speak.'

2nd *The world of testimonials and references can be unintentionally hilarious.,,, like this one from a willing but inexperienced assistant superstore manager writing about a part-time student shelf-packer:*
'I am not sure that Mr X has had the requisite administrative experience you are looking for. I remember that he is responsible for the student union bar three nights a week. Could be useful, I suppose.'

A colleague headteacher received something similar.
        'I can certainly confirm that Miss Z shows promise as a drama teacher. All her lessons are full of it.'

And then one that excelled in enigma:
I find that her pupils pay scrupulous attention to her every word - not out of intellectual enquiry but more out of curiosity as to what she is going to say next.'

3rd   **Doctor Foster**

                    Doctor Foster went to Gloucester,
                            In a shower of rain;
                          He stepped in a puddle,
                          Right up to his middle,
                      And never went there again

                                    SO
                    Doctor Foster went to Worcester.
                      And had no puddle trouble;
                          He parked in the street,
                          And with mudless feet,
                      Did his shopping at the double.

                              HOWEVER....

The good doctor, bored with Worcester,
Decided his career should prosper;
He made the grade,
Of the highest paid,
And found himself back in Gloucester!

4th   *An Aussie pal reminded me of these remarkable collection of proverbial sayings – 'ockerisms' - in 'The Jumbuck Stops Here' by Philip Adams, Here are but three of, well, plenty…..*
'One good turn gets all the blankets.'
'He who laughs last didn't get the joke in the first place.'
'He's too big for his thongs.'

Try making up your own!.... It's not so easy.

5th   *One Advanced Level student I taught many years ago was intrigued by the variety of interpretations his fellow students had of the enigmas in Shakespeare's Sonnet 18.*
To appreciate his brilliant modern sonnet you need to be reminded of Sonnet 18, so here it is.

Shall I compare thee to a summer's day?
Thou art more lovely and more temperate.
Rough winds do shake the darling buds of May,
And summer's lease hath all too short a date.
Sometime too hot the eye of heaven shines,
And often is his gold complexion dimmed;
And every fair from fair sometime declines,
By chance or nature's changing course untrimmed.
But thy eternal summer shall not fade
Nor lose possession of that fair thou ow'st,
Nor shall Death brag thou wand'rest in his shade,
When in eternal lines to time thou grow's.
So long as men can breathe or eyes can see,
So long lives this, and this gives life to thee.

The student wrote:
The Lower Sixth were puzzled by Shakespeare,
Sonnet eighteen to be pernickety precise.
Who 'thou' is in the poem was not clear;
To know for sure would be quite nice.

Some plumped for the shadowy Dark Lady;
Some insisted it was an even darker man.
The Bard's motif for penning it was shady;
Was poesying for patronage his plan?

By guile their furrowed brows you diverted;
You squeezed their understanding over time.
It struck them how meaning is converted
By imagery, by rhythm, and by rhyme.

So, to grip young readers, setting minds on fire,
Know, problems dismay, challenges inspire.

6th *Mr. Ivor Bang, a long-standing 'company man', made the following report to the company's Human Resources Department.*

Incident: I was winding up the office venetian blind with the cords provided when it concertinaed, trapping my fingers. On whipping my fingers out, the blind fell from the window onto my legs, giving me a sharp blow on the shins.

Fortunately, I had the presence of mind to leap back and avoided being impaled by shards of glass from the shattered window pane…. but in so doing fell over my office chair. At this point all would have been well. Instead disaster struck.

My secretary, on hearing the noise, rushed in too quickly and tripped over my prone body. To steady herself she thrust out a leg and an arm, thus breaking my nose and two ribs…. quite unintentionally. I wish to record that she apologised profusely but I was unable to express any thanks as I was short of wind. But I will do so in a timely fashion on my return.

I shall be off work for a day or so…. or even more. I would be grateful if you would replace the window and blind.

7th   **A Good Question**

What happened at school today,
Dear daughter, dear daughter?
What interesting things did you do at school?
Dear daughter, what?

Nothing happened at all today,

Dear mother, dear father;
I did nothing very interesting today,
Dear mother, dear father, as usual.

Were there no comings and goings,
Dear daughter, dear daughter?
No ups and downs or to's and fro's?
Dear daughter, nothing?

One interesting thing did happen today,
Dear mother, dear father;
A new girl arrived from some Stan or other.
Dear mother, dear father, a Stan.

Is she from Afghanistan,
Dear daughter, dear daughter?
Or Uzbecki,Turkmeni or Paki - stan?
Dear daughter, which Stan?

I know nothing at all about Stans,
Dear mother, dear father;
The only Stan I know is Stanley Mee in 4C.
Dear mother, dear father, Stan Mee.

Do you know where the Stans are,
Dear daughter, dear daughter?
Do you know if they are in the west or east?
Dear daughter, where?

I have no idea, not an inkling,
Dear mother, dear father,
But if I think very hard I do have a hunch.
Dear mother, dear father, a hunch.

And what is your hunch, do tell us
Dear daughter, dear daughter?
We are very interested to hear your hunch.
Dear daughter, this hunch.

I don't know exactly where she came from,,

Dear mother, dear father;
But it can't be far, as she went home for lunch.
Dear mother, dear father -
She… went… home… for…her… lunch.

The Great Magician

A group of comedians were waiting to record a TV programme, and only the ventriloquist hadn't turned up. They were sitting around in the 'green room', waiting for him. At the last moment he burst into the room, apologised for his lateness, saying it was traffic.

'I must grab a quick coffee,' he said.

He quickly opened his case, took out a puppet and hung it from a coat hook on the wall, then closed the case and exited. The top comedian said,

'We mustn't look in his case – it would be very unprofessional.'

So they immediately sneaked a look in the ventriloquist's case. There were all sorts of strange things inside – a snake with rolling eyes, a frog with a protruding tongue, and so on. "We shouldn't be doing this," said the top comedian after a moment, so they closed the case. Then the ventriloquist came back in the room. And the puppet on the wall said:

'They've had a look in your case, Bert!'

9th   *Car insurance claims are notorious for the frequent convolutions in drivers thought processes as they seek to prove they were victims of circumstances beyond their control!*

A driver, after being found guilty of careless driving when he rammed the back of the car in front, sought to gain the judge's sympathy by claiming that the victim driver was partly at fault because he had said at the time that this had happened to him twice before.

10th   In another car insurance claim a driver wrote, ' I could not avoid the damage to my car because it was a very foggy night and I drove into the wrong house drive and hit a tree I have not got.'

11th   *Over the centuries many famous writers have had a go at summing up 'schoolboys' not schoolgirls, as they had not been invented yet.*
Plato, the 5th century BCE philosopher was puzzled by them:
'Of all animals in the world the most unimaginable are boys.'

Two thousand years later William Langland in his immortal poem 'Piers Plowman' took a much more relaxed view but did not deny that schoolboys were something of a problem:

'Schoolboys are not so different as before.'

Two centuries later Shakespeare spelled out what that perennial schoolboy looked like in Jacques's 'All the world's a stage' speech in 'As You Like It' He could be describing certain pupils even today, 450 years later…. But would this co-describe girls?

> *And then the whining schoolboy with his satchel*
> *And shining morning face, creeping like a snail*
> *Unwillingly to school.'*

What is actually learned by the schoolboy and schoolgirl will, of course, depend on time, place, circumstances, need and resources. Many questions put to Dr Samuel Johnson in the 18th century were met by his good sense and characteristic wit. He was asked once what subject a child should study first. He replied:'

'It is no matter what you teach them first any more than what leg you shall put in your breeches first……but if you put both legs in at the same time you will certainly fall over.'……' You can't argue with that!.

12th *During the 2020 and 2021 pandemic lockdown parents learned a lot about the problems of teaching their offspring, and the experiences that teachers go through every day:*

Mrs. Rivet learned that sometimes you can try to over-refine your offspring's language. She was doing some sums with her daughter, four-year old (and a half, actually, mummy) Tracy, when seven year-old brother, Colin, burst in and announced, 'Mr Frost next door has just let me see his peacock.…'

Tracy banged her pencil down, 'You should wash your mouth out, our Colin, shouldn't he, mummy?…. He is so rude…..'

Mummy, smiling, 'It's not rude, darling, a peacock is a rather colourful and elegant bird…'

Tracy: Then he should say wee-cock. Being polite is what you've taught us, mummy.

13th As a blind person I have met countless wonderful strangers who have offered help in one way or another. One or two have been slightly embarrassed and confused my disability. One lady guiding me to a station lift said apologetically, 'I'm sorry, I don't speak Braille.'

'That's all right,' I replied cheerfully. 'I don't read it.'

14th *The school magazine's Listening Ear caught the following conversation in the School Office:*

'I've lost my raincoat.'

'Is your name in it?'

'No.'

'How can we find it then?'

'The lining's missing.'

15th

Success at being a manager is successfully concealing the truth about yourself.

16th I overheard a conversation on a park bench that can add fuel to any argument about whether the art of conversation is dead.

Bert to Horace: I met a super girl at the disco last night….

Horace: Was she pretty?

Bert: Pretty what?

A Pause

Horace: ….. Pretty.

Bert: Pretty WHAT?

A Pause

Horace (very deliberately): Just… pr…et…ty…..

Bert: Yeah, but pretty WHAT….pretty cool or pretty nifty…..or pretty likely…. or what?

I decided that life was not long enough…. and left.

17th **College Daily Bulletin**

PLEASE NOTE: Mrs Old has postponed her EMBROIDERY EVENING class because she is still tied up in her knitting.

18th *In 1868 the Western Australia Governor wrote to the Colonial Secretary:*
'The fact that many of the teachers are drawn from the convict class speaks for itself….it must be admitted that the convict class are not as a rule fitted for the education of the young, either morally or intellectually, nor is their employment as schoolmasters calculated to raise the moral sense of the colony.'

19th *In the log book of one school in the Australian outback there is a 1906 letter from the Head to one of the teachers;*
'Re your request to sleep in the lavatory. I can agree so long as during school hours there is no visible trace of your occupancy.'

20th *A wealthy friend, CEO of a large company told me that*
despite his lengthy education in economics, one lesson has been with him from his Sixth Form A Level days.
        I'll never forget those hilarious Economics lessons with Dr. 'Magnus' Opus on marginal returns….. 'Remember this,', he intoned whenever we were straying, 'You can't have a mass market in sauerkraut…!'….
I've never forgotten that…even when I am negotiating multi-million-pound deals in textiles machines…. this vision of mountains of menacing sauerkraut always appears….'

21st And, my friend continued, 'It was Dr. Magnus Opus who brought all the high theorising of economics down to the ground level…. He was fond of telling us that there are three types of economists…those who can count and those who can't!

22nd Just as sharp as Dr. Opus was Miss Erie, Head of Music,' said my pal…….. I still chuckle when I think of Pauline Proctor telling her that she hadn't done her violin practice…. because she had heard on the radio that the world was going to end! What a great excuse!..... But, quick as a flash Miss Erie said, 'O dear. That will be very inconvenient!.. I tell you what…. if it does end before the lunch bell I shall cancel orchestra practice…..!'
'Wish I was half as quick!'

23rd *My friend completed his feminising:*
Yes, Miss Erie was one of the brightest, I must admit….. She told us the story of going into one of the local primary schools to play the cello and talk about it. She told the kids it was 300 years old. 'Wow,' said the kids, of course….. They did not have much idea of what 300 years was except that it was very old….. One kid apparently put up his hand and asked her if she had had it all that time. 'No,' she answered….. 'I had another one before this,'

24th *There have been many versions of this favourite nursery rhyme 'Jack and Jill'. Even the spelling of 'Jill' has changed from 'Gill'. The first verse was the original 18th century rhyme. The rest of the story was added later –with more pain for Jack and Jill*!

Jack and Jill went up the hill
To fetch a pail of water;
Jack fell down and broke his crown
And Jill came tumbling after.

Up Jack got and home did trot,
As fast as he could caper;
Went to bed to mend his head
With vinegar and brown paper.

Jill came in and she did grin
To see his paper plaster;
Mother, vexed, did whip her next
For causing Jack's disaster.

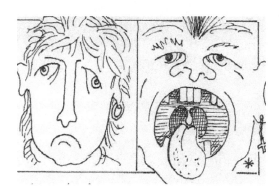

I think we should spare both Jack and Jill the pain and hurt…
with a modern version.

Jack and Jill
Climbed up a hill
Even though it was raining.
They both tripped over
On slippery clover.
But were saved by their
Safety training..

25th Little Helen was an inveterate questioner …. overendowed in inquisitiveness.
One day as the family sat at the tea-table she suddenly piped up, '
'Why can't you see stars in the daytime?'
Her sister, eleven-year old Sandra was also inveterate…. an inveterate
putter-down of little sister. She lifted her eyes and declared,
'Because stars are nocturnal.'

26th *A lawyer assured me that the following story is true…. so it must be….*
During a long case in a north of England city a judge discovered to his horror
that on his return from a weekend break at home in London he had left some
a vital document out of his briefcase.
He apologised profusely to the waiting barristers, who were eager to get the
case over and done with.
'I am so sorry. We will have to adjourn until the papers can be brought to the
court,' wailed the judge.
These were the days before the internet and emails, but during the time
when documents could be sent by 'fax' machines….. a technology with
which an elderly judge was totally unfamiliar.
'Fax it up, Your Honour,' said a bright young barrister. 'Fax it up, sir.'
'Yes, it does rather,' sighed the judge.

27th *Some years ago a newspaper expressed outrage at bad-tempered teachers,
as follows:*
The public discussion on school management boards in the local Council
was accompanied by loud laughter from teachers…it makes one doubt
whether the Education Department has secured the right type of teacher.
While state schools contain bad-tempered teachers school boards will be
found necessary, so that parents have a safety valve of to express their
feelings. These will then be properly dealt with by the managers.

28th **Mother:** What did you learn at school today?
Bernard (after some thought): We learned that in the old days seamen used clippers to cut through water quickly and circumcise the world faster than ever before…

29th *More Aussie 'ockerisms'.*
Remember the sabbath, and keep it for lawn mowing!
The strewth, the whole strewth, and nothing but the strewth.
Dr. Livingston? long time no see!

30th *A Victorian summary of contemporary education:*
We do not want a race of youth who can translate the odes of Horace and quote harmonious Virgil from memory. These may be desirable accomplishments, but we want practical workers, not accomplished drones.

31st   **Carry On Suffering**

Like war, pestilence and disaster, hospitals can be sources of comedy and good humour….. sometimes through nervous banter, but mainly, I think, because of the advertent slapstick opportunities they afford.
Take catheters, for instance.
   Catheters are not a normal subject for literary attention. I can't recall a single novel or poem or even opera that broaches the subject. I have also scoured through my legal tomes and found no specific offences of 'misuse or abuse' of catheters, or hoarding catheters 'with intent'…… even intent to avoid using them! The subject has been, quite simply, taboo.
Maybe the silence is because catheters are considered serious….. er… intimately private…. objects, albeit obnoxious and necessary evils. Those of us who are catheter-carrying members of the 'Urinary Challenged' know, or have known, all too well the whispers in the corner and the conversations behind the hand…. about…. ahem, you know what…. 'those things'.

But like the army, prisons and schools they have their comic dimension. My personal acquaintance with the topic began when I woke up in the City General after a bladder and 'urinary tract' operation – my 'Youtee Op' (I think I will call it) . My three other alcove companions also sported these life-changing carrier bags…. and made light of them….. to such an extent that the first time I left my bed, about five hours after waking up from the anaesthetic, to go to the toilet in order to attend to the other bodily function, I had, of course, to take my carrier bag with me. Holding it out in front of me in my right hand, somewhat gingerly and in a rather mincing manner, I tip-toed past my left-hand companion-in-misery. He eyed my bag and in a rich north midland accent growl greeted my passing. It was my new pal, Lefty.

'Eh up, mate, are yer goin' up Tesco?'

Priceless! It made what I had to perform in the next five minutes infinitely more bearable…. though not actually pleasurable.

Hospitals contain much tragedy and misery, but as in wars and disasters people find time for wit and humour. It is a human trait, thank goodness.

At the following tea-time Lefty distinguished himself again, but this time unintentionally. The ward assistant who was taking orders for the evening meal asked Lefty what he wanted.

It says 'ere on the menu card, Beef curry, Spaghetti Bolognaise, Hungarian goulash…. I dunner want any of that foreign rubbish! What else have you got?' Lefty was a bit disgruntled.

'   Well, we do have one piece of quiche left.'

Lefty broke out in what was, in his terms, smiles of joy. 'I'll 'ave that. That's proper English. We get that in the delicatessen.'

Me and his other three ward companions crawled under our covers chuckling away. O joy!

I wasn't surprised when he told me he was a Port Vale supporter. There are not many of those…. And you have to have a well-developed sense of gritty self-flagellation to keep on being a Vale supporter year in and year out. But that's a Stoke City supporter's view….. in much the same vein as a Liverpool supporter's view of Evertonians …. to be acknowledged but not necessarily applauded!

APRIL

1st   A solicitor was sitting outside a courtroom waiting for his case to be called. Two magistrates who had been hearing in a previous case came out of the court and stopped in front of him.
'That chap was lucky to get off with a suspended prison sentence,' said the younger one.
'He certainly was said the other. 'If we had been really sure that he had done it we would have sent him down straightaway!'

2nd   *A colonial Board of Education recorded in 1893:*
'Girls are in future to take the same arithmetics as boys, but separate and easier questions will be given to them.'

3rd   However, it seems that some progress had been made by 1893 from the kind of schooling offered by Mrs. Highfield in 1838. She had advertised that her School for Girls would *'present the art of Plain and Ornamental Needlework, English Grammar and Storekeeping.'*

4th   *About 100 years ago 'equal rights' was not a big issue.*
This afternoon Mr Bligh will be starting his round of lessons for the Lower School on Basic Physiology and Social Purity. Girls need not attend. Only boys aged 12 and 13 years of age will be admitted.

5th

The Would-be Adviser

I don't want to be a teacher,
I don't want to face the hordes'
I would rather make my pile,
With an enigmatic smile,
Lecturing on the virtues of the Core Curriculum.

I don't want to see a classroom,
Don't want facts to cloud my view.
I just want to be a pundit,
And hope the State will fund it –
Then I'll lay down the law to such as you!

6th   Young Bagshot of Year 8 informed the world in his Religious Education 'essay on his favourite character in the New Testament' that a taxi driver, Saul, had a conversation on the road to Damascus, with some lord wanting a lift. This Lord had revealed himself to possums, who were amazed at what he did. So, Saul thought it best if he changed his name…. before the lord or one of the possums told his story round the town.
There is no record of the marks he obtained.

7th   Miss F. Craddock reported to her manager that while eating a salad sandwich in the works canteen she bit through a caterpillar. Half of it dropped on the table. Aaron Scarum sitting next to me screamed causing Miss C. to fall off her chair. She said that although she was bruised and shocked, her real complaint was that the canteen did not routinely check for creatures (edible or not) in the lettuce and other salads, instead of leaving it to chance or the paying customers to do the job for them.
Sadly there is no record of any action taken, although I have ascertained that the whole factory has since closed – a misfortune which probably did not owe its provenance to a caterpillar.

8th   *This reference is also enigmatic in its way – as the referee gets carried away with enthusiasm.*
Miss Y excited us all last year with her attractive exhibition of fashionable underwear. This year she has done some fantastic things in boots.

9th   *I defy anyone reading this health and safety incident report to be absolutely sure what had actually happened in the leisure centre.*
After some intense physical activity with Miss Rochester and her group in the small gym I have suffered from severe muscular pain and periodic groin discomfort. I believe it has to be attributed to the vigorous nature of the demands made on me by Miss R…. and her group.
My consultant has not yet determined if my injuries are permanent or temporary pain which will gradually disappear now that the activity in the gym has been curtailed.
Miss R told me at the time that she was horrified by the experience with me. I consider that as an agency worker I should have been given more practical guidance the physical nature of what I was expected to do.

Rustic Ruminations: Spring

Spring springs, doing its burgeoning thing
Thrusting nature out with a triumphant zing.
While my hand is constantly up a sheep's backside,
Urging little lambs from inside outside

11th *The Grand Old Duke of York', a rhyme which is usually sung to a version of 'A Hunting We Will Go, has been a favourite marching rhyme for over 300 years. It is not clear which of the plethora of Dukes of York is referred to; whichever it was, he has brought some amusement to the boring act of marching hither and thither.*

Oh, the grand old Duke of York,
He had ten thousand men;
He marched them up to the top of the hill,
And he marched them down again.

When they were up, they were up,
And when they were down, they were down,
And when they were only halfway up,
They were neither up nor down.[[]

No Duke of York has the privilege of marching troops anywhere today, but an elected politician does and professional senior soldiers do, and that is right..... but soldiers have always moaned about not knowing what was going on and still need to point a finger of fun at somebody.

The Secretary of State for Defence
Had a hundred thousand soldiers ,
He moved them here,
He moved them there,
He moved those soldiers everywhere.
And when they were here, they were here,
And when they were there, they were there;

And whether they knew where they were,
Was neither here nor there.

12th During a visit to Les Invalides in Paris where Napoleon Buonaparte and his brother Joseph, are laid to rest in stone tombs, the Guide spent a long time going through Napoleon's exploits. After questions she pointed to the next tomb. , 'That's Joseph'.
One of the party gasped in surprise. 'Gee, and I always thought Joseph was buried in Palestine with Mary…..'

13th *An Incident Report by Grace Fuller (Ms) to car park proprietors:*
I put out a hand against the car park wall to steady myself and it fell down, destroying my car and three others. It was not my fault.

14th *Gloria Duemonte reported to her company Complaints Department about an unfortunate entanglement:*
I was standing on a table removing a display. I thought I noticed my manager, Mr Brush, behind me. To save his embarrassment at unintentionally looking up my skirt, I quickly brushed the skirt down and in so doing fell off the table, knocking Mr. Brush down onto the floor. He, inadvertently, fell on top of me….. Luckily Mr. Hawke came into the office and saw us. He will be able to testify that Mr. Brush and I were quite innocently entangled on the floor….... I'm sure.

15th *Miss Ethel Spratt reported to her headteacher:*
As part of the Science curriculum I was in the process of demonstrating to a Year 3 group in the local 'Zoo and Aquarium' how timid fish were, by swishing my hand in a tank of water when one of the fish jumped up and bit off the end of my thumb. It turned out to be the piranha tank and apparently they get anxious when their water is disturbed.
I think in future you should provide piranha training.

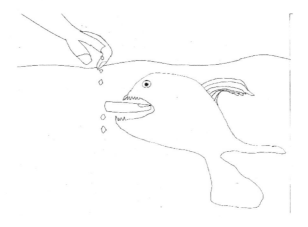

16th *The school magazine's Roving Eye caught sight of Mr. Paltry in the corridor waiting to complain to the Deputy Head about his Year 11 Physics group. He could not stop moaning.*

'I don't believe it….it's just what I thought they would do….. just typical of that lot….. Before the exam I kept on telling them to 'Look at the question.. always look at the question!' And that is ALL they did – Look at the question!'

17th The European School Heads Association (ESHA) with support from the European Commission organised a rally - cum - conference of 16-19 year old school students in Venice. It was specifically designed to bring together able and disabled students.

One group consisted of deaf and hearing students from England, Italy, Belgium, Luxembourg, Germany, Spain and Ukraine, listening to lectures and discussing a variety of topics they had chosen and with the full translation and with the support of all the deaf signing that the European Parliament could produce. There was a great deal of animated chatter and signing. On the last evening when all the large gathering was enjoying a social evening out in old Venice, Charlotte, a deaf student from England came and sat by a group of hearing and deaf teachers. She was excited by it all, and feeling rather smug about one aspect.

'Look,' she said. Can you see all those hearing students from the different countries all standing in their own groups, with just a few daring to speak to students from other countries…. And now look at the deaf students all mixed together…. signing away happily to each other….. Belgians, Spanish, English…. All of them chatting together in sign language…. So who now are the disabled students and who are enabled, eh?'

From an early 20th century school inspection directive:
'In forming an estimate of the efficiency of a school the competency and usefulness of the headteacher's wife in teaching needlework will be taken into account.'

19th   **Ode to a Very Modern Football Manager**

(With apology and gratitude to W.S. Gilbert)
I am the very model of a modern football manager;
I am a leader to success, and not a measly passenger.
I know the moves and tactics and can quote the rules categorical
I can recite the club's results of all matches historical,
I am well acquainted, too, with scores mathematical,
I understand formations both triple and quadrilatical.

Of 4-2-4 and 5-3-2 I know a lot of theorem,
I revel in triangulation…. on paper and in model form.
About defence in depth I teem with latest news,
And can describe how to beat a man on the square of the hypotenuse.
I know more of tactics than a monk in a monastery,
And can show the team what football is in managerial honesty.

But when the team can close the wings and defend at centre back,
And revels in quick passing and thrusting counter-attack,
When players know when to keep the ball or dribble and carefully thread it,
And some can even cross the ball while others simply head it.

THEN, I'm sure that when we get around to using this practical strategy,
   We might actually win one match, and follow it with two or three.

20th According to Astrid Murgatroyd of Year 9 - Noah built the ark for his wife
Joan of Arc who, unlike most French women, did not like plain steak, so
Noah served up animals in pears.
'It turned out to be popular,' said Astrid, ' and the take-up became quite a
flood.

21st *The late Barry Cryer was one of the funniest raconteurs of his generation. He
always held firm to the view that jokes and funny stories were universal and
did not belong to any one person. He told me once it was a great pleasure to
hear one of his stories retold by another comedian who could add a personal
tone and a different twist. He loved to tell parrot jokes. Here is one out of the
dozens.*
     A man saw a parrot on sale in a pet shop for just £1. It was a
  magnificent -looking bird with bright red and blue and yellow plumage,
  called Jack. He couldn't understand why it was only on sale for £1.
'Because it is on sale 'as seen…. and as heard',' said shop-owner. 'It's
language is dreadful; it's rude and nasty. It will annoy your family, friends and
neighbours. All in all a right pain. '
'I reckon I can deal with it,' said the man, 'and it is so beautiful I can't resist
it.'
 So he took it home and put it in a cage in the front room and opened the
window to let the air in. His elderly neighbour, a large widow dressed in
black, passed by. Jack leapt up and down squawking.
'My goodness! You are so fat and ugly!'
His owner rushed up to the cage and admonished Jack. 'Never let me hear
you say such dreadful things again! Understand?'
Jack hung his head and looked at his owner through one eye.
An hour later the elderly widow came past again.
'You're still fat and ugly!' Screeched Jack.
The owner rushed in again.
'Right! That's the last straw! If you ever make such dreadful comments again
you're going back to the pet shop….. Understood?'
Jack hung his head again. It is only through one eye.
Next morning the old lady past again.
'Oi,' screeched Jack.

The widow turned and stared at him. His owner rushed in again. Jack looked at him and then at the widow. He peered at her through one eye….. then looked back at his owner and then back to the neighbour. Eventually he looked at her directly and said,
'You know what I'm thinking.'

22nd A friend tells me that for a whole year after they had taken in Boris, a golden retriever puppy, they were unsure whether he was a bit slow on the uptake or just biding his time.
He took some time to respond to commands and to distinguish between e human right dog wrong. But he did learn quickly that he was not allowed upstairs. He observed this rule day in day out…… until, that is, just after his second summer.
Son had ordered a pizza to have with his friends in an upstairs room. Boris bided his time until everyone was out of the way, bounded upstairs, threw himself at the bedroom door, which was opened by one of the friends, and rushed into the bedroom. He dashed up to the table, grabbed the whole pizza with one deft swipe of his mouth and ran off with it…. downstairs, out of the back door and into his kennel.
He knew what he was doing!!

23rd During the Cold War years after the Second World War Britain had a civil defence force whose task was to keep us all safe. One of the booklets that was issued to all households contained advice on what to do in the event of nuclear attack. One famous piece of advice was that citizens who survived the initial blast of an atomic bomb should immediately climb into a brown paper bag! It wasn't pantomime advice; there was scientific evidence that brown paper absorbed a lot of the deadly radiation that hung around after nuclear explosion. The main problem was that 50 million citizens could not find any brown paper bags!
Warnings of imminent attack in the 21st century will be delivered by sirens in cities and towns and via radio announcements.
On St George's Day 2023 the government gave the nation a test warning via mobile phones. There was no mention of what to do after the warning……..
but rumours of a run on large sacks of potatoes in local greengrocers were unsubstantiated.

24th It was a Monday morning in late April, just after the Easter holidays. In the town hall offices. Two elderly spinsters, long-standing heads of service departments, were sipping early morning coffee in a corner A very excited young female teacher burst in followed by two friends, both junior administrative assistants.

'Hey, everyone….do you know….Mavis has gone and got married on Saturday….and is back at work on Monday…..how about that…..!'

Amid the chatter and congratulations that did the rounds…. One of the Heads was heard to mutter to the other…

'Goodness me, Flo, can you think of anything worse than getting married at the weekend and coming back to work on Monday?'…..

There was a short silence, and then a wistful reply.

'Yes…..coming in on a Monday…. not having been married at the weekend……'

25th Just before morning school in a London suburban school a long-standing Head of Religious Education positively bounced into the staffroom like a trampoline, seething with anger. She attacked her cup of real coffee with a silver spoon …..kept under lock and key in her common-room cupboard…. with the vigour of an irate builder's labourer mixing cement.

'That's the last time I help Mr Spring with his trip to Madame Tussaud's!' she muttered through clenched teeth. '….. 'He insisted…. insisted, I tell you….that I came at the back of the line of pupils off the coach……me, a rear-end?…. outrageous….! I do not do rear-ends….I have always been the head of a crocodile, I told him…..and head of a crocodile I will remain….Well, by the time we had finished arguing…. and he inevitably agreed to do the rear bit…. all the pupils had dashed off upstairs….I rushed upstairs after them….. and found they had all run down the other stairs on the opposite side…When I got halfway down those stairs I found a security man and engaged him in conversation….

'My good man….have you seen a party of children in blazers pass this way?'…. He just stared blankly at me…..

'Don't just gawp, my man,' I said…. in the politest voice I could muster,. 'Have you seen them?'….

I was exasperated with the lack of help, you see….. and then this young boy with a foreign gentleman…. I think he was from Birmingham…. stopped and I heard him ask his father,

'Dad, why is that old lady talking to a Tussaud's dummy?'…..

Well, you can imagine how humiliated I felt…..'old'!……..and, anyway it was a very lifelike dummy policeman… it is all that man Spring's fault…..a crocodile tail indeed….!'

26th In the middle of the last century when see-through material became available in great quantities a fashion designer was asked by a BBC interviewer what the rationale was for introducing such a bizarre piece of fashion as a see-through blouse.
'Well,' said the designer, 'there are two points of view……'

27th   Noah's wife to Noah, as she checked his loading manifest for the Arc,
    'I don't think woodpeckers are a very good idea.'

28th A news editor from a local newspaper gave a talk to a school sixth form on his career as a journalist. He told them that he began as a cub reporter one August many years ago when news was slack. The editor complained that everyone was on holiday, no one was doing anything wrong or brave or calamitous. It was a disaster for the news industry!
 'For goodness sake start a rumour,' the News Editor told me and the reporter who was inducting me into life of a journalist.
So we did. My senior rang the city mainline station and asked the station manager, . What's this rumour about a strike amongst the carriage cleaners?'
    There was silence at the other end and the stationmaster finally muttered, 'I've no idea! I'll ring you back.. We sat by the phone for half an hour and sure enough station manager rang back..
    'There is no strike,' he wailed. 'There hasn't been one for at least 10 years.'
    That was all we needed to hear, of course. We were now able to write a substantial column beginning, *'The rumour that railway carriage cleaners were striking for better pay and conditions was denied today by senior manager, Mr. So-and-So.'*
    We filled this out with several inches of comment on pay and conditions of railway workers and a bit of history of striking railway cleaners from ten years ago!

I tell you this,' said the guest speaker, 'because two months later there was indeed a cleaners' dispute – and they quoted our article!. I do not take any pleasure out of being the unwitting instigator of an industrial dispute…. but I do warn you to take a sceptical view of what you read and hear in what is dubbed news'. Much is 'faction', if not 'fiction'. If you approach journalistic outpourings in a critical vein you will learn to pick out the absurd and enjoy the genuine….. and there is lots of that.'

I thought it made sound sense and so did the Sixth Form….. until ,that is, some ten year's later I read in the local paper an article about industrial unrest in the city, which began '*The rumour of an imminent strike was denied by …..*', written by a reporter who had been the senior pupil who had given the Vote of Thanks to our guest speaker ten years previously….

A Load of Trouble

After three days in the 'Urinary Recovery Ward', it was time for preparations for my departure ceremony.
'Right, come into the toilet. I have to show you how to insert and remove the catheter.' This was the ward sister, a kindly woman, but with a rather too professional approach to her job for my liking….. no flexibility…

When I protested that I did not need any lessons in catheter-insertion, she snorted and said, 'Don't be so troublesome. The doctor says it has to be done, so do it I will…. and do it you will, too …. so listen, and take note.' Having served as a trade union negotiator for some years, I knew when negotiation would be futile.

I will skirt over the next few minutes…. on the grounds of decorum. Suffice it to say that in a surprisingly short time the catheter was going in and out as smoothly as I remember my pull-through and 'four-by-two' cloth went up and down the barrel of my rifle during National Service in the army…. keeping the barrel clean and highly polished.

'Excellent,' said Sister. 'I will now order you six month's supply. They /will arrive at your home within the week. Here is the first week's packet.'
I took the green bundle without demur, but also in total stupefaction.

'What do you mean? Six month's supply? I've only got to keep my urinary tract…. my UT… open for the next day or so. It will be all right after that… That's what the doctor said…..'

'I don't know what the doctor said to you. What I do know is that my written instructions are that you must use them '*until further notice*'.'

'Well, I'm giving you due notice now,' I croaked, a certain desperation entering my voice, as it is prone to do when you have no idea what is going on.

'Not YOUR notice! …. ….. Stop being a silly boy and get on with it. Keeping the urinary tract open will prevent you having to come back here, and that is what you want, isn't it?'

I suppose it was, but I was quite clear that the doctor had said that once the tract had been opened up it shouldn't close for years…… 'and you might be dead by then,' he had added…. In his surgically-inspired cheerfulness.

I thought of appealing to the consultant about 'waste of public money' and 'no need to cure someone who is well' and 'I would like to donate these to the needy', but something told me that I might be storing up trouble that would not suit my needs if I had to return. Best let events take their own course.

So I did. And I had almost forgotten about my burden…. having by now expended the useful life of the green shoots I had been given on departure…. When, one sunny Spring morning, a pantechnicon drew up outside our house.
Out stepped a jaunty driver.

'Where dryer want them, mate?'

'What?' I asked querulously, though the sinking feeling in the pit of my stomach told me that I knew very well what 'them' was.

'I've got three cartons here…. with 180 separate packages…. Tubes and bags…. to be delivered to this address… so, where-do-you-want-me-to-put-them?' He spoke the last sentence slowly and with emphasis on each word, as though he feared he was dealing with the village idiot.
'Er… I think you have got the wrong address…. I think you had better take them back….'

'This is the address on the carton and this is where I am leaving them… If you have any queries there's a telephone number on the delivery note. Ring the company…. Now sign here and I will trundle them into your garage for you….. that's where people usually put them.'

I could sense that further protest was useless. The goods were going to be delivered, come what may.

And so the menacing cartons remained in the garage, gradually moving back into the inner recesses as Spring turned to Summer and then into Autumn. I really had forgotten all about them until five and a half months later when I took a call from a number I did not recognise.
'Just letting you know, sir, that your next six months-worth of catheters will be despatched today.'

Now, I am not very good at instant responses, and I probably should not have attempted one at that moment, but I did.

'You've got the wrong person, I'm afraid.' I simpered….. 'The catheter chap is my son and he's gone abroad… to Papua New Guinea…. up in the jungle….. for three months…' I lied.

There was what is called 'a pregnant pause'.

'I see, sir. I hope he took enough with him.'   'Oh yes. Boxes of them…. wouldn't be without them….'   'OK. I will stop the delivery…. But I will have to inform the hospital, of course.'

And there the matter rests. Five years of blissful silence. I am beginning to sleep more easily.

And if you are of a Doubting Thomas nature, and if you happen to be passing through my part of the world, may I invite you to pop in and poke around our garage….. right at the back. There is only one proviso…. as an entry fee you must agree to purchase a bundle of 'green straws', ideal for sipping summer cocktails on the terrace….. or sucking sherbert from a plastic bag…. which I can also provide.

30th   *Having read my painful account above yet another friend sent me a description of his own well-remembered hospital experience.*

I was in a side ward of 6 beds recovering from a joint replacement. As is the case in these situations we all soon established friendly relationships. Except for one….

Arthur was in the bed opposite to me. He was much older than the rest of us and hard of hearing. We were all orthopedically compromised and therefore unable to shuffle across to Arthur's bed side to have a chat. The only way was to shout, as a result conversation soon dwindled.

The next morning a striking and young Australian locum came in to see Arthur. She was there to assess what needs he might want in his support package when he went home. She began by asking him if he was Arthur Fenwick (No reply. Realising Arthur was hard of hearing she repeated the question in a much louder voice. This time Arthur nodded.

"G'day Arthur I am here to ask you a few questions"

This was the signal to the rest of us to sit up and take notice. Arthur got off to a confident start with his name and date of birth. The day of the week was more of a challenge. Then came the killer question. *"Can you tell me the name of the Monaaaark?"* In print it is apparent what the question was but when asked with a strong Aussie accent it was not so obvious. We were all stunned including Arthur.

For a few seconds we didn't understand the question. I briefly thought a Monaaark might be a variant of the African spiny ant eater. The penny soon dropped but not for Arthur who had to endure several more testing questions. Eventually the Australian vision finished, closed her notebook and left. Poor Arthur was a crumpled man. No A* for him, his grade was almost certainly a low 'F'. He had not impressed the vision of beauty with his cognitive abilities. The rest of us were saddened that Arthur might go home to his lonely home only seeing his social care workers twice a day.

We discussed between ourselves sotto voce what we might do to help. But then visiting time intervened. In came Arthur's wife, his daughter, his son-in-law and two grandchildren. They gathered cheerfully around his bed chatting and making a fuss of him. He didn't after all need a support package. He had one. Ready made!

MAY

1st   Benjamin Rogers was organist at Magdalene College chapel, Oxford from 1665 to 1686. Traditionally, his *Hymnus Eucharisticus* is sung at the top of the chapel tower at 6am each May Morning. This is an event renowned internationally. Within the college he is remembered in another way.
The celibacy rule for Fellows of Oxford colleges remained in place until the late nineteenth century, despite religious reformation.

      The college records indicate that Benjamin Rogers lost his job in 1686 because his daughter, who lived with him in the college, became pregnant by the college porter, having previously 'been known by the Fellows'. Tut, tut…..

2nd   *I was told that May Day anecdote by an Academical Clerk, i.e. a student member - of the choir of Magdalen College, Oxford. He also told me of an encounter with a tourist, anxious to demonstrate his ecclesiastical knowledge.*

      Our scholar was accosted one day by an enthusiastic tourist, who asked, 'Can you direct me to the university?'

      'Before he could reply the man's wife pointed to the college name board and asked, 'Why is this place called Magdalen College?"

      And before the scholar of Magdalen could reply the husband butted n….. 'It is named in honour of the Blessed Virgin Mary Magdalene, obviously.'

It isn't, of course. Mary Magdalene was present at Christ's death, not birth.

3rd   *Another quip, or even quiddity, to complete a Magdalen May musical medley:*

A former organist of Magdalen College was playing the accompaniment to the choir singing of the psalms when he heard an unfamiliar voice joining in from below. A visiting clergyman in the congregation had dared to participate in this worship. The organist reached for a large hymn book and tossed it from the organ loft onto the offending head.

      At the end of the service the clergyman accosted the organist and remonstrated that this was unseemly behaviour in the House of God.
The organist replied, 'And this is Magdalen College Chapel and "Don't you forget it!'

4th   A headteacher had a long-standing policy of seeing the work of students who were not working to the standard they were capable of.

One day Dean knocked on his door and brought in his English exercise book, a ritual that happened often. The head flip through the exercise book, while he discussed the teacher's comments with Dean before looking at more pages. Suddenly his eyes widened and he looked to Dean.

'My goodness, Dean, this little poem of yours is brilliant… You must have had some deep emotional crisis….. Do you want to talk about it?'

'Yer what?' said Dean, puzzled.

'This little poem here….

Deceit, deceit, deceit;
Grief, grief, grief;
Belief, belief, belief;
Relief, relief, relief.

It's very moving, Dean.'

'Nar,' said Dean, 'they're my spelling corrections.'

5th   *These were the first lines of poetry I ever learned -in 1944 at the age of 6: The lines were composed anonymously and read out on the radio. They are included in The Random House Book of Poetry for children (1983)*
I eat my peas with honey;
I've done it all my life;
It makes the peas taste funny;
But it helps them to stick to the knife.

6th   On the day of the coronation of King Charles III I was in England but thinking of what might be going on in a small village I know in 'France, far from sophisticated towns and cities.

It comes to a halt whenever there is a British or other monarchy's ceremonial occasion on the TV. Farmworkers come in from the vineyards…. the baker, the grocer and the winemaker pause …. the priest considers it ideal time for private contemplation in the vestry, the 'mairie' shuts temporarily, while on the other hand the bar with its huge screen is crowded.

The railway bridge on the edge of the village is called *'Le Pont de la Reine',* the Queen's Bridge. No-one knows why, nor when, nor who chose the name….. nor which queen it is… but no-one enquires either. It is quietly enjoyed by these proto-monarchical denizens of this village in *'France profonde'* as it is called, hidden from prying over-zealous republicans. They enjoy a bit of the ceremonial. They sense the importance of ritual. … or maybe they are puzzled by it…. but whatever it is that moves them they cannot help peeping at the live … and free…. show.

The village mayor told me once that he was mine-boggled *(ahurissant)* by seeing millions turnout for the late Queen Elizabeth's 90th birthday. .'If the French President drove down the Champs Elysees in Paris on his birthday only half a dozen people would know. You certainly know how to do it!' he chuckled. Then, he added ruefully, Your rulers know the value of patronage. We gave up Aristocracy Inc. centuries ago. Republicanism works but it is nothing like as joyful.'

I thought about his summing up of the British monarchy. It woks all right, but it is a bit *'ahurissant'.*

7th   Grozny was a peasant from land high up in the hills of a country east of the East of Europe. His farm was right on the border of the neighbouring rich country and the nearest town to hi was on the other side of the border. By an agreement reached many years before, Grozny and fellow peasant farmers were able to cross the border once a week with a handcart full of their produce to sell in the market and then depart via the exit gate.
For the past 30 years the chief of the border police was certain that Grozny was a smuggler, on the basis that all the other incoming farmers were smugglers and had been caught at one time or another. But nothing had ever been found in Grozny's cart. They had searched for plants for drug making, precious stones from the mountains, military weapons that were sold by gangs roaming the mountains, and even human-trafficking. Nothing had ever been found. Grozny had paid duty on all the items he brought into the country.
On the day Grozny announced that he was retiring, the chief of police stopped him at the border once again and leaned against the loaded cart. 'You must have been smuggling, Grozny. Please tell what you have been smuggling. I promise there will be no reprisals. I am just desperate to know……. For old times sake, please tell me.'
'Handcarts,' replied Grozny…. 'and this last one is for you……'

8th　　　　*This day marks the anniversary of the end of the Second World War in Europe in 1945. Many countries nark this day officially with parades, church services and national holidays, but in the UK we do not, possibly because our war was still raging in the Far East. It was another three months before that conflict came to an end.*

I thought it would add a different kind of smile to share the reminiscences of a former 'enemy soldier', though actually a 15 year old schoolboy at the time of being conscripted, who wrote the following account for me… at the age of 93. In his letter he reminded me how little we know of 'the other side'.

'About the time of the beginning of the war we lived in Bruchsal, near Karlsruhe. I was 11 years old, my elder brother13 my younger one not yet born.

My father, a moderately paid inland revenue civil servant , had planned the first holiday journey with his family for this wonderful summer 1939: a real thrill for us down to the Lake of Constance by train at the beginning of the August school holiday, on the beautiful Black Forest Line and a flight over the lake in a hydroplane as a highlight.

But the holidays were marred by the looming danger of war. All pleasure flights around the lake were cancelled and we had to set out on our homeward journey before schedule.

Unlike my parents I think I kind of enjoyed the general suspense and unrest , not understanding a bit what was going on. The exciting feeling of drama was enhanced as the train passed through the village stations, which had been so quiet on our outward journey and were now teeming with horses, which had been confiscated to support the war effort from the Black Forest farmers, who were standing by, sadly watching their animals being laden into goods vans.

Back home again, it must have been on one of the first September days ,my father was drafted into the army ….. no enthusiasm from him! (No wonder as he was a WWI veteran). Obviously war didn't only mean peasants parting with their horses, but fathers with their wives and children as well !!

However, after a few weeks he was discharged again without having been in action and it was only toward the end of the war that he was drafted again.

After the defeat of Poland in 1939 the war seemed over. At the western front, which at its nearest point was less than 70 km away from our town, everything remained absolutely quiet for almost a **year. Life** was back to normal.

But normalcy in Nazi Germany, of course, meant constant indoctrination and suppression of non-conformity of all kind like Christianity. Our family was rooted in the Catholic church, and as such in an inner opposition to the Nazi Regime. My brother and myself were members of the illegal catholic youth Organisation „Neudeutschland", which was detected by the Gestapo (the secret police)in early summer 1940.

My brother was punished with three weekends in prison and provisional exclusion from school. Myself…. being under 14 I escaped sanctioning then. Sometime later, however, our art teacher at the Gymnasium (my grammar school), who was a member of the Gestapo, asked a classmate of mine to observe my behaviour clandestinely and report anything suspicious to him…… But my friend did not do so and on the contrary we developed friendly relations between each other which have persisted to the present day.

With this background, my brother and myself became more and more aware as we grew older that we could not really wish for Nazi Germany to win the war. but Germany was our „fatherland", and patriotism was another stream in our socialization! We had no alternative but to do our duty.

Soon after the 1940 defeat of France, Germany annexed Alsace-Lorraine, which France had lost to Germany in 1871 after the 1870 - 71 war and which she had won back again under the Versailles Treaty 1919.

We had learned in our history lessons that this area by culture and language rightly belonged to Germany. We did not question it. And so it was that my elder brother and I in 1940 set out on a cycling-tour to explore this beautiful bit of land on the other side of the Rhine.

The population was not unfriendly toward us two boys, but they also had to be wary not to show too much sympathy for us Germans. I remember that we caused a lot of head shaking and sneering when we asked people to help us find our way – because our map was so brand new that all place names had been Germanized. Quite obviously they did not wish to be Germanized as well!

9th   (continued) In 1943 my friend's father was sent to the eastern front to fight against the Soviet Union. He was never seen again by his family. His elder brother was called up at 16 and sent to fight, and was finally made a French PoW. My friend was conscripted at 15 and served in the Anti-Aircraft defence.

I hope that his recall of small but significant events of 80 years ago will add something positive to your thinking about war and peace…. and about people's knowledge of other people.

10th *Every day millions (yes, millions) of employees are too ill to attend their workplace. Apologies are sent and excuses given….. but not all are as intriguing as others, such as this one received by a school explaining the non-attendance of little Clara:*

'Clara could not come to school as she has a coleslaw.'

11th And then there was Glen, who could not come to work that day, apparently, 'because he ran into a wooden fence which was a brick wall…'

12th *A good Aussie friend likes to mix his salutations. Two he uses frequently are:*

As we slide down the "Banister of Life", may all the splinters point in the same direction!
and
As we journey along these pandemic virus times, may the A.G.E. virus treat you kindly!

13th **Presence of Mind**

I jumped from an airplane with my parachute,
It did not open – so downwards did I scoot.

I was kind of nervous, many a hasty prayer I made,
I was breaking wind too, like a Dyson Airblade.

When suddenly up flew a man from miles below;
We met half way, and paused to say a very brief hello.

I said 'Friend, do you know about parachutes?'
He said 'No. Do you know anything about gas ovens?'
Colin Sell

14th *More plaintive notes from insurance claims.*
The bus driver did not see me coming round the wrong side of a roundabout and failed to stop.'

15th 'I had to break the driver's-side window in order to open the car door because my key wouldn't open it. It was only then that I discovered it was not my car.'

16th *And in the same vein:*
'I saw my wife in her blue car passing me on the other side of the road. I blew her a kiss and only then realised it was not my wife. The lady driver swerved and hit me.'

17th Define "*Manhood Suffrage*" demanded a teacher of his Politics Advanced Level class, full of robust but non-political, teenage boys........'
'Shortage of women'   Sir   !!!' cried Oliver without hesitation.

18th *A friend told me that he had once flirted with the idea of a career as a teacher, but gave up the ambition halfway through his first 'probationary' term.*
'In exasperation I ordered a rather large boy with loutish tendencies to stand outside the door. With considerable reluctance he did so. The lesson perked up after that but Carl was noticed in the corridor by a visiting County Adviser, who did not take kindly to seeing the boy there. He mentioned that to the Head he called me in for 'a chat', with the adviser alongside him.
'What on earth are you playing at throwing a boy out of your class and ordering him to stand outside in the corridor - in full view of visitors! Mr Wright, our area adviser, thinks it very inadvisable.
Some thing snapped inside me!
        'I see,' I said through gritted teeth, 'and what you have preferred it I threw him out of the window instead?.... And while I think about it what advice has this adviser ever given to me!, and come to think of it what advice have you ever given me??
Unwise as I knew it was, I found that I was enjoying myself.
'This is outrageous...... We shall have to consider your position at this school!' cried the Head.
'I've already considered it,' I retorted and took my favourite fountain pen out of my inside pocket.
        'Show me the form and I'll sign it!'
        I felt more in command of the situation then I had ever done with year 10 C group. I had not felt so happy for weeks.
The Head stopped my hand in mid-flourish.
        'Let us now start again......' he said, 'That was a false start....'
    And so we did, but I only lasted a term. I did not need an adviser to tell me a teacher's life was not for me.

19th *An Incident Report by Miss Ava Flutter*
'   I was looking for a Bible in the Deputy Head's desk drawer. I found a pistol, a guillotine and length of rope.
       I dislocated a finger when I shut the drawer too fast and forgot to take my hand out….. because I was in a state of shock.

20th 'Everything is possible in the most possible of all possible worlds. ….. .' so I'm told.' Somebody said it….. and it sounds very profound…… but meaningless. Perhaps that is true of all profundity….. (Discuss)

21st   **Making It All Plain**

Now for something radically different – a chant, a plainsong parody explaining the education law as it then was, and its implications for schools. It should be solemn, but not serious…. although, of course, the government's legal requirements are really serious…..

Here is a summary of the Law of Education, as enacted by the Queen's most Excellent Majesty…. with the advice and consent of the Lords Spiritual and Temporal and of the Commons….. on the proposals of Her Ministers Temporary and Disposable…. and anyone else who wants a go at it….

All Maintained Schools will be Academies…. except those that are not…. and will become by Order, independent and, therefore,…… successful….. 'like the great Public Schools are, and were and ever shall be…..

All Academies will be in Trusts… with Trusties…. who will be entrusted…. and trusted …. so that no Man may put them asunder… except the Secretary of State….

Headteachers of Academies are principally Principals, and may, or may not, be unprincipled…. but must pursue Principles principally provided to promote Progress in Pupils….. in principle.

Ordinary Principals may become Executive Principals…. if the Trusties require Something to be executed……. or Somebody…..

In order to provide tactical know-how, due diligence, superior knowledge, executive management and strategic leadership….. Principals are required to follow all the 'doing' verbs to be found in the English Language…. except the rude ones.
They must, according to their Conditions…. (of Service, not their physical or mental conditions)……. lead and manage, organise and develop, maintain and support, secure and supplement, foster, appraise, promote and ensure…. and even on occasions………teach…. even if not very often….. or indeed very well….

Headteachers and Teachers will be paid according to the Schoolteachers Pay and Conditions Order of England and Wales …… or not, if the Trusties so determine…

It shall be the solemn duty of every Trusty, every Governing Board, and every Headteacher, to exercise their Functions…. professional as well as natural…. on a daily basis…….. as conferred upon them by law, with respect to Religious Education…. Religious Worship….. and the Curriculum, National and Otherwise….. with a view to securing that the School Curriculum satisfies…….Someone…. or Something……Somewhere…. Sometime…..

The Curriculum must be balanced and broadly based….. and prepare Pupils for the Experiences of Adult Life…… but not the sort that Darren and Sharon are contemplating, at this moment…..

Headteachers may no longer cane Pupils in order to chastise, and thereby improve them……. but may instead use their Functions to relieve themselves of the Burden…. by disappearing them into an Exclusion Zone…..

And Pupils …… and Teachers …. and Schools, but not Ministers….shall be tested, appraised, and examined according to the Rites of the Secretary of State …. who will be forgiven their trespasses, as they know not what they have done….. nor what will be done to them….

Parents may complain about…. anything….. so long as they use the appropriate Forms, follow the agreed Procedure, revolve in ever tighter Circles, go through smaller and smaller Hoops…. and thank the Board for its final Decision…. whether or not they can understand what it is…

Then the People will rejoice…..All will be hunky-dory…. and the word of the Government will be satisfied…. and Pupils will no longer be sore .

Let us praise Ministers, Prime and Otherwise, Parliament and Monarch…. now and for ever and for Something or Other …. all the days of our school life ….. which were and are and ever shall be… the happiest days of our life.

22nd   **A Meaning for Life**

A philosophy professor stood before his class with some items in front of him. He wordlessly picked up a large, empty jar and filled it with golf balls. He asked his class whether the jar was full, and they agreed it was. He then pic ked up a box of pebbles, and poured them into the jar, where they into the spaces between the golf balls. He asked again whether the jar was full and the students agreed again that it was.
The professor then picked up a box of sand and poured it into the jar. Once more he asked whether the jar was full, and received a unanimous "YES".
He then produced 2 glasses of wine from under the table, and proceeded to pour the entire contents into the jar.
"Now," said the professor, "I want you to recognise that this jar represents your life. The golf balls are the important things – your family, your health, your children, your friends, things that if everything else was lost, your life would still be full. The pebbles are the other things that matter, your job, your house, your car. The sand is everything else, the small stuff. If you put the sand in the jar first, there is no room for the pebbles and the golf balls.

The same is true of life. If you spend all your time and energy on the small stuff, you will never have room for the things that are important to you. Pay attention to the things that are critical to your happiness – make time to relax with your family and friends, there will always be time to go to work, to clean the house, to put out the dustbins. Take care of the golf balls first, the things that really matter, the rest is just sand".

But then, one of the students asked what the wine represented. The professor replied, 'I'm glad you asked. It just goes to show that however full your life may seem, there's always room for a glass or two of wine!'

23rd   In a house at night a burglar suddenly hears: 'Jesus is watching you!'
Terrified, the burglar calls out: 'Who's there?'
Again – 'Jesus is watching you!'
He switches on his torch. The source of the talking is a parrot. The burglar says, 'You frightened the life out of me! Who are you?'
'I am Satan the Parrot,' comes the reply.
The burglar asks: 'Eh? What sort of houseowner calls his parrot 'Satan?'
The parrot answers: 'The same sort of houseowner who calls his rottweiler 'Jesus'!

24th   *In 1918 the Western Australian Sanitation Department issued a decree to schools.*
The amount for sanitary service stands at 1 shilling per pan. Teachers in schools where a higher charge than 1 shilling is made should endeavour to make a reduction. Teachers should make every effort to cut costs.

25th   *Mr. Arthur Braine reported to the headteacher:*
'I refuse to do any more supervision of pupils on the school field. This morning while looking for pupils smoking, as per your directions, I was viciously attacked by a squirrel (grey), suffering severe scratches on my legs. To my mind it is beyond the call of a teacher's duty.'

26th   *Miss Flo Chart sent a note to her headteacher:*
I drew a chalk circle on the blackboard and it fell on me. I received severe injuries.
An hour later she received a note from the Head:
'Thank you for the information. Please describe the damage caused to the blackboard.'

27th   M*r Jim Epstein also wrote a note…. to his departmental manager in a
pottery factory,*
While I was helping one of the apprentices to use the pug mill I asked her to
pass the handle. She did but released it before I had got hold of it. It fell on
my foot, thus breaking it.
The manager replied: 'I am not sure whether it is your foot or the pug mill hat
is broken. If it is the latter, please replace it and carry on with the training.'

28th   Two burglars spent a lifetime in thieving and were never caught. One day
fate caught up with them. They fell off a roof together and ended up at the
Pearly Gates in front of St. Peter.
St. Peter scrutinised both the Good and the Bad Book but could find no
reference to them. He said he would have to seek the advice of Higher
Authority.
After half an hour he returned saying, 'Good news! No one can find anything
against you…….' He looked around…
They had gone …. And so had the Pearly Gates.

29th   **Why We Love Old People**

A farmer left his truck for repair at the garage and decided to walk home. On
the way he stopped at a hardware store and bought a bucket and a can of
paint. He then stopped at a feed store and bought two chickens and a goose.
However, he struggled to carry everything, and while he was wondering what
to do, an old lady approached him to ask if he could direct her to an address.
The farmer said the address was close to his farm and he would walk her
there, but he was struggling to carry his goods.
'Why don't you put the can of paint in the bucket and carry it one hand, put a
chicken under each arm and carry the goose in the other hand?. said the old
lady.
'Oh, thank you,' said the farmer and they proceeded on their way.
After a while, the farmer said they could take a short cut down an alley. The
old lady looked cautiously at him. 'I'm a lonely old widow, with no one to
look after me.' she said 'How do I know that you won't hold me up against
the wall, lift up my skirt, and have your way with me?'
'How could I possibly do that" said the farmer "I'm carrying a bucket, a can
of paint, two chickens and a goose?'
The old lady said 'Well, you could put the goose down, cover it with the
bucket, put the paint can on top of the bucket, and I'll hold the chickens.'

Song of the Senior Management Team

Boss:	I'm the boss.
Deputy:	I'm the sub.
Boss:	I'm the big wheel.
Deputy:	I'm the hub.
Worker: And…	I… am… just… a worker.

Boss and Deputy:	Together we make up stories of our glory and renown, Put them on the website and spread them round the town.
Worker:	And.. I.. just ….. work.

Boss:	How well we plan
Deputy:	How well we plot.
Both:	We do it quite a lot.
Worker:	And… I… just carry on working.

Boss and Deputy:	Together we are managers and manage all the rest. We deploy staff here, and money there; We always do our best.
Worker: And…	I… just pick up the pieces.

Boss:	I'm the Chair.
Deputy:	I'm the Vice
Both:	We cut the mustard. It's very nice.
Worker:	And… I… am… just a worker.

Boss and Deputy:	Together we've the making of a really perfect team. We give out good advice, And paper by the ream.
Worker:	And… I… just… get… buried deeper.

Teacher's Pet

'Right, off you go now.' Becky Smith signed the class register and watched with a smile on her face as thirty chairs were pushed back with maximum scraping. Desk lids were banged shut like rifle shots and 3A bustled out of the room on the way to morning assembly at Much Knowing Primary School.

She liked this moment of repose, short as it was, to compose herself, brush back her golden hair and have a last brief thought about the day ahead, before joining her Year 6 charges in the school hall. She knew that at the back of the hall she could listen with joy in her heart to the particular rendering of favourite old hymns, sung sweetly by some; bawled with raucous enthusiasm by others; and growled out like distant rolling thunder by the rest. It was how it was and how it had always been, and hopefully will always be, she thought.

She came out of her reverie. The noise in the corridor had died down. She could see Old Rob, the caretaker, sauntering past her door, brush in hand. Time to go. She had better hurry. She shut the attendance register, stood, straightened her dress…. and then she saw it. It was just a slight ripple of movement at first, then a sound of scurrying past chairs, and then half view under a desk.

A rat! Or was it just a mouse? She was unable to decide. But whatever it was it paralysed her.

Whether it was musophobia or murophobia was not relevant for her at that moment. She could not move. Her revulsion for rodents was not rational. She knew that. But it was real enough. It consumed all sense, and roused half-hidden sensibilities. She leapt on the nearest chair and began to shake. She must have screamed because the door burst open and Old Rob dashed in, brandishing his yard brush like a medieval broad sword.

If she had been in a state od cool reflection she might have wondered how Old Rob had got there so quickly. He appeared as though out of a magician's top hat. She did not know that sixty year Old Rob had the kind of crush on Becky that affects some middle-aged romantics.

There was nothing he would not do for the gorgeous Miss Smith. He wished he was half his age, but as he was not he could only do the chivalrous thing and make sure that Becky, Miss Becky, his Becky, received his special attention. So, quietly and unobtrusively watching her back, fending off any recalcitrant pupils and leery male colleagues had kept him going since Becky had arrived in the school a year ago. He was 'on call' now. Becky had let out a piercing shriek. Someone, something was frightening her. That was sufficient. Like Sir Lancelot Old Rob *'burn'd like one burning flame together'* as he sought to defend his Lady of Shalott.

'What is it, miss? What's goin' on?' he cried as he twirled round in front of her chair, the brush held firmly in front of him.

'It's a rat, Rob! Over there. Under the desks! Quick! It's making me tremble.'

'Hang on, Miss,' he cried in time-honoured chivalry. It was knight against foul commoner, right against wrong, Rob against the rat.

Thrusting desks and chairs aside, he caught sight of the rodent cowering in under a desk.

'There it is! Got yer,'' he yelled as he brought his weapon down with a crash. But he had paused a millisecond too long. Rat had ratted, feinted left and scuttled right.

'Missed it! Dammit.' He pushed more chairs aside.

'It's in the corner, miss. I've got it in my sights.'

Becky had not got it in her sights. Her eyes were tightly shut. In the distance she could make out the strains of *'All things bright and beautiful, All creatures great and small....'*

'Just get rid of it, Rob!' she cried with renewed vigour.

And Old Rob did. The bristles on his brush picked up the creature so that Rob could swing it into the air. He aimed to throw it out of the classroom window, but the body slipped off the brush and fell right below Becky's chair.

'Yeeow……. Move it, Rob. Throw it out!' Becky could feel her feet stamping up and down on the chair. It was stupid, but she could do nothing about it. Uncontrollable shudders took over.

Rob did not hesitate. He scooped it up with one sweep of his arms, marched across the room, flung open a window and deposited the rodent in the shrubbery below. He turned and beamed at Megan.

'It's all right now, miss. All over.'

Becky took a large intake of breath, and held out her hands to be helped off the chair.

Rob thought it had all been worth it. Heaven was his.

'Off you go now, miss.

'Thanks, Rob. I am so grateful. I wish I could just accept rats and mice and things for what they are, but I'm not made that way. That's how it is.'

'I understand, miss. I'll see to everything, don't you worry.'

Becky made for the door.

'And it'll be our little secret, miss. Just ours,' was Old Rob's parting shot.

By the time she had crept into the Hall and slipped into a seat near the back, the deputy head was just finishing her reading of the plague of frogs in Exodus Chapter 8.

'Thank the Lord I missed all that,' thought Becky. 'The day's started badly enough as it is!'

It was time for the Head's reading of daily information and notices. The Head, Mr. Cheshire, looked rather troubled.

'Now, everyone,' he said a solemn voice, 'I just have one piece of rather distressing news this morning.' He paused, and appeared to wipe a tear or some grit from his eye. ' I brought in my family's pet gerbil to show the first year infants. We have only had her for a week so she is rather precious to us. Well, I am sorry to have to tell you that little Gemma has somehow escaped from her box and is roaming around the school.'

There were audible sighs and groans from the youngest classes at this point. Mr Cheshire hurried on.

'She is a greyish colour, with a tail like a mouse, and is rather timid. Hides under chairs a lot. Could you all keep your eyes open and when you spot her tell one of the staff immediately. Thank you. Now school, dismiss.'

A crestfallen Head left the stage brandishing a large white handkerchief, closely followed by Miss Terry

As the classes filed out in orderly fashion Becky sat at the back, paralysed, unable to move a muscle. The world seem to have stopped and left her in a cocoon of terror.

She had just witnessed… no, aided and abetted, the murder of the Head's own pet gerbil! The Head's !! It must be….no, it can't be. Surely she would have recognised a non-mouse or a non-rat?... No, she would not. She had no idea what a gerbil looked like, she confessed to herself. She had always kept as far away as possible from little creatures.

What on earth was she to do?

No decision on this was possible at that moment because her class had to be rescued from sitting alone and puzzled in the hall in front of her, waiting to be escorted back to the classroom. And on top of that she could do nothing for the first hour and a half up to morning break . She was taking her class for English and though more grammar and punctuation was on the syllabus she just did not have the heart nor inclination at this moment. So, 'silent reading' was ordered…. and silent it had to be. She was in no mood for any banter from Jacob, nor irritatingly clever questions from Renu. She wanted to be alone with her thoughts.

When the children had been dismissed for morning break she knew she had to brave the interview with the Head. It could not be put off, even though she could think of fifty different reasons for delay.

Eventually she took a deep breath and marched purposefully down the corridor, staring straight in front, oblivious to the various greetings from children in her class. She passed them by leaving them not a little bewildered. Miss Smith was never like that. What could be wrong? Her own anxiety became matched with theirs. They had no idea why they were worried for her – but they were.

She decided against knocking and then waiting outside the Head's door. She just knocked and walked straight in.

'Oh dear, what's the matter, Miss Smith?' said the Head looking up from his reading. 'What on earth is the hurry for?'

Becky took a deep breath. 'Well, Mr Cheshire, you know that sad news of yours at Assembly?' Mr Cheshire nodded. 'Yes, I still haven't…'

'Well, it's like this,' cut in Becky, 'I have a….'

Before she could continue the door burst open and there stood Old Rob framed in the doorway, for all the world like a wild west sheriff entering a saloon bar. His hands were stuffed into his pockets as though he was about to draw two revolvers. He was panting and finding it difficult to speak.

'There… er… there….' Another deep breath. ' There you are.' He was looking at Becky but realised he should be addressing the Head. 'Oh… you, sir…. You…'

'Well, of course I'm here,' said the Head, 'it's my room!…. what on earth is the matter, Mr. Potter?'

'I've done it, sir!'

'Done what?'

'I mean I've *found* it! I have found your gerbil!' And with that he withdrew his clenched hand from his right pocket and held it out. Poking out of his clasped fingers was a little nose sniffing this way and that.

'Gemma!' cried the Head in delight, leaping up from his seat.

'Crikey!' muttered Becky in disbelief.

'Well done, Rob! That's brilliant!' 'Where did you find her?'

'It's a long story, sir. I will tell you one day, but now I think you had better take her and see she is all right, and gets a square meal, I expect.'

'Yes, yes, you are right, of course. Plenty of time to fill in the details.' Mr Cheshire gently accepted into his hands the little Gemma, who seemed, and probably was, oblivious of all the fuss about her welfare. She seemed sprightly enough.

Becky had sat transfixed once more, not quite believing the unfolding drama. Her mouth was open; she was lost for words. This is what deliverance feels like, she thought.

Mr Cheshire remembered she was there. 'Oh, sorry Miss Smith, please excuse us. You will appreciate all the euphoria I am sure. Now…. You were saying…'

'It was nothing important, sir. It will wait. I can see you have some important and pressing tasks to perform.'

'Thank you so much, Becky. That is very understanding of you. Come back at anytime this afternoon and we will continue our little chat.'

There had been no chat, but Becky was not going to quibble. All need for a chat had disappeared anyway. As she fled through the study door Old Rob called after her.

'I'll call on you in your classroom shortly, Miss Smith. We have some things to discuss.'

But Becky had gone.

Back in her cosy and beloved classroom she sat in her teacher's chair and put her head in her hands. She was trembling. The pace of events was too much for her. What had been going on?

That is how Rob found her a few minutes later.

'Now, miss, no need for fretting. All's well.'

'Oh, Rob, You are a real treasure! I don't know how to thank you,' said Becky lifting her head from her hands.

'Well, you can start by reimbursing me a tenner for young Gemma there,' replied Rob with the hint of a smile.

'What do you mean, 'give you a tenner'…what for?' Becky looked blankly at him.

'Well, to tell you the truth, that's what it has cost me to sort out this business.'

Becky made to interrupt him.

'No, just let me explain. I couldn't bear you despairing like that at the end of Assembly. I tried to find Gemma's body in the shrubs but it had gone. Could have been my cat, I suppose. Never shirks a free meal. But never mind. Something had to be done. So, without thinking very much I got into my car and drove into the city. I knew there was one in the shopping centre because I bought our cat there.'

Becky did manage to intervene at this point. 'Don't tell me you bought another gerbil!'

'Yes, I certainly did! There was only one left. The shopkeeper said he had no idea what gender it was. So, Miss Becky, our little Gemma might now be little Gerald!'

'Oh, goodness me!'

'I wouldn't worry if I were you. Mr. Cheshire was happy enough. I can't see him or his wife and daughter worrying about any gerbil progeny just yet! And look on the bright side. I've saved our bacon, haven't I?'

'Oh, Rob, you certainly have. You will get the tenner, I promise you. But will you make do now with a kiss from me?'

Would he?!!! Becky's brief but heartfelt peck on the cheek made old Rob's day… even week….even ever!

He left the room with a red face and a glow. Becky sat still, staring out of the window, gathering herself for what she hoped would be just an ordinary afternoon, her and her thirty kids.

Before the bell went for afternoon school Rob was there again at the classroom door. He knocked and entered, hands thrust once more into his trouser pockets, a sheepish look on his face.

'I don't know how to tell you this, Miss,' he began.

'If it's the ten pounds, Rob I….'

'No ,no. It's this.'

He took his right hand from his pocket and opened it. There in the palm of his hand was…. a gerbil. Becky stared at it and then at Rob.

Rob was stroking the little creature's head gently. 'I found it on the front door mat of my office. I dunno how it got there really. I can only think my cat must have brought it back. I saw the little thing was moving her legs so I gave her a drink of water and hey presto she started moving around. Not exactly running, but definitely 'with it'.

He looked up at Becky and grinned. 'First there was one, then none, then one again, and now two! I don't know whether to laugh or cry!'

'I suppose it has to be Gemma?' said Becky lifting her eyebrows.

'Well, it's difficult to believe there is a third gerbil hanging around the school waiting to be found, so I reckon we can be absolutely sure….. And I'm absolutely sure what I am going to do! But don't ask me, miss. It's perhaps better you do not know the full details…'

'You are not going to kill it, Rob, are you?' Becky showed genuine alarm.

'No, I'm not, miss. Just let me give you a hint. Mr Cheshire is teaching this afternoon and he has asked me to look after Gemma. Enough said, eh? Gemma will be back….well fed and watered!'

'OK, Rob, enough said…. But what about the 'other Gemma'?'

'No problem there. The Pet Shop allow you to return a pet if you decide against it… within twenty four hours. A sort of 'money-back guarantee', you see. Leave it to me. Just get on with your teaching…. That'll be good for you…. and them.'

He smiled and turned to leave.

'Oh, one other thing. Have you noted that the last time Gemma was in this room you were screaming for me to catch her and bash her… and you were trembling all over? You have not batted an eyelid this time. No shaking at all….I think you might even be able to stroke her.'

And so saying, Rob held out his little bundle of fur. Becky did not hesitate. Rob was right. She felt none of the old anxiety about rodents, no tingling when she thought about running fingers through fur. She took Gemma and stroked her. No reaction, no trembling, not even the slightest shake.
'My, my, we've seen changes today,' said Rb. 'Come on little Gemma,….just one more change.'

JUNE

The Museum's New Collection

This is the knob off the head of the bed of Marie Antoinette,
If you haven't heard anything of this,
You haven't heard anything yet.,,, oomph, tarara, oomph, tarara.

In the Tudor Room we are sure to find Henry Eight's betrothal pledges,
Rumour had it, quite unfounded, that he'd lobbed them over hedges. Tarara.

Here is the cloak that Ralegh used to protect our Good Queen Bess; He
draped it over a puddle to stop her stepping in a mess. Tarara.

You mustn't miss old Charlie's head, struck cruelly from his shoulders,
By Cromwell and his Parliament, a right lot of bounders. Tarara.

And in the old colonial section, wrapped in a cotton rag,
Straight from the Boston Tea Party comes a freshly used tea bag. Tarara.

Here's a paper in the manuscript room, that you might have missed;
Whenever Grieg went CHOPIN' he always took a LISZT…. Tarara,

Because we always think ahead, we've cut a little slack,
So last of all, in 'The Exit Hall', we've added a Union Jack.

Oh, this is the knob off the head of the bed of Marie Antoinette,
If you haven't heard anything of this, you haven't heard anything yet.,,,
oomph, tarara, oomph, tarara.

2nd   When I was President of the European School Heads Association I had the
privilege of inaugurating the Ukrainian school principals association. During
the visit the ESHA delegation was taken to a secondary school in the middle
of a huge army camp near Kiev. I heard a military band in the distance as we
entered the gate.
        'Can I go and watch the parade?' I asked.
        'You are not only watching it,' replied my host. 'You are taking the
salute.'
        And so I did. One year previously these soldiers had been part of the
Soviet Red Army. Now here was a school principal from rural
Northamptonshire acknowledging their salute.

At the end of the march past the commanding officer approached me and said something in Ukrainian. I was told by my host to say 'Tak dyakuyu'. I know I was thanking them, but not sure whether or not I was giving the 1,000 troops a day's leave. I shall never know.

It was an extraordinary moment and such a show of pride at sharing with us their celebration and enjoyment of their newfound freedom. One can only wish the nation all good fortune as any oppressors try to knock the joy out of their lives.

3rd   On Trinity Sunday towards the end of May one year, a vicar gave a sermon on the meaning of the 'Trinity'. It would be long, said the Reverend, because the explanation was complex. But he hoped they would find it very useful to them, enabling them to contemplate the relationship between Gad, the father, Christ the son, and the Holy Spirit. He hoped it would increase their understanding and have a great effect on them.

At the end of the service, as he was saying goodbye to his parishioners, one elderly farmer, who had never been known to say anything about the sermons, shook the vicar's hand vigorously while remarking, 'Very interesting, Vicar. You were right, I did find it useful. When I woke up at the end of your sermon I felt very much netter. Extraordinary! Keep up the good work.'

4th   *There are some situations where understanding where your adversary is coming from may be a matter of life or death! I was once involved in one such confrontation.*

I was in Northern Ireland, sometime before 'the 'Good Friday Agreement'. I was travelling by car between two appointments and my Irish companion decided to show me the views from up in the Mountains of Mourne. We were motoring along a country lane, close to the border with the Republic of Ireland, and just beginning to climb the foothills when suddenly, at a crossroads, numerous men in camouflaged uniforms with grass and weeds poking out of their berets and small packs, rose from the ditches on either side of the car. From their hat badges I gathered that they were British soldiers. I decided that my Irish colleague knew best what to do and so I just sat still.

A soldier motioned me, on the passenger side, to wind down the window. I opened it an inch or so.

'*Stewer poot!*' he shouted thrusting a rifle to within an inch of my head. It was an accent I could not immediately place, or quite understand. I think it could have been honed on Tyneside or Clydeside, neither of which areas was I familiar with..

I wound down the window…. slowly…. and poked my head out.
'Did you say, *'Stay put'* or *'Step out'*? In the present circumstance, sergeant, it is rather important to get it right.'
He smiled…..We survived….

5th   *Continuing with the 'communication' theme. The importance of knowing your audience'…. understanding where they are coming from, is just as important as finding expression for your own demands and concerns, as this little anecdote demonstrates.*

The legendary Scandinavian king, King Hagbard, had been out a-plundering with his brother Haki and needed to recruit further human lambs to the slaughter. He travelled round the villages making impassioned pleas.

One day he arrived at this little village in upper Sweden, gathered all the menfolk in the village square, and from his horse waved his sword and exhorted them to join 'the good fight'.

'I want men who will rape, plunder, pillage, murder, massacre and otherwise cause mayhem… and have a good time…..

The crowd greeted this with wild applause and cheering

King Hagbard continued, warming to his theme….. 'I see that you are just such men…. warriors….. men of steel, men with guts… who are loyal, brave, ruthless, not afraid of wounds, not afraid to die….in my just cause …. …….. so join me NOW!....

Wild cheering again….

Any questions?' cried the king waving his sword over his head.

There was silence. Then a hand went up at the back…. An old man spoke.

'Do you provide free dental treatment?'

6th   *Bringing this theme closer to home here is another take on the variation of perspectives.*

A long-serving and long-suffering teacher at a staff meeting that had already gone on for two hours suddenly remarked,

'Principal, if you were just to make a decision sometime it may not change the fortunes of the world, or shake the national economy, or even affect the country's Gross Domestic Product…. but it would enable us all to go home.'

7th   One of the most telling little stories illustrating the importance of 'the *point of view of the participants'* was told to a seminar of young headteachers to stop them bleating about how their staff were continually arguing with them about the reforms they were intent on introducing. The lecturer listened politely and attentively and then said,

    'There was once a baby elephant who was suddenly confronted by a little mouse, grey like him, but ever so tiny. Very perplexing. He had never seen such a creature before.

    'My goodness….. you are very small and thin…' he said, shaking his trunk in disbelief.

    The little mouse drew himself up, puffed out his chest, put his paws firmly on his waist in indignation, and yelled back, *'Well, I've been poorly!... and anyway Fatso, seems to me you should be on a diet….!'*

8th   After a virtual stalemate in a Danish referendum on whether to leave the European Union or not, a Danish delegate told a Conference of European Business Leaders, that you people in Great Britain enjoy Hamlet, the Prince of Denmark, saying, *'To be or not to be, that is the question'.* Well. here in Denmark itself we have different expression, 'To be or not to be, that *is the answer."*

9th   One of the most perplexing excuse notes I ever received was one that informed me that:
'Billy was in the toilet and fell over a stool…'
I didn't query it.

10th   I was mountain-biking, for the first time in my life, after some fruitless protests…. with a group of colleagues in the Alps. We had ascended a steep hill where I learned that 'mountain-biking' actually consists of scrambling up steep dirt tracks carrying a bike on your back. I looked forward to the descent….
Three hours of going up finally led to a going-down. While descending an equally steep downward slope at a steady but impressive speed, a Belgian group suddenly appeared over the brow in front of us.
I did not panic, as some of my pals still claim. I simply pulled on what in the UK is the rear brake but which in France is not. It is the front brake.
The front of the bicycle came to an abrupt halt …. I did not.
I sailed over the handlebars, severely scraping my nose and cheeks. I survived that with reasonable equanimity, but then the bike, still upright, slowly rolled over the top of me embedding tyre marks in my brow and causing substantial damage to my nose.
Even then I might have laughed the whole thing off, but for the Belgian group to a man and woman crying, '*Bravo….!..... Encore!'*…. while at the same time my own colleagues broke into uncontrollable laughter.
I consider that to be unsociable behaviour – and have never stopped upbraiding my friends about it…. and I have never ridden a mountain bike again.

11th   Mrs. Mollie Coddle, School Lunchtime Supervisor, reported to a Deputy Head that while patrolling the playground she saw a large boy was hitting a much smaller boy.
'I tried to stop him by talking gently to him,' she said, 'as I was taught on my recent conflict resolution course that you ram….. However, the boy just stuck his finger up and said 'b…. off' and then hit me, causing me to call for assistance. … Mr. Great and Mr.Tuff held the boy down. He then said he would stop hitting the little boy.
I suggest you reconsider your conflict resolution guidance…..'

Tree

This poem surely fails to be
as lovely as that tall beech tree,
displayed against a clear blue sky.
Magnificent! But here is why
despair creeps in when winds are strong -
I know this fussiness is wrong –
and flowers and nuts and leaves all fall
on our side of the old brick wall.

Its splendour in the early spring -
when leaves uncurl, and blackbirds sing -
is marred as each bud's sticky sheath
flutters to pathways underneath.
(Above the tree stands strong and proud
whilst I below curse long and loud.)
They fill the pond and drift around
and carpet all the new-swept ground.

So beds are raked, stonework made clean
and soon the garden looks pristine.
The breeze has dropped, the sun is out -
I wonder what I swore about.
But lo! What's this? Flowers downward drift -
such blossoms are but Nature's gift –
I grab a broom, and start to brush,
and wish that Nature weren't so lush.

There is a conflict, and some stress
in Nature versus Tidiness.
The Spotted Woodpecker's decline
Is blamed on habits such as mine;
no rotting wood to forage in –
it's swept up, put into the bin.
So when the nuts, then leaves should fall
and I rush out to clear them all,
perhaps good Fagus, God of Beech,
will stay my hand before I reach
for brooms and brushes, *house*work tools;

make me observe some Eco rules.
Jill Rhodes

An Apple A Day

Inactivity did not sit easily with the Stubbs Walks kids.. It was five years into the Second World War. Fathers, uncles, brothers were away at the war or nursing injuries at home. By now nervous energy, ceaseless schoolwork and hours of play hid the heartache they all felt but could not articulate. There was only so much running about as cops and robbers, cowboys and Indians, or German and British air aces, that young legs and lungs could take, and so a prolonged sprawl on the park benches was necessary.

In addition here was only a short span of time before boredom set in again and, for Charlie at least, that span had been reached. Something exciting had to happen soon. He lay with his feet drawn up on the bench, looking at the fence of the High School field that backed onto the Walks. He noticed that a couple of branches loaded with large green apples were overhanging the fence. That gave him an idea. He straightened up, then sat up and announced.

'Let's go picking apples.'

The gang all stared at him. What had got into 'the Chief?

Charles Short, nearly-10 year old Charlie, was after all the leader, the self-appointed leader of 'The Kids', mainly because he volunteered himself and no-one else did.

Then there was Gary Gough, known as Gee Gee, also nearly ten. Adults thought his nickname came from his initials GG, but the gang knew it had originated when Gary kept on telling them that he was 'slow' - slow at thinking and slow at making up his mind. 'But I get there eventually, my mum keeps on telling me,' insisted Gary. And so he became *'Get there eventually Gary'* – alias Gee Gee. He had been known as this for so long that even the other members of the gang were forgetting how it first came about.

The next eldest, Pinkie Pat Evans, was from the outdoor pub. Only take-away bottles and bring-your-own jugs of a thin brown ale were dispensed there from the back kitchen. At nine – going ten - Pat was, you might say, self-sufficient…. some would say 'self-centred' and some 'wild and wayward'. But she wouldn't agree. She just loved life, the great adventure, full of things you could do that people told you not to. No-one disputed she was a bit of a tomboy, who stood up for herself and was not averse to stretching a point or two – like tucking her skirt up in her knickers to do cartwheels and handstands, which she did frequently – especially when boys were around, because none of them could do these gymnastics as well as Pat. And they did not have pink knickers to show off like Pat. She was Pinkie Pat, and she loved it. Her parents did not.

But Hattie – now there was someone who was going places – a born king-maker, with just the disadvantage at that time of being a girl. Harriet Mason, daughter of pottery modeller dad and ceramic painter mum, was rather clever and knew it. She played hard and with a cunning none of the others could match. She just liked instinctively to work in the background, influencing front-man Charlie, but not wanting to take the limelight. Charlie was always wary of this little nine-year-old.

Hattie found her voice first.

'Just one problem, Charlie. There are no apples in Stubbs Walks.' She slithered back down on the bench. 'So how do think we are going to pick any?'

'Ah,' replied Charlie, 'Maybe not exactly *in* the Walks, but look over there. Loads of them.' He pointed to the orchard over the fence. 'I bet there are thousands more in the orchard there.'

The gang followed the direction of his wagging finger.

'Charlie,' said Hattie reprovingly, 'That's the high school headmaster's garden! You know it would be stealing. And we may get caught.'

'Well, that's all you know…. It is *not* 'stealing'…. I know it is called 'scrumping'. That's different… and everyone does it. Read the *Just William* books.'

'I don't read books about stupid boys.'

'They are not stupid books.'

Hattie put her hand up to stop his growing agitation.

'I didn't say they were…. I said William was stupid, just as stupid as Billy Bunter in *The Magnet stories.*'

'I agree. Bunter is stupid,' admitted Charlie, 'But he doesn't scrump apples. He isn't adventurous enough for that…. Anyway, I thought we could get some apples….and just eat a few and then sell the rest, and give the money to that Mayor's Fund the head was telling us about last week. Do you remember Shirty Shelton said we would get army ranks depending on how much we raised for people made destitute by war? Five bob and we'll be majors; one pound and we'll be generals! Sounds a good idea to me. Selling apples is better than asking parents for money again, isn't it?'
Pat thought it was time to stop Charlie's flow, She now piped up.

'All right. I agree. I fancy being a general. I'll come with you. It could be fun'

'And if Pink…if Pat is going, then I will go, too,' said Gee Gee. 'And I don't mind which rank I get. In fact, I think I prefer to stay a soldier. I didn't like being that German Hitler bloke this morning.'

'OK. Let's go then,' said Charlie. Then turning to Hattie. 'As chief of the gang I give you permission, Hattie, to stay as rear-guard.'

'Yer what! You don't order me about when we are not playing games, Charlie Short. I decide myself what I do. And I may….or may not, follow you.' Hattie put her hands on her hips and glared.

'Suit yourself,' said Charlie with a shrug. He did not really know how to deal with the strong-willed Hattie. 'Come on then. Let's get through the broken fence behind the bushes.'
It may have been 'breaking and entering', but no actual 'breaking in' was necessary as the wooden fence had disintegrated in parts, and 'entering' was not a problem.
Once inside they stood in awe of a bumper crop of apples, Bramleys and Granny Smiths. Charlie knew what these types looked like as they were the best-sellers in the family corner shop, run by his mum and invalid dad.

'Cor,' exclaimed Gary. 'How are we going to collect this lot, Charlie?'

'I'll run home and get some bags,' said a voice from behind them. They whirled round in fright.
It was only Hattie. Curiosity bordering on bravado had got the better of her.

'Pick what you can and put them by the fence. We'll collect them from there,' she whispered. Then she was off. Charlie smiled to himself. 'Good old Hattie. She's a real sport when it comes to it.'

'Right then, men…er… man…and girl, let's get cracking.'
The three of them set to, picking the fallen apples from the ground and stuffing them into their pockets, or in Pinkie Pat's case into the skirt of her dress and down her knickers.

They scampered back and forth to the fence, and when Charlie judged that there were no unbruised ones left he began tugging them from the lower branches. Each of them selected a tree, but it was hard going, so much so that Pat stopped and said, 'How about you shake the branches, Gee Gee, and we will pick up the apples that fall.'

'Good idea, Pin… Pat,' said Charlie, though he wished he had thought of it.

Gary shook the first branch with inordinate force and the apples flew off in all directions, one of them clonking Charlie on the head.

'Ouch,' cried the injured chieftain. 'You daft b…..' He got no further. There was a loud yell from the groundsman's shed on the other side of the orchard.

'Heh, you lot! What do you think you are doing? I'll get you, you little blighters.'

They could see a large figure lumbering towards them. He was hampered by having to use a walking stick but he was still moving at a surprising pace.

'Crikey,' cried Gary.

'It's the Red Baron,' cried Charlie, not caring at that moment for historical exactitude. The First World War German air ace, the Red Baron, was an all-time favourite in their games..

'This way,' he yelled pointing towards the back of the Headmaster's house on the other side of the trees.

Pinkie was already ahead of them, still carrying an apple in each hand. Charlie, relishing the chase, quickly overtook her but came to an abrupt halt when the backdoor of the house was flung open and there on the steps above them stood the man himself, tall, stern, imperious, jet black hair flowing behind him - and in striped pyjamas, a brown raincoat….and a black academic gown draped over the top! And not only that – wearing flying boots for slippers.

It was the Headmaster. He pointed a crooked finger at the gang.

'Stop right there!' he ordered. They did.

Pat let the apples slip from her hands. Gary kept muttering,

'O crikey, O blimee.'

Charlie found himself caring less about the romantic Red Baron, seeing instead a wounded second world-war soldier and current head groundsman bearing down on them from behind – with a stick. And in front of them stood the equally frightening figure of the headmaster, looking for all the world like a Stag beetle about to launch himself from a windowsill.

The fast-hobbling Red Baron arrived on the scene and grabbed Charlie and Gary round the back of their necks. Charlies had never felt a grip so strong.

'What is going on here?' asked the beetle wafting his arm at them.

'O God,' said Gary in a small but clearly audible voice.

'Not quite God, young man,' came the stentorian reply. 'But it might be the closest you ever get to him if I don't get to the bottom of this. Now, who are you?' he demanded pointing at Gary.

'Monty,' said GG completely flustered. The beetle's hand shook and his mouth twitched.

'So…. I suppose you are General Eisenhower then, eh?' he roared, turning and waving at Charlie. Before Charles could open his mouth Gary pointed straight at Pat,

'No, he's not, she is, sir. Charlie is Biggles…. This afternoon…you know, the ace pilot in the Biggles books.'

There was a complete silence, for what seemed an age to Charlie. 'O Lor',' he thought. 'That's done it. Now we've added lying to stealing.'

'Well, I'm simply Doctor Sweeney, not as world- famous as you three, but just as well-known round here as you, Field Marshall.'

He turned his attention to the hapless Charlie.

'Biggles!....you would not like things to be stolen from your home, would you, eh?. Well, this is my home, Biggles, and I do not take kindly to having my apples stolen.'

'We haven't stolen any, sir. They are all still in your garden,' pleaded Charlie. 'Anyway, we were only scrumping them. For a good cause, you see.'

'Really? And what might that be?'

Charles explained that they wanted to contribute to the Mayor's Fund..

'Hm. How old are you, eh?'

'Nine, all of us,' answered Charlie, not adding the 'going- ten' bit that he usually did.

Another 'Hm', a pause, and then the Head turned to the groundsman.

'Mr. Jackson, do you know Monty's impersonator and Biggles here? And what do you think we should do?'

The groundsman released the boys' necks.

'Yes, I know who these little beggars are, headmaster. This is Charles Short, and this is Gary Gough.' He re-applied his grip to the back of their necks. And this is Patricia Evans. They are all from Castle Street over there. I have had trouble before with people stealing apples and pears from your orchard, sir. I expect it was this lot. We could make an example of them and hand them over to the police.'

Dr. Sweeney scratched his chin.

'I think he has a point there, even two points, perhaps.

'What,' cried Charlie, now thoroughly alarmed. '…. For trying to do some good? And we haven't ever scrumped before.'

Doctor Sweeney eyed the gang.

'It is certainly wrong to steal. You know that, don't you?' he demanded, still retaining his stentorian tone. But without waiting for an answer he added, 'You might be young and you may not have transgressed before, but I expect an apology from you here and now, and a promise not to do it ever again. Now each of you apologise and promise in turn.'

They did.

The Head's face softened just a little.

'Well now, I admire what you are trying to do, but this is not the way to do it. I'll tell you what we are going to do…. Mr. Jackson is going to fetch his wheelbarrow and you are going to load it with as many apples as you can pick and take away. You will then come back as many times as you like till exactly four o'clock this afternoon and collect more. But, as punishment, you must carry away at least ten loads. But you must not, and I repeat must not, climb any of the trees. You can only have what you can reach. Understood?'

They understood and muttered their thanks.

'What about their parents, headmaster?' asked Mr. Jackson. 'Shouldn't they be informed?'

'Good point, Jackson. But I am going to leave it to their consciences. They can decide whether to tell their parents what has happened.

'Do you understand that as well, eh?' The headmaster, now looking more human addressed Charlie who was clearly the leader.

'I dunno about the others, but I always tell my parents everything,' said Charlie with some defiance in his book. 'We are a loving Christian family, see.' He had heard the vicar refer to this once and it had impressed him. He thought now might be a good time to resurrect it.

'Well, be that as it may. Off you go now to your work. Mr. Jackson will keep me informed on progress.'

' With that the headmaster drew his coat round his body, transmogrifying back into a beetle, and disappeared through his back door.

The Head Groundsman, alias legendary air ace, rubbed his hands. 'Right. Now you will do as I tell you. You two, start picking up apples and, Gary, you fetch the barrow with me.

There was no arguing with Mr. Jackson. They recognised the value of just getting on with it. As Charlie and Pat picked up fallenapples they heard a whisper from the bushes. Hattie was back.'

'Pssh. Have you been captured by the enemy?'

'Well sort of,' replied Pat in a whisper. 'To tell yer the truth, I 'aven't got a clue what's going on. The 'eadmaster has got us working t' clear 'is garden of apples. Then I think we can go 'ome.'

'Working on his garden!' cried Hattie in indignation. ''E's got no right to do that. It's slave labour, that is. There's a law against it. My dad says workin' for posh people is always slave labour. And a a grammar school 'eadmaster is definitely posh - definitely.'

'Oy you, girl.' The groundsman's voice cut in from just beyond the bushes. 'Is that Hattie Mason, eh? Come here. I want a word with you.'

But Hattie had slithered through the undergrowth and had gone, whispering, 'I'll tell the police.'

It was no good Charlie crying out, 'No!'…. She'd already gone.

Jackson, no longer 'Mister' in Charlie's book, still kept his hand firmly on the Chief and his temporary deputy Gee Gee. Pat walked behind dejectedly, with two more bags of apples hanging down loosely. Before they got to the shop Jackson bent down and whispered to the boys.

'Just you wait till you get a place at the High School. I'll be watching for you, and I may have a gammy leg but I have A1 eye-sight, see.' And he opened his eyes and rolled them round.

Gee Gee thought he looked daft but Charlie shuddered involuntarily. Jackson looked sinister to him. He decided there and then that wild horses would not drag him into seeking a place at the High School. Gary was much happier.

'No chance of me getting a grammar school place,' he said later. 'Too slow, you know.'

Outside Shorts Stores on the corner of Castle Street, Jackson addressed all three of them.

'Right. In you go Charlie Short, and tell your parents all about it and then come back to the Headmaster's garden. I'm taking Gary and Patricia home and then back to the orchard. I expect to see the fourth gangster, Harriet Mason, there, too. See you in ten minutes. OK?'

Charles sighed, took a deep breath and stepped inside. His mum was behind the counter. No sign of dad. He had been invalided out of the army just a month ago and needed to rest his shattered leg.

'I was wondering where you had got to,' said his mum brightly. That did not last long, as Charles explained what had happened, putting the best gloss he could on the debacle, and emphasising they were wanting to support the mayor and help the wartime destitute. That was the noble ideal. Apples were merely a means. He was about to explain the reward of army ranks, but decided there was no real need. That might be confusing.

Luckily Mrs. Short was minded to be sympathetic. She did not tell her son that she, and her husband, David, had both scrumped apples in their youth – from the same place. She tut-tutted about how the Shorts had always done 'the right thing' and kept on the right side of the law. She knew that was the right thing to say.

'You'll take note of other people's feelings now, won't you, Charles. Then we'll say no more about it. Get off and finish the picking. I must say there's a huge number of apples. Dad will certainly put them on display in the shop, and any money he gets for them will go to the Mayor's Fund. I will make some apple puree and apple juice from some of them and sell those as well. How many do you think there will be?'

'Hundreds, mum. At least ten barrow loads full, even after Gary and Pat have their share. And Hattie has already got some, too.'

'Goodness me! We'll be selling jars right up to Christmas. I don't know if the Mayor's Fund is open that long, but we'll find a good cause. Off you go.'

'Will you be telling dad, mum?'

Mrs. Short contemplated the request. 'He'll have to know where so many apples come from, but I am sure he will understand your good intentions. Don't worry.'

But Charlie Short did worry. Up to then he had not faced a stranger giving him a right talking to. He was not used to being taken to task at all. His mother and father were loving people and believed in talking to their children, not hitting them. So, no-one had gripped his neck like Mr. Jackson. More facts of life were revealing themselves to young Charles Short.

And the facts revealed themselves a bit more when on his second trip back with a load of apples he found local bobby, P.C. Embley, talking to both his mother and now his father in the shop along with Hattie Mason. He couldn't run away because he had gone through the shop door with his barrow. He could only stand and stare.

'Is this the boy what captured you, Harriet?' asked P.C. Embley.

'No. I told you! He was the one captured. There were these two big bullies grabbing hold of him and beating him up. I saw it all happening. One of them called him names. That's terrible isn't it? Are you all right now, Charlie?'

'His name's Charles,' said his mother rather haughtily.

His father held up his hands. 'Whoa, whoa. This is getting out-of-hand. Charles, you and Harriet wait in the shop. Constable, just come into the sitting room for a moment and we will sort it out.'

And, of course, dad did sort it out – much to the amusement of the constable who had been asked to give the Castle Street Kids a 'little talking to'.

That was something else that Charlie did not like either. It meant five 'talking-tos' by three strangers and his mum and dad in *one* morning.

'Could be a record,' he thought ruefully.

That same evening Dr. Bertram and Mrs. Cynthia Sweeney were guests at dinner with the school's chairman of the governing body, Hugo, and his wife. Daphne.

As she put down her spoon on her empty dessert dish and wiped her mouth on the linen serviette, Cynthia became ecstatic.

'That's the nicest apple charlotte I have ever eaten, Daphne. The apples were simply delicious….where on earth did you get them from?

'From Short's Stores, Cynthia. Jackson hasn't picked this year's garden crop, so I was lucky to find these. But they were expensive….really expensive. Mrs Short told me they were very hard to get hold of.'

'Well, They are as good as the ones in our garden, I expect…'

well nearly as good as our garden Bramley's aren't they, Bertram?' said Mrs. Sweeney, turning to her husband.

Bertram Sweeney smiled. 'Yes, dear….nearly.'

14th *On dull mornings teachers can rely on pupils to get them smiling. Here are more bons mots.*
'The advantages of growing plants in a greenhouse are it stops them getting the wind.'
'One breed of cattle is the Little Big Horn.'
'This week we were listening to music by the well known French composer, Bidet.'

15th To get a 'B' Teaching Certificate in 1899 a candidate had to :
1. Distinguish between collateral and co-ordinate sentences and give examples:
2 Mention any changes which have taken place in Latin words passing into English through French.
A sobering thought!

16th Anne was the wife of a country vicar. She helped out in the parish where she could, tea and cakes etc. She particularly enjoyed anything musical, having a moderate ability to 'tickle the ivories'. She liked to cover for the regular organist when necessary.

Mary, a local elderly widowed lady met and fell in love with Bob, a retired farmer, also a widow of some years. They became engaged and planned a very traditional church wedding, requesting that Anne play the organ. Anne agreed and practiced at length the lovely Wagner 'Here Comes the Bride' from Lohengrin, and Mendelssohn's popular 'Wedding March' from 'A Midsummer Night's Dream'

Anne asked John to signal to her when he saw the bride arriving. She was playing some simple bits of Handel and glancing over her shoulder for the right moment.

Eventually Mary arrived escorted up the aisle by a smart gentleman (whom she assumed to be her brother or friend) There had been no signal from John, (she would deal with him later) She moved the swell to maximum and confidently struck up with 'Here Comes the Bride' and the whole congregation rose to their feet, turning round to look. As the couple walked forward, there were gasps and mumblings. As Anne looked again over her shoulder she saw clearly that this was not Mary but her sister.

The bride did arrive moments late but Anne's 'Here Comes the Bride' no longer had the verve and lilt of five minutes ago.

She apologised, of course, but the bride assured her she had no need to.... 'After all it gave the congregation something to talk about at the reception...' Anne never played for a wedding again, but was in great demand for her funeral music.

17th *More unintended humour from school examination papers.*
Q. What kind of fish is a kipper?
A. One that swims.
OR
In France you can get your frog's legs rare, medium or well done.
OR
In those days was a gutter in the middle of the street where all the slobs and undesirables were thrown.

18th *And some more:*
'Inflation is a time when lots of babies are born.'
'A Mansfield spade is broad at the top and sharp at the bottom so that you can push it into the sod easier.'
'There are two forms of sugar, granulated and castrated.'
'Hertz Van Rental played for Holland in the World Cup.'
And taken from a letter from a French pen-friend) .... .
'I like very much athletics and often have the runs.'

19th *It is the comic triumph of the English language to stem from so many sources and to be prone to comic double-entendres!*
Teacher: Name two classes that existed in 16th century Elizabethan England.
Simeon: History and Religious Education

20th **Teacher**. What have Gouda, Edam and Gorgonzola in common?
Simeon again. They all played in the European Cup.

21st **Maths Teacher**: At your friend Billy's birthday party there are six slices of cake, one slice on six of the nine plates on the table. What are the chances of getting a plate with a slice of cake on it?
Sheila: None, if Bomber Bates has been invited.

22nd   **The Actress and the Bishop**

The actress and the bishop were walking down the Strand,
reflecting on their working lives - and both were rather grand.
How good to see you once again, it's been at least ten years
and much has happened in that time, not least in our careers.'
The Bishop gave a modest smile, 'We both have our vocations, you've trod
the boards to great acclaim, awards, standing ovations
We've laboured in the vineyard as curate, vicar, rural dean;
and that is where I thought I'd stay – promotion unforeseen.'

'With me work came in fits and starts, with endless weeks of 'resting
I must admit to feeling low – an actor's life is testing.
But then a breakthrough came at last - Ophelia, then Kate;
most critics thought me quite sublime, my future prospects great.'

'I too have had despondent sloughs,' the bishop gave a sigh,
I must admit that now and then I've wondered how and why.
Dog collars, cassocks, PCCs, so many grim privations,
the rectories with leaking pipes; the job has its frustrations.'

'Performing in the provinces - imagine how things were;
those dressing rooms, the b&bs, I'm quite a connoisseur.
Of course, nowadays I get the best, the hotels are five star.
it's flashing lights and interviews, champagne and caviar.'

'How lovely,', said the bishop, remembering 'Bring and Share',
the quiches and the sausage rolls; fine dining was most rare.
'Though since my elevation, the conditions have improved,
requests to lecture on cruise ships, I really am quite moved.'

The actress yawned, and looked away; the subject rather boring
'I have to move on now, you know, my public's so adoring.
Impatient fans awaiting me, the stage door will be busy -
but first I'll pop into the bar; a glass of something fizzy.'

'And when the call from Lambeth came, I was quite unprepared;
Pull up a pew,' the Primate said, 'and please don't look so scared.
The vote in Synod, as you know, gives women the green light
and, Lucy, you are just the one to carry on the fight."

They parted near to Soho, the actress waved goodbye;
'Fancy old Luce, a bishop now, her prospects all awry.
She could have been a lawyer - her future so much brighter -
but now she's stuck with gaiters, cope, a crook, large ring and mitre.'
Jill Rhodes

23rd As the result of a bad telephone line and scant knowledge of the classical
music repertoire a local newspaper reported that the town choir's
programme on Saturday included *"The Flight of The Bumblebee"* by *Rip
Your Corsets Off.*

24th Our golden retriever I introduced you to earlier, Boris, continued to ne a
sweetie, loving to be loved and loving to love others, be they animal or
human. He was naturally fast and vigorous, relishing chases and being
chased. He was particularly fond of with great speed at anyone he saw in the
local park. There were usually shouts and barks of pleasure.
  But what amused me most and me the greatest pleasure was when I
watched a group of rough looking yobs, who had been rather raucous for an
hour or so, running for their lives being chased by a happy golden retriever
who was loving every moment. The faster they ran the more he yelped and
barked….. such fun…..

25th My old pal, Dai, is a wholehearted Welshman from the north of that principality. He spoke only Welsh in his youth and did not learn English till in his teens. Needless to say he had, and has, some conflicts with the nuances of the language. In particular he has never grasped the meaning and provenance of English proverbs. They tend to get mixed up – in a quite delightful way…… so subtly that you have to stop and consider whether he has got it right , or not.

For example, one of his favourites is: *'I've got a bone to grind with you……!'* and another is, *'let lying dogs sleep.'* They seem so natural that they make you pause… while another of his gems - *'if he doesn't watch it the smile will be on the other foot'* is clearly a mutilation, but so delightful that you wish it was a true proverb…. as indeed you do when you hear Dai intone in all earnestness that *'Many hands spoil light broth'.*

26th The apotheosis of Dai's struggle with correct usage came at a lunch in a Cambridge college Masters Lodge when he was a guest of the Master and his wife.
Dai, already an international athlete at 19, had a hearty appetite, but even he was beaten by the huge lunch. When asked if he had enjoyed it and would he like a second helping of pud he rolled his eyes, patted his stomach,
'No, I can't take any more….. I've had a dearth of it, and am really fed up….'
The Master's wife had to go and lie down.

27th   An old friend told me that at the 450-year-old school where he was head, they decided to scrap the old-fashioned single desks with graffiti-infested lids in favour of easily movable small tables.   One teacher immediately lamented:
'What a shame! Towards the end of a lesson, with five minutes left, I used to say 'Carry on reading your desks.'

28th *Taken from another insurance claim form:*
I slowed down at the roundabout and had almost stopped when the back end of the car I front banged into me.

29th *A famous reply to a request for a reference. It reflects a world-weariness with 'management'.*

Dear Colleague,

You ask my opinion of Ms. Freda Inglenook's contribution to the development of this organisation. I can tell you with all the enthusiasm I can muster that her contribution has been indescribable.

30th **You Are Never Too Young to Learn**

Management training, Management development, Management degrees, research into Management...... plenty of such help and support these days..... but in the early 1970s when I became a headteacher and was deemed, to my astonishment. To be a 'manager'.... there was no such luxuries. It was 'seat-of-the-pants' stuff and you got help from wherever you could.

I realised early on that the best and most reliable help I could call on came fifteen years previously, from my two years' National Service in an infantry regiment.

My 'trainer', my lecturer, my mentor, was my platoon sergeant, whose fate it was to draw me in the lottery of life, when I joined my infantry regiment in 1957 as a newly commissioned second lieutenant. We served – and in his case, suffered, together in the British Army of the Rhine (BAOR) during the 'Cold War' years.

Think of it.... a teenage officer leading a platoon, a group of up to forty young regular or national service soldiers, with a second-in-command, the sergeant, a thirty-year-old veteran of the battle of Arnhem in September 1944. When he was barely twenty he had fought in one of the most savage battles of the Second World War....

Me.... I was just out of the school sixth form and a sixteen-week officer-training course. He was supposed to, and did, take orders from me.... but I took advice and know-how from him.

I learned from him three very important principles that were down-to-earth and straight to the point. These are what stayed with me as my bottom-line personal management guidance for the rest of my working life.

The first lesson came on a large exercise involving the whole of the British Army of the Rhine. It was just after the 'Suez Crisis' when some of the British Army were engaged in skirmishing in Egypt. We wee told that we might have to join in, or alternatively, go to face crises in Cyprus or Africa or Malaya. We needed all the training and advice we could get.

This was a preparatory exercise…. It made a change from imaginary battles against the armies of the Soviet block to our east.

During the big exercise the battalion was placed along the bank of a tributary to the mighty River Weser. We were going to practice paddling our flimsy little wood and canvas craft across the water and then 'attack the 'enemy' on the opposite bank.

My platoon sergeant took me aside.

'*Listen 'ere, sir'*, he muttered to me, '*I don't want any 'eroics from you. I had enough rescuing gung-ho subalterns during the war. Put your revolver away and your Sen gun on your back and just let us blokes get on with the job we are trained to do, right?'*

'*Right.'* There was no disagreement from me.

Luckily, I never had to test this theory in action, but it was great advice. Forever more it was ingrained in me that if people are well trained, expert at their jobs, and raring to go, then they should be trusted to get on with their work. Teachers and Teacher support staff are no different from soldiers in that respect.

The second lesson came when my platoon was dug in on a hillside '*somewhere in Germany',* overlooking the River Elbe, the border between 'us', the West and 'them', the East.

We had been there for three days and nights, freezing cold under the single woollen blanket that was still the standard issue in the British Army…..doing precisely nothing.

Sometimes our rations were cooked behind the lines and brought forward….. h, if you were lucky. But often you carried your own tins of stew and vegetables and packets of biscuits, called 'composite rations' or 'compo', and you either heated them in your mess tin via a little throw-away stove, or you ate them cold. It was quite normal to eat our breakfasts of bacon egg and porridge all together in the same mess ti! The other mess tin was for tea. A tin mug was actually part of a soldier's kit but many considered this to be just added weight and left it behind.

My sergeant, being an 'old soldier' knew how to 'acquire' things…. and things knew how to find him….straight into his pocket.

I, on the other hand, was far too green to know how to intervene, and in any case it was all done with panache and savoir faire. Usually we all benefited from his antics anyway.

And so, on this particular night my batman (a sort of servant and wireless operator) was heating up his and my fodder in our trench as best he could, while I crawled from trench to trench seeing how the rest were faring. I was suddenly aware of the smell of delicious hot food unlike any I had experienced before. It was coming from my sergeant's trench in my rear, the traditional place for the platoon sergeant who would have to take over if the platoon commander was incapacitated. I crawled over and peered down.

There was the good sergeant lying in a thick kapok sleeping bag eating from AN American self-heating tin of sausages. He had profited again from his cultivated friendship with our American infantry neighbours! *'Sergeant,'* I muttered plaintively, *'I'm supposed to be the officer around here. Don't I get any?'*

He looked up from the warmth of his bag waved a fork at me and growled – slowly and deliberately with a slight nod of the head, and in a North Staffordshire accent that cannot be replicated in print,

'No offence, sir, but any fool can be uncomfortable!...

Perhaps I should have bridled, but I could not help breaking out in a huge grin. It was another unforgettable lesson.

His final lesson came on the same exercise. In the middle of the night I was ordered to take a fighting patrol of some twenty soldiers to 'attack' the defences of Brigade Headquarters which we knew was in a wood just over the top of the hill about a mile away opposite our position. The Brigade HQ Defence Platoon was made up of some infantry soldiers and some semi-soldier refugees from the Eastern Block who were drafted into the British Army to serve in various non-combatant or sentry/guard duties. Usually they wore a navy blue uniform.

Our orders were to leave at twilight, get there before dark and take one of the defenders prisoner during the night.

I plotted a circuitous route just under the ridge of our hill and down a gully which we could just discern in the distance and then up the other side through a wood of small trees and over the top to our target. So, having checked weapons and kit, to ensure nothing jangled, off we went.

Now, actual terrain is never the same as it appears on a map, or even as it appears from a mile away! The small wood of trees turned out to have dense clinging undergrowth. Progress was slow. In the gathering gloom I could see down below us a green sward which ran right up to the start of the final hill we had to climb. I made a rapid decision. I stopped the patrol and signalled to them to go down the hill and across the field. We accomplished the first part, going down the hill, easily, but then our troubles began.

The green sward turned out to be green slime over a bog! Gradually we all began to sink in, to the waist. My sergeant struggled from the back to come up alongside me. He was not a happy bunny. Being somewhat shorter than me he was up to his chin in slime.

'*I'll say just one thing to you, sir,*' he gurgled, pointing yet another finger at me.

'*Time spent on reconnaissance is never wasted!*'

Indeed it is not. I have never forgotten that principle.

JULY

"Some human said recorders had gone out of fashion."

1st   It was the custom of St. Thingies School to oblige all Years 7 to 9 pupils t watch, and dutifully applaud, the annual School First Team cricket XI versus The Old Boys.

It was also the custom of the English Department on the following day to set all Year 9 pupils an essay on the glories of the national game. It may have taken nearly a century in coming but one girl, not normally a rebel but driven on that day by some primeval force, wrote:

'Watching paint dry is in my experience ten times more exciting than watching cricket. It is truly the most boring of past-times. (It is often mis-described as a sport.) It begins slowly, gets slower, pauses when a batsman is out and stops for a tea break when the players are exhausted with doing nothing. It is enlivened only by incomprehensible shouts and grunts, takes five hours (Test Matches five days!) and usually ends as it started with no winner.

There is no more to be said.'

2nd   **Parent of a prospective pupil**: 'Head, I understand that your school has a strong policy on drugs.'

Headteacher: 'Absolutely. I can assure you, all our pupils can get anything they want We cater for all their needs…..'

3rd   Mr. Thomas Wott, History teacher, wrote a note ithe Incident Book:

Incident: My right-hand inadvertently hit Tracy Tallon while I was demonstrating how Hitler's forces had swept through Belgium in 1940.

Result: I dislocated a finger. (No injury to Tracy, who said she was used to it)

4th

Rustic Ruminations: Sheep

Sheep bleat plaintively long and loud,
Mooching slowly like a summer woolly cloud.
Racks of lambs In mint condition,
Leap up and down as is their tradition,
Fashionable cuddly sturdy white jumpers
Playing leaping, chasing and bumpers….
While muscular rams with energy to burn,
Chase around trying to make a ewe turn!.

Checking Farjeon's Cricket Bag

Herbert Farjeon's mortal innings closed over 75 years ago. This great cricket raconteur campaigned all his life for certainty in the Laws of Cricket. It is a fitting tribute to assess how successful his mission has been. After World War Two the MCC clarified who was *out* when two batsmen are lying prone equidistant from each wicket, a dilemma that had occupied Farjeon greatly between the wars. The MCC is to be congratulated.

Less clear is the MCC's response to Farjeon's niggle where a batsman hits a full toss with extreme force, splitting it in half. 'If one half sails over the boundary for an apparent six; and the other half is caught by the bowler, *'Is it a six? Or out caught?'* he asked.

My friend Max, a cricket guru if ever there was one, was certain that the ball is dead as soon as it split. I do not possess that level of conviction. The Laws are disconcertingly silent on this point. I suspect the umpires will seize the way out offered by Law 20.1.2 and determine that the fielding side and both batsmen at the wicket have ceased to regard it as in play. That would be a relief….

But what if one of them says they do not? What then?

Farjeon on another occasion recalled his high leg pull was once caught on the boundary by circus acrobat brothers playing for an Invitation XI. One climbed on the other's shoulders and took the catch inside the boundary. Farjeon thought it was a six; the umpire gave him out. My pal, Max, was sure that was wrong.

'It should be treated as Not Out in the same way that being caught in a fielder's cap is Not Out,' he pontificated.

I hesitate to disagree with an 'Over 70's' county player but I take the view that Farjeon was correctly given out. The top brother took the catch; the bottom brother had his feet inside the boundary rope. That is all there is to it. The MCC has not seen fit to rule anything else in the interim…..

But there yet remains a danger. The Law says that it is not a fair catch if 'either of the catcher's feet is beyond the boundary.' So what would be the position if the bottom brother's foot was outside the boundary line while the top brother's feet were inside the boundary? Clearly the MCC has not finished its post-war deliberations on this point. The last 80 years have brought no new thinking on this ticklish issue.

In these days of advanced athleticism in cricket urgent action is still needed

7th   Finally Farjeon asked for clarity when a fearsome bouncer glances off the bat handle onto the striker's temple; whereupon the batsman drops dead before the ball is caught.

Max told me that custom and practice dictate that a striker can be caught out after he/she is dead. I am more inclined to the correct decision being 'Retired Hurt', or better still a new category of 'Retired Dead'.

A speedy MCC decision is called for here, too. After all, it affects both the deceased's season and lifetime averages. …..

Cricket retains its eternal fascination…. For those nations that have stumbled across it.

8th   **Little Lotty Regrets Rien**

The pantheon of great songs contains many which are as popular today, not only with the aficionados, but the general listening public, as popular as fifty to a hundred years ago.

One of these icons has to be Edith Piaf's 'Je ne regrette rien'. This is a tribute to her memorable song.

Edith, known as 'the little sparrow' because of her waif-like looks, wrote hundreds of her own songs, but this one was composed by Charles Dumont with lyric by Michel Vaucaire. Piaf launched it in Paris in 1960. She said it was the song she had been looking for, and it has never stopped being sung all round the world ever since. It has also featured as background music in dozens of films and shows over sixty years.

It hints powerfully at the tragedies that dogged her life….. but ends with an enigmatic note of hope, which ironically presages her last words as she died of multiple organ failures in 1963, still only 47…. 'Every damn thing you do in this life you have to pay for'.

As a supporter of the forces wanting to keep Algeria as part of France she dedicated the song to the French Foreign Legion, part of which had spearheaded opposition to Charles de Gaulle's wish for an independent Algeria. To this day the song is sung by the French Foreign Legion.
My quixotic mind pondered on how today's 'little sparrow' might have composed such a song...... someone who had regrets, but not Edith's extreme angst. You can even sing it to her original tune, o create your own. It deserves to be sung.

Non, rien de rien,
Non je ne regrette rien.
Not the bad that I've done,
Nor the good that I have not.

Non, rien de rien,
Non je ne regrette rien.

I chased, and loved, my Duane
Fought off Dolores in vain.

I have never lied,
I thought Dolores was a fool.
I followed her round, and tied
Her pigtails to a stool.

We tossed and I lost,
I cried all day in the rain.
I counted the cost,
Said au revoir to my Duane.

Non, rien de rien,
Non je ne regrette rien.

It was my good fortune,
I could sweep away all the bad.

Non, rien de rien,
Non, je ne regrette rien.

I stopped fancying the riff-raff,
Because.... Freddie Dupont joined the staff.

9th   *This notice appeared at the entrance to a campsite on the Continent. Its owners are to be commended for their diligent attempt to render the warning into four languages.*

> **PAS DE PIQUE-NIQUE**
> **KEINE PICNIC**
> **GEEN PICKNICK**
> **NO FALLING OUT.**

It turned out that the owner had looked up the English for the French word 'pique' and found it meant *'falling out with someone'*. It illustrates the danger of believing everything a dictionary tells you!

10th

Rustic Ruminations: Summer

In summer I'm stung by a wasp or a bee;
Ironic, I have just had honey or tea;
I remove sandbags that kept out the water,
And mouth expletives I didn't oughter.

11th   Sitting on a beach near Calais in northern France a French friend of mine saw a young English pupil sitting next to a teacher, with her head on the teacher's shoulder. The teacher was rocking her back and forth muttering,

'Soon home, Maureen. Mummy and daddy will be waiting with a nice hot cup of tea and your favourite dog.'

My French pal said to the teacher, ' Zat is very nice, seeing you comfort zat little Maureen.'

He English teacher smiled and sighed.

'You've got it wrong,' said the teacher, 'She's Zoe. I'm Maureen.'

12th   Aunty Gert came home from an Easter service at church seething with indignation.

'Well, I've never been so insulted,' she said through gritted teeth, 'I know I haven't managed attending for a few weeks, but really!'

'What on earth went wrong,' replied sister Flo.

'I had no sooner got through the door when the choir burst into song, with that Handel song from The Messiah, *'Hardly Knew Yer'*.

13th   *A primary school teacher set her class a task to write a short description of a wild and stormy night. At the end of the lesson she asked Maud to read her attempt.*

Maud: 'It was a wild night. The clap of thunder shook the houses and the forked lightning lit up the forest, sending all the little animals scurrying for cover.'

Teacher: That's a really good description, Maud…. Very vivid. Now, Shane, I wonder if you can match Maud's colourful vision.

Shane: *'It was a shitty night and the rain was pissing down'.*

14th   In the third of the 2020-2021 Covid pandemic lockdowns Constance's mother finally discovered the forces of infant self-interest that teachers have to face every day, and screamed at daughter to *'be quiet, and pay attention to what I am saying!'*

Constance (quietly and with reproving finger), instead of shouting, said, 'Mum, why don't you try to be a real teacher and just ask me to put my listening ears on?'……

She then walked out of the room with a suitably haughty toss of her head.

15th   Demure and infuriatingly clever 12 year old Sally-Ann put her hand up in an English grammar lesson just before Christmas, and asked Mr. Shelley if Santa's little helpers are subordinate clauses.

She was immediately invited to join the school magazine permanent staff.

16th   *Browsing through an old school magazine I came across a number of quips and quiddities that amused teenagers the……. 60 years ago… and I wondered idly whether they would still raise a smile today.*

Answers to a questions in an end-of-year English test:

What is the meaning of:

Put the cart before the horse: *So the horse can pull it backwards.*

Straight from the horse's mouth: *a racing tip from the one who is likely to know best.*

Lock the door after the horse has bolted: *lock the door after the horse has bolted it.*

17th   **Song of the Operatic Thespian**

Best sung to the tune of the Major General's song in Gilbert and Sullivan's operetta 'The Pirates of Penzance' – or make your own tune.

We are the very models of modern opera thespians..
We sing operas from Gluck to Ralph Vaughan Williams.
We sing on stage and in our baths and anywhere else we can.
We are known to smile at conductors, even the avant-garde director man.
We revel in the lyric mood; twelve notes can make us bristle,
We make money with Offenbach, but not with Harri Birtwistle.

BARITONE

I croak and growl and trill and bawl like any jobbing baritone;
I don't sing high; I don't sing low, I prefer to be a demi tone.
I'm rarely exuding evil like the deep bass's throbbing drone,
Nor ever quite as sickly as a tenor on a stage alone.
When I got a chance in the prime of life to sing a little solo role,
I spent a month on words and notes; to make an impact was my goal.

I rushed on stage to sing and shout, carrying my trusty silver sword,
Only to have my one line drowned - by a loud, crashing orchestral chord.
My aim in life has always been to star as Mozart's Figaro.
To get there I tried Germont - and for Macbeth I had a go,
I sang Schaunard and Posa, too, - and even Stankar in Stiffelio,
And then failed to reach the heights of singing Rigoletto.

CHORUS

He sang Schaunard, and Posa, too, - and even Stankar in Stiffelio,
And then failed to reach the heights of singing Rigoletto.

BARITONE

I've strutted the stage while murdering suitors in Turandot;
I've studied Oberto until ultimately I lost the plot.
I stumbled then through Berg's Wozzek, but gave Iago a sniffy miss,
I had to leave Boheme in haste, when I gave Mimi a sloppy kiss.
It wouldn't have mattered but she screamed and made such a fuss,
Despite my protestations I had to catch an early bus.
.
I could tell my voice was fading fast…. and knew I'd missed a biggy;
I waved goodbye to Mephisto; I knew I would never play Figgy;
Then one day I tripped on stage, fell headlong into Gloriana;
It's something you never ever do in any opera seria.
I was heard to curse my flippin' luck while the crowd cried bravo, bravo;
My career was assured for ever more - as a famous basso buffo.

CHORUS
He was heard to curse his flippin' luck while the crowd cried bravo, bravo;
His career was assured for ever more - as a famous basso buffo.

18th   *The Listening Ear section of the school magazine claimed to have heard of*
Mr. Grump's remarks to his Year 10 Maths group last Monday..
'Last night I looked gloomily out of the window at the clouds and rain; I gazed in despair at my bank balance/ I reflected on the state of the nation...... and then I marked your books…..and I asked myself…..if pessimists can't be happy now when can they be?'

19th   Anna Misha's mum informed her boss that Anna, was too poorly to attend that day, but, she added with confidence, 'she is under the doctor now but expects to be over him in a couple of days..

20th   *It is always prudent to check your emails before sending them.*
A man on a 'Gun, Game and Golf' holiday abroad sent an email from his mobile phone to his friend back home..
'Had a bit of a disappointing day today. We were supposed to be shooting peasants but they refused to come out of the undergrowth despite the strenuous efforts of the land owners and their beaters.''

21st   The next day the sporting holiday-maker messaged his pal again.
'Better day all together'. We were up on the local golf course.
I shot five birdies, an albatross and narrowly missed an eagle.
His friend wrote back immediately: 'Wow, Congratulations. What was your final score?'
Man on golf course: I've just told you… five birdies and an albatross.'

22nd   At a Management Conference the lecturer, a dapper and clearly successful exponent of management, chose as his subject '*Style is Everything*'.
He, then, strode through all the characteristics of managing and being managed. At the end he summarised all the various styles of management that he had observed on his illustrious journey.
THE '*BEN HUR*': which relied on rushing around collecting followers to take on the reviled opposition – who might be rival institutions, or even the customers or fellow managers down the corridor. The prime aim is to gather quantity rather than quality behind your cause.

THE *'JULIUS CAESAR'*: apparently a much-used approach….. where you are so wrapped up in your own sense of righteousness that you do not see the daggers raised till too late.

THE *'VAMP'*: favoured by the more narcissistic leaders….male and female…..characterised by a charismatic presence, alluring , but without substance…. and yet always forgiven if found out to be wrong.

THE *'SPACE STATION'*: a style favoured mostly by the captains of the larger ships of business, the grander institutions ….. so far away from the real world that you can do anything and no-one will notice…. However, it is important that there are competent underlings who know-how to bring you safely to earth when your orbit has got too much for you.

THE *'NEW TESTAMENT'*: a very much olde-worlde style, developed in the Victorian era, but refined right through the twentieth century….. based on St Matthew chapter 8 v 9:. *'For I am a man under authority, having soldiers under me: and I say to this man, Go, and he goeth; and to another, Come, and he cometh; and to my servant, Do this, and he doeth it.'*

THE *'BUFFALO BILL'*: an approach he had noticed was particularly prevalent in academic institutions and government organisations - where a ruthless rounding-up of the opposition to your plans, corralling them, branding them…. and finally getting rid of them, prevails.

THE MARX AND ENGELS': collective, coercive and collective – but some leaders are more collaborative than others, some more coerced than others, and some collect much more than others.

Choose wisely; your career depends on it.

23rd   A brigadier was being shown round a regimental kitchen during a territorial Army unit's annual camp. The kitchen and cooking was presided over by a veteran cook sergeant, whose day-job was a lorry driver.

It was a hot summer and the kitchen was swarming with flies-as happens so often in the countryside. The brigadier frowned. The sergeant came to attention with a sharp bang of his left boot.

'There are too many flies in here, sergeant.'

'Thank you, sir…. And how many should there be, sir?'

24th   **Joy Confined**

Jump for joy! Jump for joy!
Joy defined. Joy unconfined.
At the top of the mountain
I jumped for joy.

An octogenarian
Leaping like a boy;

What could be more thrilling,
Than an ambition fulfilling?
Than treading hallowed rocks,
In red mountain socks?
O joy, O joy, Unconfined joy.
It's like hugging a new toy.

Then I tripped over a boulder,
Broke my left shoulder,
Fell on the scree,
Dislocated a knee;
Tried to roll over,
And cracked my right elbow;
Banged my head,
And felt half dead.

So now I'm in hospital care,
Only able to lie and stare;
Toes pointed at the ceiling,
Waiting for the healing;

O joy. O joy, Eternal joy.
Joy now defined. Joy now confined.

25th

'By all means marry; if you get a good wife, you'll become happy; if you get a bad one, you'll become a philosopher.'
(Socrates)

26th   *Throughout the ages writers on educational issues have recognised the eternal clash of 'the young' with 'the old'. We can all agree, I think, that while the young hate being constantly told how to behave by the 'old', it is equally true that that the 'old' do not like being lectured to by the young, either Novelist Mark Twain is purported to have recognised the tension between old and young in this famous summing up of relations between children and parents.:*

'When I was a boy of fourteen, my father was so ignorant I could hardly stand to have the old man around. But when I got to be twenty-one, I was astonished at how much he had learned in seven years.'

It is a brilliantly witty saying….. but sadly one that Twain did not say. No trace of it has been found in Twain's works….. and Twain's father died when Twain was elevenish. But enjoy the humour! Somebody said it!

27th   Prime Minister Tony Blair famously made education the focal point of his long government. His mantra was 'Education, education, education'….. neither difficult to remember nor easy to forget…. Education…… schools, colleges, universities…. they were central to national progress, according to Mr. Blair…. A truism if ever there was one, you would have thought. Not so 170 years earlier when dear old Prime Minister, Lord Melbourne, could not understand what all the fuss was about. Bumbling as he was, he kept himself in power for some seven years…. as he did not have much to do as PM, other than school Queen Victoria in her first years as fledgling monarch. He thought his personal schooling was quite enough 'education' for a queen.

I don't know, M'aam, why they make all this fuss about education. None of the Pagets can read or write and they have done well enough. (Lord Melbourne to Queen Victoria)

28th   *Thomas Carlyle spent much of his life extolling the virtues of 'Great Men' and the importance of 'Heroes' in shaping history, and also lamenting the fact that he was not a very good Mathematics teacher.*

'It were better to perish than to continue schoolmastering,' (Thomas Carlyle 1795 –1881

29th   Liz and Al, in their eighties but with 25 year olds' sense of get-up-and-go, set off from their Gloucestershire home on their 'adventure' to stay with friends in *'France-profonde'*, remote France high in the Cevennes. With 'Disabled 'Assistance.' doing its best and Eurostar on time all went exceedingly well….

'Assisted train change' at Lille was no problem and the TGV was on time. But by the time they reached Lyons for their next connection, things took a turn for the….. well, not the worst, more, the bizarre!
Firstly, the TGV was late, not very late, but late enough for the next one to have departed.

'Number one 'Assistance man' said there was no other one due. Number two 'Assistance' man assured them a stopping train would stop …. but in an hour's time…. to take them on to their final stop, Nimes. To ease the pain they would be put into the first class compartment.

The 'Stopping' train arrived and set off. Liz and Al relaxed in First Class…. Too soon.

Back in England Liz's sister was tracking sister Liz's progress on her App and was surprised to see the train from Lyons on its way south east when it should be going due south. She rang Liz on her train, as you do these days, to inquire if she knew she was going in almost the opposite direction to Nimes!

WHAT!' cried Liz…. But just as panic set in, the stopping train stopped, with juddering screech of brakes.

A man was seen jumping off a Lyons platform and puffing his way along the side of the train. Whether he had anything to do with the subsequent change of direction is uncertain but the train lurched backwards, set off South, and duly arrived in Nimes. It was, however, two hours later than scheduled and there were no more trains or buses up into the Cevennes, to their final destination. 'Assistance' in Nimes was just as helpful as at Lyons; a taxi had been ordered and Liz and Al were escorted to it. 'Assistance' had done all it could….. and a damn fine job, too …. If only someone had told the taxi driver where he was to take them, all would have neen fine!

The driver had been told to take them to the village railway station but the driver had no idea where either the village or its station were. in any case the station would be firmly closed at this late hour.

Liz and Al had their friends' village address o but without a satnav and map a simple address was not sufficient in the dead of night….. The taxi driver just waited for instructions from these mad foreigners who could not understand him, and he them.

A final phone call to friends from an almost dead mobile got friends and helpers out into the village streets… but unable to stop a taxi-emulating-a-Ferrari hurtling past them three times before spotting them.. The last they saw of the taxi was it, too, setting off back to the city -in the opposite direction!

Liz and Al wanted an octogenarian adventure. They got one.

The Search for the Facts of Life

In the great line of Jason's quest for the Golden Fleece and Galahad's search for the Holy Grail, and Bunyan's Piers Plowman's quest for the true Christian life, comes s Charlie Short's search for the Facts of Life, which I tell below.

A strange fact - it took less than four hundred years to translate the teachings of Christ with all the accompanying complexity of ethics, morals and rituals into an international movement with its written biblical guidance, but it took 2,000 years before there was any formal written guidance on sex education in British schools.

It is obvious that Aristophanes and his 5th century BC colleagues, and Geoffrey Chaucer and his 14th century contemporaries and William Shakespeare and his 16th century rivals and Henry Fielding and his 18th century scribblers all knew all about sex and procreation and how to describe acts and feelings in a way that their readership could understand and engage with – and not be offended by.

But it all came to a stop in Victorian Britain in. Victoria and Albert themselves had an active and profitable, and by all accounts thoroughly enjoyable sex life. They knew what they were doing and how to do it. But 'the Victorians' put a stop to anyone else talking about it. Doing it was OK…but teaching about it?.... oh dear no.

The politeness about hmm… sex, which partly characterised the 18th century now developed into an all-out taboo. Ordinary dictionary words, never mind ordinary human acts, were snuffed out of literature and theatre and sanitised in the pictorial arts. The use of censorship in sexual matters was not changed significantly, until the decision in the 1960 *'Lady Chatterley's Lover'* trial paved the way to explicit sexual scenes in the arts and public discussion. There will be differences of opinion about whether this was a good or bad thing. My purpose here is simply to note the difference.

Schools in England and Wales have a moral, social and legal duty to do what they can do to foster healthy and respectful peer-to-peer communication and behaviour and provide an environment, which challenges perceived limits on pupils based on their gender or any other characteristic.

My generation of teenagers – in the fifties - was told, even by the great singer Ella Fitzgerald that:

Birds do it, bees do it
Even educated fleas do it
Let's do it, let's fall in love

However, it was apparent to all of us was that what birds did was no guide to human activity. Even the great comedian Bob Hope had been disappointed. He once memorably remarked that his dad had told him all about the birds and the bees. 'What a liar,' he said. 'I went steady with a woodpecker till I was 21.'

And no-one had a clue about how bees did it. So the search was on. And some 50 years after Ella's plaintive plea the government have advised us all on 'how to do it'.

For historic and nostalgic reasons you could keep a copy of Guidance to Relationships Education, Relationships and Sex *Education (RSE) and Health Education 2019* next to your copy of Richard Burton's 1880s translation of the ancient Sanskrit sex manual, the '*Kamasutra*' – if it has not fallen to pieces by now.

The following story could be matched by many others from the pre-1960 Lady Chatterly's Lover era. It was inspired by my re-reading of Muriel Spark's '*The Prime of Miss Jean Brodie*', where her little group of young girls in her class speculate innocently and wonderingly on sex. Yes, we really were pretty well totally ignorant compared with 10 year olds today.

31st   **Charlie's Quest for the Facts**

In the late 1940s the bench in Stubbs Walks - the one by the old bandstand and the Russian cannon captured at Sebastapol in the Crimean war - was definitely the HQ of the Castle Street Kids. They met there every afternoon after school, and at weekends, too.

Ten-year old chief Charles Short was the self-appointed leader, ship's captain, cavalry colonel, aeroplane fighter ace, or pirate king. Then came Gary Gough, Gee Gee to friends and even his family; then Pinkie Pat Evans (on account of her preference for pink knickers that she used to tuck her skirt into; and Harriet Mason, just 'Hattie' because no-one could think of anything else. She considered herself to be second-in-command but had never been officially appointed – by Charlie. He had never really thought about it.

Across the park roamed the Garden Street Gang, led by Bomber Bates, so called because no-one could bowl a cork ball faster than Bomber. Bomber ruled the Stubbs Walks' roost with his four henchmen, or really henchpersons, Nicola 'Nickers' Bailey, Chalky White, Gritty Kitty Murphy and Wham Bam Sam Evans, Pinkie Pat's elder brother.

Bomber and the Garden Streeters had hijacked the one pair of goalposts on the brown patch of clay at the end of the Walks, and they held the best bushes for hiding and jumping out from. Smoke could occasionally be detected from their camp-fire in the marl hole, from which pottery clay used to be mined. A camp fire was the envy of the Kids. The Kids were never allowed matches. Too dangerous.

The Kids' bench in its time had been a wild west United States 7th Cavalry fort; an Indian camp; the bridge of Nelson's flagship; or, if they fancied a modern battle, an enemy machine gun position to be overwhelmed. But at this moment it was just a bench – somewhere to lounge on in order to catch their breath and recuperate before the next great battle.

'I'll choose the next game, Charlie' said Hattie. 'It's my turn. We'll play Florence Nightingale nursing soldiers. I'll be chief nurse, Florence Nightingale."

'What!' cried Charlie. 'That's a cissy game! We are not
doing that! I'm chief, and I decide.'

Hattie glared at Charlie. 'Watch it, Charlie Short,' she hissed. 'One day girls will rule the world and I'll be chief – and you
will not be a chief nurse….or any nurse…., Charlie Short, you'll be a patient!'

With that she had stumped off with Pat in tow.

'See if we care,' was Charlie's limp parting shot….. But they did care. They did not know how to show it.

'Girls!' muttered Charlie.

'Yea, girls, Chief. I can't understand them,' added Gee Gee.

They sat for fully ten minutes on the bandstand bench without saying another word – and that was light years of restraint for ten-year old boys. The trouble was that Charlie wanted to talk, but just as he was about to pipe up Gee Gee would take a deep inflow of air and breathe out in an exaggerated long sigh. And then he scraped some clay from beneath his feet and kneaded it into a ball, spitting on it now and again to make it flexible.

'Don't do that,' Charlie, irritated by Gee Gee's constant
squeezing and pulling. 'It's disgusting,'
Gee Gee persisted.

'Helps me think and concentrate' was his excuse.

So Charlie whiled away the time by lobbing bits of gravel at the cannon, to see if he could get a piece down the barrel. Eventually he could stand the boredom no longer. He threw a last pebble over the top of the cannon and then turned on Gary.

'For goodness sake, Gee Gee, what's up with you? You are

making me nervous with all this heaving your shoulders up and down and gasps and wheezes.'

GG slowly raised his head. 'I'm werrit abite Tracy Lane next door.'

'What!?' Genuine surprise from Charlie. 'Then you must be the only person in the world that does. No-one else worries about Tracy. She's in and out of everybody's house all day long. Some evenings, too.'

'Well, Charlie, I 'ave to tell yer….' He paused not sure whether to spill the dramatic news. 'Tracy's in the family way, my mum says, She's 'aving a baby, and I'm werrit.'

Charlie contemplated this piece of new and perplexing information.

'Well, I didn't know that, Gee Gee. Thanks for telling me. But what's there to worry about? There's plenty of women have babies. If there weren't we wouldn't be here, would we?'

Gee Gee thought about this, took a deep breath and then asked in a low voice, 'Charlie….where do babies come from, anyway?'

Charlie turned slowly towards his pal. He had half-expected this question. Now it had to be faced. He wished he knew. Perhaps as chief he should have known. But he did not. However, he could speculate, and in so doing perhaps gain some time.   'Well, Gee Gee, I think it is quite complicated…. It's possible that there is more than one method. I remember my mum used to tell me they were brought by storks. But I ask you, Gee Gee. How many storks do you see flying over Stubbs Walks, eh?'

I haven't seen any at all, Charlie. Well, not lately. There was a white bird thing flying over the Lyme brook yesterday. Could have been one. But it wasn't carrying a nappy with a baby in it.'

'I saw that, you twerp. I was with you. It was a seagull.' Charlie shook his head disparagingly.

'Well,' said Gary, 'I was only trying to be helpful. Actually I've no idea what a stork looks like. Do you?'

Charlie gave this some consideration. 'No, not really, but it must be a big thing to carry a baby the size our Ian was when he was born. And, anyroad, all we get round here are blackbirds and crows. They couldn't carry a woolly glove.'

'So, shall we knock them off the list, Charlie?'

'Yea. I think so. Makes no sense.'

There was another pause while both of them collected their thoughts and wracked their brains for a solution.

'Should we ask the girls?' GG enquired sheepishly.

'What! Ask Hattie and Pat. No way. You'd never be sure they told you the truth even if they really knew. We'd still have to make sure. Forget girls.'

'OK,' sighed GG. Another pause. 'I've heard they've been discovered under mulberry bushes,' said GG.. 'Do you know what a mulberry bush is?'

Charlie shook his head. 'Naw, no idea.' Yet another pause.

GG had another try. 'Another possibility I've heard, Charlie… though I can't remember who told me…. is that you can find them in cabbage patches.'

Charlie stared at his friend, wondering if Gee Gee knew some secret he did not. He decided not, and so shook his head emphatically.

'How gullible can you get, Gee Gee. How many cabbage patches can you see in the middle of the city?'

'There's allotments, Charlie! And all those new back gardens. And my Uncle Gareth has got cabbages growing in a box in the outside loo,' Gee Gee countered. 'But I'm not happy with it, I must admit.'

'And how many babies have you seen being wheel-barrowed along Castle Street, eh?'

Gee Gee scratched his head. He could see the difficulty but he was determined not to give in too soon.

'Well, I did see Ma Laws pushing a pram along Marsh Parade yesterday - with a cover over what looked like babies' clothes. That's a bit suspicious-like, innit?'

'Gee Gee,' said Charlie shaking his head, ' we all know Ma Laws collects old clothes from neighbours and sells them at Wednesday's market. You and I were both clothed by Ma Laws when we were born. You know that.'

'All right, all right,' said Gee Gee. 'And we did offload all the clothes back to Ma Laws when we grew out of them. If Ma Laws 'ad a baby in a pram she'd sell it, pram and all. She'd sell anythin'.'

' You are right, Charlie. Babies don't come from Ma Laws.'

They both became wrapped in their own thoughts.

Eventually Gee Gee turned to Charlie. 'I 'aven't told yer summat because I don't know what it means.'

'Well tell me now, Gee Gee. We need to know everything.'

'I 'eard my mother tell me dad that Tracy was going to have the baby with a Sicilian operation on her stomach, or summat.'

Charlie grimaced. 'Crikey, Gee Gee. That sounds bad. Who's this bloke Sicilian that's operating? Never heard that name before. There's a Cedric bloke down in Marsh Parade.'

'Yea, but he's an indertaker….and there's Dr. Cecil in Lancaster Road,' said Gee Gee perking up.

'Right, Gee Gee. That's more likely. A Cecilian operation. That's what it will be. I think you heard wrong.

Gee Gee was very happy that they had appeared to have cracked it. It must be the answer. Tracy's baby will come out of her tummy courtesy of Cecil.

Another pause. Both were thinking that this got them no further in understanding how babies got into the tummy in the first place, and how exactly you got them out.

Charles made up his mind. 'Seems far-fetched to me, Gee Gee. It's only a baby, not an illness. Can you imagine Tracy with a doctor brandishing a great big knife? She'd give him what for.'

'Yea, she would,' agreed Gee Gee, then clicked his fingers.

'Yer know what we've forgotten, Charlie. What about those old nurses that go into houses when babies come along. Mid-somethings. Perhaps they bring 'em with them.'

'What?' said Charlie laughing, 'from cabbage patches or from storks nests? Is that what you are saying? I thought we had chucked those out already.'

'Yes, of course we have Charlie. But they could be from hospitals, Charlie. It's wheer your little Ian came from after all.'

'No,' replied Charlie, 'he was born in the hospital, that's true. And we know that some come out of mothers' tummies. But what we are trying to discover is how he got made. How did he get there in the first place?'

That was a killer question for GG He thought long and hard about this. 'So, what do you think we should do, know-all? You haven't come up with anything useful yet. It's me trying to find an answer.'

Charlie said nothing. He knew Gee Gee was right but he had no convincing theory to offer.

The silence was broken by another musing from Gee Gee.

'Tell me something, Chief. Something has bothered me for a long time.'

'Well, what is it? Spit it out.'

'Why is it that we are taught how to use a potty and find our way to our mouths before we are one year old; and how to stop peeing in our nappies and use a toilet and then to crawl around the house before we are two, and then we are taught to walk and run, throw balls, climb walls, ride bikes and push carts, but never, never does anyone tell us where we came from and how we got there in the first place. Don't you think that's strange? It's very mithering, Charlie.'

Charlie looked at GG in amazement.

'Blimme, Gee Gee, for someone slow like you, you do a lot of thinking. Why are you thinking of this now?'

'I don't know. Sometimes I don't think of anything for ages, and I start dreaming of things. Sometimes I don't hear my mum and dad asking me questions and tellin' me to do jobs, so they get a bit mad at me. But then at other times I can see clearly what has to be done, and I do it. That's why my mum says I am slow…. but I get there. I do get there, Charlie ….. usually. But this baby thing has stumped me.'

'It has stumped me, too, Gee Gee. The answer is staring us in the face. And we will get to know, otherwise there would be no more children in the world….. If it is any comfort, Gee Gee, my sister, Dotty Dot, told me she knows…… but she isn't going to tell me. When I mention it she says, 'You'll find out soon enough, our Charlie,' and then runs off giggling….. And my mum just laughs and says, 'All in good time, Charles'. Well… I haven't got the time. A bomb might fall on me any time, and then I'll never know.

'The war's over, Charlie. And I don't think the Russians or Chinese are going to be bombing Castle Street.'

'You know what I mean. There's something strange going on, Gee Gee. We've got yo get to the bottom of it.'

'Then you'll need expert help,' said a voice behind them. They turned quickly. It was Castle Street public enemy Number 1, Bomber Bates. Two years older and ten years more worldly wise…. with six elder brothers and sisters. Bomber and the Garden Street gang were now in their first year at the secondary modern school. He reckoned that gave him an advantage over the castle Street Kids.

He slipped onto the bench beside them.

'Yes, at the big school we are into proper science,' he said. 'So, me and the Gang have been considering this mystery…. scientifically. Science begins with observation, you know.'

Bomber was showing a rather superior air. Charlie thought he ought to try to get back some authority, but did not know how. Bomber seemed clearly way ahead of them.

'Yes,' continued Bomber, 'We have been observing dogs and noticing how they chase bitches and leap on them. We reckon that has something to do with it.'

'What!' yelled Gee Gee. 'Are you trying to tell us that our dads prowl around waste grounds waiting to leap on unsuspecting women! I'm not stopping here to listen to this twaddle.'

GG, pushed himself off the bench in a huff. 'It's disgusting. My mum and dad wouldn't be seen dead leaping around Stubbs Walks or on the waste-ground next to our house.' He was nearly in tears now.

'We are decent folk in Castle Street, Bomber, not animals,' added Charlie.

'Don't take on so,' said Bomber holding up his hands. 'I didn't say humans did the same, now did I? You can't deny we are animals, but we are superior animals, so it's not the same, Gee Gee…. My mum say so, and she works in the City General Hospital. She says we make new life like all other animals, so there must be something in it. It stands to reason. So, sit down, Gee Gee. I didn't intend to upset you. This is serious stuff. We're all in it together.'

'In what together, Bomber?' said GG retaking his seat.

'Finding out about life, of course. My dad says there has been so much about death and hate during the war it is about time we thought about life and love and getting on with people.'

Charlie thought it was ironic that Bomber, renowned for his wrestling skills amongst other things, should be talking about getting on with people, but he let it pass.

'Come on, Bomber. Do you know exactly how mums and dads get babies, or not?' asked Charlie.

'Well, maybe yes, and maybe no…. I've heard rumours, mind…. We're doing Biology at school. There's a bottle on the shelf in the lab with a baby's feet, or something like that in it. It looks very small, but it definitely looks like a baby.'

Charlie and GG stared in wonder at Bomber, who was looking straight ahead as though directly at this magical bottle. He had fascinated himself, let alone Charlie and Gee Gee.

'Anyroad,' he said, facing them again. 'we are only cutting up dandelions at the moment, but we'll get round to rats next year and it won't be long after that before we are onto humans.'

'We can't wait two years, Bomber! Can't you give us a hint?' Charlie pleaded.

'Well, perhaps I can. As I say, I don't know everything. But I know - roughly,' replied Bomber carefully, 'I can't say I have all the details. But I can tell you for sure that it involves something called hanky panky. My eldest sister, Ethel, told me.'

'Hanky panky!' cried Charlie and GG.together. 'What the heck's that?'

'I don't rightly know. That's what she told me. I saw her coming out of the air raid shelter with Big Bert. He's been drafted into the army and he's on leave again. He was fastening his tunic, and she were a bit red in the face . I didn't like that, so I asked her if she was all reet. 'Perfectly all reet, Brian,' she said. 'I'm not Tracy Lane. We haven't been up to any hanky panky, you know.'

'Hanky panky,' Charlie repeated scratching his head. 'That's a new one on me.'

'I think it's summat like kissing and smooching behind the bike sheds or in the air-raid shelters,' offered Bomber

Charlie now had a sudden thought.

'Heh, Bomber, did Ethel kiss Bert?'

'How the 'eck do I know! What are you getting at, Charlie? I don't like that language.'

'I didn't mean any harm, Bomber. It's just that Pinkie Pat told me at the weekend that her mum had forbidden her to kiss boys. She said that girls who went around kissing boys were sure to have babies.'

'Blimme!' Gee Gee gulped before Bomber could respond. He was already counting how many times Pat had given him a quick peck. It did not bear thinking about. He could scarcely breathe.

'Blimme,' he croaked again. 'I must be real lucky not to be a dad already.'

The other two stared at him.

'How many times, Gee Gee?' enquired his pal Charlie slowly and deliberately.

Gee Gee took a deep breath. 'Must 'ave been abite three times last week. I tried to run away but she and Hattie collared me. Crikey! I kissed Hattie once, too. I could be swimmin' in babies at this rate! O bloomin' 'eck !'

There was another moment of reflection.

'Bomber, have you ever heard of someone becoming a father while at primary school?' asked Charlie. He was responding to his urge for logic and reliable information

Bomber thought hard. It was not clear whether this was to give some thought to his answer, or for dramatic effect. Eventually he nodded sagely a couple of times and turned to Gee Gee.

'No, in my view you are too young, Gee Gee. You have to be at secondary school at least. Me and the gang 'ave kissed lots of girls in primary school and we don't 'ave any babies.'

Gee Gee let out a sigh of relief.

'Mind you,' added Bomber, hedging his bets, 'I'm not saying it could never happen. I expect you would have to ask an expert to get a proper answer. But I could give you a bit more information from Ethel. It's a bit hush hush so it'll cost you though. A penny up front – each. Can't say fairer than that. Take it or leave it.'

Charlie and Gee Gee looked at each other. Neither was convinced that any information from Bomber was worth as much as one penny. Charlie made the decision.

'I think we'll leave it, Bomber. Maybe tomorrow – after school.'

Bomber shrugged. 'Suit yerself, but you may regret it.'

Lost in their own thoughts they watched him saunter down the Walks towards his Garden Street Gang headquarters.

'Blinking heck, crikey and blimee,,' Gee Gee was muttering to himself, vowing never to meet up with Pinkie ever again. It had been too close a shave, he thought.

'We are no nearer the truth than an hour ago', Charlie was thinking. 'You can't really believe Bomber.' But there was no other tenable theory on offer.

'Right,' he said, standing up. 'At school tomorrow, Gee Gee. you and I will ask Miss Jones straight out.'

Gee Gee was less sure. He tried to keep his head down in class, in case he went into one of his reveries.

'You can do eet, Charlie. Leave me out. You have a way with words. And Miss Jones likes you. And don't forget to ask if primary school kids can have babies.'

'Yea, well, maybe.'

The opportunity to tackle the baby question came late in the afternoon. There was no chance in Arithmetic with Mental Martin nor Music with Tin Pan Allen, but afternoon English with their class teacher, Miss Jones was ideal.

Megan Jones was just the best thing that had happened to Charlie, Gee Gee and the rest of 3A. She had moved into the Midlands at the beginning of the war, with her South Wales mining engineer father and textile designer mum. She was now fresh from training college, back home in their city, and she was all theirs. This was her first year, and 3A her first form. She was open, enthusiastic, and still had a Welsh lilt that Charlie adored.

So Charlie waited patiently while Miss Jones entertained them with variations of punctuation for *'The cat sat on the mat. It lapped its milk.'* And then came exercises in singulars and plurals and Past and Present verbs. None of it was of particular interest to Charlie as he found he could do all the exercises easily. Words were child's play. Babies were not, so Charlie bided his time.

At last, Miss Jones tired of leading from the front. 'Now, class, let's see what questions you have today.'

Charlie put his hand up. 'Can we ask any question we like, Miss?'

'Certainly, Charles. I would welcome a range of different questions.'

'Well, Miss, how do you get babies?' There, he had done it.

Gee Gee at the back lowered his head to the desk. The class gasped.

Hattie wondered what Charlie was up to, and Pinkie Pat suddenly took a belated interest.

Miss Jones took it in her stride.

'Excellent question, Charlie. Come out to the front and you and I will demonstrate together.'

Charlie stared open-mouthed. 'You and me, Miss?'

'Yes, Charles. Come out here and we will do it together.' 'Do it?' Charlie whispered, rising out of his seat. 'Together?'

He wished the ground would open up and he could disappear down the hole, but nothing came to save him.

'Now,' said Miss Jones handing Charlie the chalk, 'write 'baby' on the blackboard so the whole class can see.' Charlie looked at her and wrote 'BABY' slowly in bold capitals.

'Right,' continued Miss Jones with her round shiny face and boundless enthusiasm and even more plentiful innocence. 'Now, Charles, how do we get babies?'

Charlie panicked, 'I was asking you, Miss! I'm sure I don't know.'

Miss Jones looked sympathetically at him.

'Well, that's a pity. I thought you of all people would have worked it out.'

She turned to the class. 'Now, I am sure one of you can tell me how to get babies.'

Stony silence, reddening faces.

'Class! Don't let me down.' She tapped the board. 'Let's say you have one doggy here, for example.' She sketched out a little line drawing of a hairy mongrel. 'And another doggy here.' Another drawing was scribbled next to the first. 'That's two of them So, how would we get doggies?'

William Kidd was the first to break the silence. 'Excuse me, Miss. Is one a dog and one a bitch?'

'Miss, puckering her brow, replied, 'Well, I don't see that it matters, William.'

'It does matter, Miss!' cried William, turning to the whole class. 'If she dunner know 'ow to get doggies she ain't going to know how to get babies.'

' No she ain't.' Chorused the whole class.

Martha, who came from an extreme religious sect went further. 'I don't think I should stay and hear this, miss. I am going to tell the Headmaster. And made for the door.

Miss J stared from side to side in bewilderment. Then pushed herself in front of the door preventing Martha from leaving.

'Martha. I don't know what is going on, but sit down and if you have any cause for complaint at the end of the lesson I will personally accompany you to the Headmaster.'

A little hesitation, but as Martha really liked Miss Jones she returned to her seat, while Miss Jones turned back to the blackboard.

Charlie was now sick with disappointment. He had had high hopes of Miss Jones. It seemed as if getting babies was far more complex than he had ever thought.

'Well,' she said, leaning against the board to steady herself. 'Well. I'm sure I don't know what has got into you all. I will show Charles here how you get babies and you can all watch.'

Martha screamed and then fell back in her seat in an apparent dead faint, but Hattie next to her could see Martha's right eye was open and Martha was looking as eager and expectant as the rest of the class.

Charlie, standing close to the board and to Miss Jones, took a step back just in case he was supposed to participate in the demonstration. He thought his knees would buckle. He did not know where to look. The rest of the class was buzzing. History was about to be made at Coronation Street County Primary.

'Goodness me,' cried Miss Jones, 'It's not difficult.'

And with a quick flourish of white chalk, she completed the task. ' You simply knock off the y like this, and add -ies, like this. There you are. That's how you get 'babies'. Couldn't be easier, could it?'

Total silence from the class. Disappointment that the knowledge they craved was denied them yet again; relief that neither Charles nor they were going to be embarrassed.

'You can all do this. Freda, give me one example'

Freda was grammar school material. 'Body becomes bodies, Miss'

'Quite right. And you, Harriet.'

'Lady turns into ladies, Miss'

'Excellent. And now what do you want, Boris?' Boris, who strove to be the class idiot, had thrust his hand up.

'What does 'willy' become, Miss?' He was hoping to trap Miss into saying 'willies' in front of the whole class, and looked around for laughs, but got none, except from his crony, Jake, who found it expedient to snigger at everything Boris said. His other classmates were all conjuring up their own words. Boris had no audience.

'Well, Boris,' said Miss Jones after a pause and a smile breaking out on her lips. 'Well, Boris, William over there is known by you all as Willy. If there were two Williams in the class we would have two what, Boris?'

Boris stared at Miss and Miss stared at Boris.

'Come on now, Boris. It's unlike you to be silent. Two what?   'Two Williams, Miss?'

'Precisely, Boris. Two Williams, one called Willy and the other Billy. Right? You might say there are two 'Billies', right?'

'Yes, Miss,' conceded Boris now anxious to move on in case Miss pressed him further.

Charles still standing next to Miss whispered, 'Well said, Miss. I think you've won that one.'

'Thanks, Charles,' she whispered back. 'Avoiding confrontation is worthwhile. 'Discretion is often the better part of valour' people say. Remember that.'

The bell for the end of the school day rang. Miss Jones could hear an excited class disappearing down the corridor practising their plurals.

'Nappy becomes nappies.' 'Oldy turns into oldies.' 'Ferry becomes ferries.' 'What's a ferry?' 'It's one of those sissy girls in short dresses in Santa's grotto in Lewis's store, stupid.'

Voices faded into the distance. 'Navy, navies, right?' ' A Cockney becomes Cocknies.' 'Yes, good 'un that!' And then the voices disappeared altogether.

Miss Jones collected her belongings and then noticed Charles still standing there.

'Oh, hello, Charles. What are you still doing here? Do you want to ask another question?'

Charles did. But looking up at Miss Jones's round shiny face, blue iridescent eyes, radiant smile and mass of golden hair, wild horses would not have dragged the question out of him at that moment.

'The bell's gone, Miss. It'll wait.'

Gee Gee and Charles escaped as fast as they could, back towards Stubbs Walks.

'That wasn't much good, Gee Gee.'

'Telling me, Chief! We're no better off. What are we going to do now? Give up?'

'Never,' breathed Charlie, 'Never,' and marched resolutely on.

They came to St Paul's Church. It towered over the Walks. They knew it well. 'Every flippin' Sunday morning,' Gee Gee complained. 'And Sunday School every first Sunday in the month. But for the moment Saint Paul was a potential saviour to Gee Gee. He suddenly stopped and grabbed hold of Charlie's arm. 'Charlie, should us see if the church is open?'

'What do yer want to go into church for? Your mum has a big enough job dragging you there every other Sunday, Gee Gee. Have you suddenly become religious?'

'We've tried everything else. This is the house of God. No harm in seeing if God's at home. I often think a lot when we are in church.'

'Well, no harm in it,' said Charlie. 'Let's give it a go.'

The boys lifted the heavy latch and slipped inside, making their way to their usual Sunday pews next to one another, and kneeling together.

'We'll say a prayer, Charlie. Like we always do. It's like asking, 'is anyone there?' the vicar says.'

They said their prayers – Gee Gee intoning the Lord's Prayer, as it was the only one he could remember, and Charlie muttering a favourite hymn from 'Songs of Praise' in the seat shelf in front of them.

'What now, Gee Gee?'

'Well, I see no harm in carrying on asking God for some answers. He made man in his own image so 'e ought to have some advice for us, I reckon.'

'But he made man from Adam's rib, not even a woman's rib,' whispered Charlie. 'I don't think that's the modern way. It's the sort of thing they do in all those old writings, like the Bible and those Greek myths Miss Jones reads us.'

'Didn't Eve do something suspicious in the Garden of Eden? A bit of hanky panky perhaps?'

'Hanky panky! All she did was eat an apple, Gee Gee'.

Charlie thought about what he had said. 'God told her not to, for sure, Gee Gee, but I don't think having a baby is a likely punishment for eating an apple. You and I, we've scrumped a few apples in our time as you well know, and we've still got our ribs and we haven't got any babies.'

'Well,' said his friend, 'I'm fed up with all the mystery and all the contradictions. I'm going to try contacting God.'

But as he muttered the first words 'O God….' the vestry door opened and in walked Reverend Tindall carrying a pile of Bibles.

'Blimme,' said Gee Gee impressed, 'That's quick!'

The vicar stopped and eyed the two small boys.

'Hello, Charlie, and you Gee Gee. Nice to see you here on a Monday. What's the reason, eh?'

He suspected it might have something to do with Charlie's dad, still suffering the effects of war. Mrs Short popped in occasionally to sit quietly in front of the altar. He knew just how much strength she got from the trappings and tranquillity of his church. He was not surprised to see Charlie. Probably Gee Gee was there as his pal. He was not, therefore, prepared for Charlie's directness and the peculiarity of his request.

'Vicar, do you know anything about getting babies?'

Before the Reverend's eyes had blinked Charlie had rushed on. 'You see, Gee Gee and I wonder why we have been taught to walk, to eat, to drink, to run, to climb, but we are never told how to get babies. Why not, Vicar? If it is important we should be told, shouldn't we?'

But the vicar was not yet over his astonishment, so Charlie continued.

'But I don't expect you will know anything about it being a vicar. You'll have to go along with all that Bible stuff.'

Charlie stopped abruptly, wondering if he had gone too far in bringing into the open the obvious restrictions on the reverend's worldly knowledge.

Reverend Tindall sat down next to the kneeling boys, placed the Bibles on a seat.

'Sit down,' he said, 'I think you need to be comfortable to think about what I have to tell you.'

They sat facing their vicar.

'Charlie, Gee Gee - I understand your frustration and admire your quest for truth, I promise you. You are right, I am a representative of God on earth, and my task is to interpret what God says to us. But I am also a father and grandfather, so you have come to the right person.'

The boys looked expectantly at each other. 'At last!' both thought.

Reverend Tindall gathered his thoughts. 'Boys, you have learned just at the appropriate moment all the things you need to know in order to make the next step in life. That is how it should be. So, now I will tell you all you need to know at your age about the birth of babies. The detail will come later, when you need to know, right?. You can play a bit of football now, but you don't expect to dribble like Stanley Matthews, do you?'

'No,' said Charlie....'Perhaps not yet..'

'So, listen to this….. You've seen seeds put into the ground that grow into flowers. Well, babies come from a seed planted in your mum's tummy by your dad. You do not need to know how at this moment. That's the Stanley Matthews bit… Is that clear?'

They nodded, a little reluctantly. Both knew what they had in their pants and what it felt like. And they knew, roughly, what Pinkie had in her knickers, but had no idea what she felt. It seemed that no-one wanted to talk about it and did not want them to know about it. Well, at least the Stanley Matthews bit made sense. They would have liked more, but what the vicar said was absolutely clear.

'Then the seed grows in your mum's tum for nine months. I expect you will have seen ladies with big tummies?'

They had.

'Then the baby enters the world between the mum's legs or sometimes out of the stomach. That's unusual, but it happens. That's it. That's all you need to know at this moment.'

'Ah, that's the Cecilian operation?' said Charles knowingly..

The vicar was nonplussed… then it dawned.

'I think you mean a Caesarean operation' Charles,' he suggested. 'It's called that because the great Roman general and emperor, Julius Caesar was born by that method, and the name has stuck.

'Blimee,' said Charles.' An emperor born that way!'

The boys were gobsmacked. This was definitely something Bomber and co would know nothing about.

The boys stared at the vicar. Eventually Charlie whispered, 'Being born by any method sounds very painful, sir. How did my mum put up with me hurting her like that?'

The vicar smiled. 'Charlie, you and Gee Gee could not hurt anyone. Just take it from me that God plays his part here. He will ease any pain. But just you two remember what your mums have to go through, and most women in the world. What we men can do is to understand the pain they bear and give them the help they need, eh? We can do that, can't we?'

They surely could.

Fortified by the wisdom of the reverend, Gee Gee put his hand up as he was used to, 'Excuse me, vicar, Can….er… primary school kids have babies?'

'No, Gee Gee. You can be sure of that.' A burden fell from GG's shoulders.

'A really good bloke, old Tindall. Fancy him knowing all that,' said GG, after they had left the church and walked slowly into Stubbs Walks. Charlie was really pleased for his friend.

Bomber and the Garden Street Gang were waiting on the bandstand wall by the cannon.

'You've taken your time, Charlie and Gee Gee. Have you got your penny - each?"

'No need now, Bomber, replied Charlie. 'We took your advice and consulted an expert, see. So we've got all the answers we need now, thanks.' He tried to look smug and succeeded. Bomber was, for a brief moment, lost for words.

''Ave yer? Well, spill it out and we'll tell you if its any good.'

Charlie suddenly felt happier than he had done for weeks. It was all falling into place. He recognised that 'knowledge is power'. He would not express it like that for many years, but he felt it in his bones, right now.

He leaned against the bandstand and crossed a leg nonchalantly. It was all instinctive.

'Bomber, get this - with the expert we have got behind us we don't need you to tell us whether our information is any good or not. Ours is hot stuff, Bomber, the best, and it comes at a price.'   'Oh aye?' said Bomber suspiciously. 'What price?'

'You can have it all for a guarantee of half-an-hour use of the goal-posts every afternoon between four and five o'clock, or instead – you can have it for a penny and a ha'penny up front – EACH of you. I can't say fairer than that, Bomber. Take it or leave it.''

AUGUST

The Ballad of Peter and Polly

My parrot, Polly, is the fiercest of critics,
Poetry her passion, but music her preference
For raucous aeriform altercation.

Britten and Bartok, bah, bah, balderdash,
Down with Birtwhistle and take with you Bragg.'
For Lennox and Lennon she cares not a fig.

But she'll bounce up and down at a Beethoven bash,
And though she considers early Handel's a drag,
She definitely thinks Rachmaninov's big

'Rubbish!,' cries Polly amid leaps and bounds,
Her view of Berg, and Henze is just the same,
As when I play some Harrison Birtwistle

'Stop those awful catatonic sounds;
That Weill, I tell you, lives up to his name;
To dissonance I could happily take a pistol'

Peter, her mate, has to take all her flak;
Assailed by Polly's thespian mincing,
He just lifts his eyes in avian awe.

He desperately wants to answer back.
But can't manage it without wincing;
Until one day he let out great 'CAW!'

At last Peter screeched, 'That's your lot!
You self-opinionated scraggy old bore,
I'm now revolting, enough is enough.

So, up with Glass and Alun Hoddinott,
Hail Frank Zapa and jazzy John Law,
Twelve-note music and electronic stuff.'

'You're right,' shouted Polly, 'you are really revolting…..
She swayed and fluttered and cried 'Melody!'
Till she jumped once too often, and fell off her perch.

2nd   During a village cricket match a phone call came to to the cricket pavilion: 'Hallo, I'm Felicity Bloggsworthy, wife of the captain, Rupert Bloggsworthy. Could I please speak to my husband?Player: 'Hallo, Mrs Bloggsworthy. Your husband has just gone out to bat. Would you like to hang on? He'll be back in a moment.'

3rd

Helping Hands

My name is Joey,
And my name is Sadie;
Yesterday we helped a little old lady;

How nice. How nice.
How very, very nice.
You are a credit to us all.

We saw her standing on the roadside kerb,
Looking up and down, a bit perturbed;
he traffic was frightening, as it sped past,
So we grabbed her hands and pulled her across fast;

How nice. How nice.
How very, very nice,
You are a credit to us all.

She told us we were kind and thoughtful pupils,
With the right sort of generous scruples;
But next time, she said, could you please just ask me,
As I was only looking for a taxi!

How nice. How nice.
How very, very nice,
You are a credit to us all.

4th   At a Management Conference in Africa a speaker from the Business School at the local university was at pains to pint out how important it was for people in leadership roles to be able to think on their feet and to have a way of confronting minor disasters in a way that carried optimism and a sense that everything is really OK despite appearances to the contrary. During the break a conference delegate, a company CEO sought her out.

'It is funny you should have said that, professor, because I think I have just demonstrated those traits that you have extolled. I have just been to the loo along with my Deputy CEO and some other delegates, who let me go first while they waited. Well, I lifted the toilet seat and found a deadly snake in the pan.

I immediately shut the lid and pulled the chain…. and then I slowly lifted the lid. To my horror, there were now two of them! So, I shut the lid and flushed it again ….. very, very carefully… and then slowly opened it. Now there were three of the blighters! I decided at this point that I no longer needed the go. I left the toilet and told the next delegate, my Deputy, waiting in the queue.

'it is free now.' That was pretty quick thinking, wasn't it?'

At that moment there was a shrill scream in the distance.

The professor eyed her quizzically.

'Quick thinking? …. depends on whether you wanted to keep that deputy or not.'

5th   *Another good friend of mine wrote to me as follows:*

When I was applying for headships I kept on keeping on …. regardless of rejections.

At one school, the feedback was: *'Unfortunately, we did not think you had the qualities we were looking for. However, we all felt that your wife would make an excellent headmaster's wife.'*

So I decided to be more assertive. At the next interview, when the chairman of the governing body said: 'Is there anything else you would like to ask or say?'

I said 'I think you should give me the job!'   And they did!

6th   For many years David's father was a widower living on his own. He made little effort to feed himself and restricted his regular diet to neck of lamb with mint sauce. My friend continued:

'Each evening the individual plate of hot food was placed in front of him.

"What would you like with it?" we asked.

'The usual.' Came the reply. This meant mint sauce.

The entire jug would be emptied onto his plate. We learned to prepare two jugs if the flavour was needed on our food.

One day we put out his usual plate of lamb, but carelessly put his mint sauce on the table next o a jug of salad dressing for our salad meal. We collected our meals from the kitchen and returned to find that father had emptied both jugs of sauce onto his plate.

He scoffed his lamb with relish and both dressings. You can't beat mint sauce…. Better than that salad stuff….. We said nothing.'

Dear Old George

We bunked off school the other day,
To visit our friend, old George.

We had visited him at home for a year before,
But our Head said we couldn't go any more,
As our dear old pal was passing a away

But we wanted to say goodbye to old George.
So, we slipped out of school at mid-day.

When we got there it was already too late.
George had passed away peacefully at eight;
Nurse said George did not want any fuss;
That was typical of dear old George.
But she handed over an envelope he'd left for us.
In it we found a fifty pound note,
With a message, the last thing George ever wrote;
We had never seen so much money before;

He was full of surprises, was old George.
We were gobsmacked; our jaws dropped to the floor;

We offered the money to help the library;.
Hoping to reduce our punishment by bribery;
The Head wanted the gift to be from A Nony Mous;

That would have fooled old George.
But we don't allow rodents in our house.

The Head tried to explain, as headteachers do,
But we said it was a right how-d'yer-do.
Naturally we refused point-blank to agree.

George would have approved of that.
We insisted the gift came from us three.

That's George, him (her) and me.

You will find in each book an inscription;
We think it is a fitting description.
In Memory of a good friend of the school;

That's our George.
From his pals who thought he was cool;
That's us.

He represented all that is good about folk.'
He was a gentleman, a really good bloke
WAS DEAR OLD GEORGE

8th   *August is the time of 'examination marking' in the UK. Although now long
retired I cant help groaning at the time and effort that is being spent on it.
There is a tradition of 'laughing at the devil's door' that is a salutary release
of frustration. My inconsequential ditty , based on those Great War sardonic
soldiers' song 'Bless 'em All', is in that tradition…. sort of.*

Test 'em all, test 'em all,
The long and the short and the tall.
Test all the infants and fifteen year olds,
Test ''em in winter when they've all got colds.

*For we're raising the standards, you know,
So back to basics we go,
No more innovation,
It's back to stagnation.
So get out your pens, test 'em all.*

Mark the lot, mark the lot,
The thickies, the average, the swot.
Mark those who can, and those who cannot, do,
Mark down those who can't even lace up their shoe.

Grade every one; grade every thing,
From school dinners to how the kids sing.
Grade those who're winning, who are top of the crest,

Don't bother about those just trying their best.

List the world; list the world,
Get all the nations' flags unfurled.
List their indicators, put them all in line,
Reward the richest, give the poor another dime.

For we're raising the standards, you know,
So back to basics we go,
No more compensation,,
To improve their low station,
Up the 'haves', down the 'nots', list the world.

9th **Question:** How many surrealists does it take to change a light bulb?
Answer: One to hold onto the kangaroo and one to fill the bath with electrical equipment.'
I think that's stupid. There was no mention of the bloke with the obligatory three eyes.

10th A group of business friends organised a trip to Paris to celebrate one of the colleague's imminent retirement.
They reached their smart Paris hotel in time for tea, a siesta followed by a stroll down through Montmartre. They split the large forty-strong party into small groups of half a dozen or so.
 The soon-to-be retiree, Hubert, an eminent local businessman and magistrate, was leading the first group, regaling the with tales of hs business prowess, when with Gallic theatricality a young Parisienne suddenly appeared directly in front of the briskly-striding Hubert. Hubert had to pull up sharply,
 'I say 'young lady…..'began Hubert…… but in reality any 'youth' she bore was partly in relation to the advanced age of the group and partly, but mostly, to the illusion created by her excessive gawdy and cheap make-up…. And as for being 'a lady' the jury was out. Her close-cropped hair and blue beret at a rakish angle were confusing.
 But it was the bright red and white plastic mac that caught the eye..Even that turned out to be not the most striking aspect of this lady of the night…. this *'grande illusion nocturne'*……

She plonked herself resolutely in front of the venerated magisterial colleague, feet astride…. as though singling him out as 'the 'man most likely to'…… and whipped open the plastic mac to reveal…… well, nothing actually!,,, She was stark naked.

'You like….?' she said peering at the hapless Hubert while shaking the flaps of the plastic mac.

It was not clear what she was expecting of Hubert, but what she got was a vision of 'Mother England'…… Hubert's wife, Mirabel…. who had been a couple of paces behind.

La grande Mirabel thrust herself *'avec une grande force'* in front of husband Hubert ……. a fearsome spectacle in brown tweed, green hat with feather……   She threw wide her arms out in a protective movement, forcing husband to peer from under her arm-pit to view what was going on.

In a strident voice that gave no room for doubt, Mirabel declared……

'Not tonight, dearie….. he's just had his tea!'

But m'selle had disappeared…. as quickly as she had appeared….. with a gesture that did not acknowledge *l'entente cordiale.*

11th *A young trainee sent a note to his manager to explain his absence   from work that day.*

My doctor prescribed a dose of medicine which I took this morning and it made me ill. The doctor says he will give me another one.

If that also makes me ill, you will know, as I will not be at work.'

12th

The first half of our lives is ruined by parents, and the second half by children. (anon)

13th   The world of opera is full of tales of hilarious mishaps. One of the most fabled is the production of Puccini's 'Tosca' where the heroine, Tosca, in despair throws herself off castle battlements when she discovers that her lover has been executed in front of her, having been promised that the firing squad's bullets were fake and that her lover would go free.

During this particular production 'Tosca' had managed to fall out with the stage manager and crew. Determined to get their own back on the last night, the crew replaced the mattress below the battlements onto which Tosca had fallen each previous evening, with a trampling!

So it was, that during the orchestra's portentous finale, the audience saw Tosca throw herself of the battlements and then reappear, arms flailing, not once but three times!

And to add to this spectacle, the firing squad of local 'extras', thoroughly confused, fired more bullets as Tosca's body rose up in front of them...... a memorable 'tragedy'.

14th

They all said the job
Just couldn't be done,
And he said that he knew it.
But he tackled that job
That couldn't be done...
And he couldn't do it.
Colin Sell

15th   William left home at 9.00am one August morning to pick up his A Level results at school. His mum waved him off… as she had done for 13 years…. And his dad grunted 'Good luck'. Two hours later his mum took a telephone call. It was William.

'Brace yourself mum…. I was knocked down by a bus on the way to school. am in hospital with a broken arm and a cracked rib and lacerations to my face…. and only half my teeth…. But the doctor reckons he can save my eye….'

His mother screamed and yelled to father who had taken the day off for the occasion…..

'Get the car out…. we have to go to the hospital…..'

She then collapsed into an armchair. Dad picked up the phone and called his son's mobile,

'Is that you William? What's going on? Your mother is gibbering away and I can't get any sense from her.'

'Sorry about that, dad….. but tell her not to worry any more….. I'm not in hospital, and in fact I'm hurt at all. None of what I told her was true….. but I have failed my Maths A Level and I wanted her to get it in perspective.'

16th   *There are many fascinating notices on Continental camp-sites. Here is one written in large script outside the site office.*

'The reglement must be paid yesterday night today before depart. '

We got the gist.

17th   On our first day at another site the whole family went off to the camp wash-room to wash the evening meal utensils and ourselves, The wash-house was a smart brick building with both indoor and outdoor washing facilities, personal at the front and utensils in the rear …. Guarded by a huge notice which told us, and everyone else;

'At the front HERE you may not wash your utensils here but you may wash your BEHIND.

Again we got the gist.

18th   A Maths teacher asked his class to work out the following calculation.

' If a local stopping train leaves Birmingham at 1215pm at an average speed of 110kph, and an express train leaves London Euston at 1315 and averages 170kilometres per hour on the 180km journey, at what time will they pass one another?'

The class settled down….. pencils in mouths…. scratching on paper…but not from Angus. He was leaning back in his chair with arms behind his head.

'Oy, get on with it ,' cried the teacher in irritation.

Angus smiled and wagged his finger at his teacher,

'Come off it, sir, it's a trick question…. the 1215 from Brum goes down the loop line via Northampton….. they never do pass!'

19th One day we refused to let our four-year-old son watch the TV during the evening as he had been rather stroppy. He took himself off to bed muttering darkly to himself.

The evening passed quietly until about 9.00pm when there was a loud knocking on the front door and in no time at all the lounge was full of a car-load of coppers.

Unbeknown to us our dear four-year-old had rung 999 from an extension in our bedroom that we needed because ironically I am part of the emergency service …. and told the police his parents had been cruel to himt.

It took a long, long time to explain to son, in the presence of the constables, that turning off the TV at 8.00pm was not 'cruelty'.

We are not sure they were entirely convinced that a ban on TV-watching is all we are guilty of.

Anyway, our son was quite chipper the following day and for weeks later as well.. We agreed with him that he had indeed chalked up a victory!

It won't stop us banning him from the TV if necessary…. but we removed the phone extension!

20th   **Ode to All Modern Chief Executives**

(With due homage to Gilbert and Sullivan - the 'song' Can be dung to the original tune to 'A Modern Major General' from their 'Pirates of Penzance', or to your own, very personal melody.)

We are the very model of modern business principals,
At managing and arranging things we are really quite formidable.
We count 'em, we cost 'em, we arrange 'em and measure all.
We leave to others the problems that are maddingly practical,
While we put our fertile brains to matters hypothetical,
And praise all those who understand matters mathematical.

We have many useful facts about the square of the hypotenuse,
About management theory we teem with cheerful news,
We're very good at integral and differential calculous,
And even better at appearing quite stunningly miraculous.

To colleagues who are falling short we are very, very critical.
W are the very models of modern business principals.

21st Answer me this said Randolph to wife Carrie when peering at a bookshop
window:
'Why is it that 90% of books for holiday reading are by women for women?'
Cannie replied without batting an eyelid:
'Well, if you don't know the answer to that I'll lend you one of my books on
the subject...... after I have read it....'

22nd *And now one received from a number of sources. Clearly a favourite!*
Prime Minister Thatcher arranged for herself and her cabinet to have an
'away day' in a hotel to discuss major policy issues. At lunch, she, as was her
custom, led the way from the front at the self-service counter, with her
cabinet queuing sheepishly behind her.
'Madam, what would you like as your main course?' asked the member of
staff.
'Beef stew', please, said the PM.
'Potatoes?'
'Yes please - boiled.'
'And for the vegetables?'
'Oh, they'll have the same as me.'

23rd **Apologia for the End-of Year Exam Results**

*A brief acknowledgement of the masters of the iambic pentameter, rhyming
in pairs, John Dryden and Alexander Pope, back in the late 17th and early
18th centuries.*

Laugh not again, O thou of the gown,
Who feareth not with wit to tread us down.
Spend not the time we wretched ones to scoff,
O wearer of the academic cloth,
For now we have entered transcending heights,
To join there other unfortunate wights,
Who failed this year thy subject to pass
And must spend another year with us, the mass.

We who in hope for knowledge now do strive,
Away from the Lower Sixth, senseless hive,
To listen no more to thy bootless wit,

With which thou at our ignorance dost hit.
We have reached those realms above thy head,
Where knowledge is rife, or so it is said.
There, to live, to learn, to gain is our aim,
Thus to succeed to immoderate fame.

Ideals, thou mayst say, that cannot ensue,
Nor can they if one trusts to thy value.
But happily, dear sir, we have left thy haunts,
No longer to suffer from thy base taunts.
Bacchus no more can be our god, for we
To Helicon now have risen, to see
The Nine, to follow submissive their ways.
Star seeking Uranus some will obey,
While others to Thalia idylls will sing.
It is not expecting too much of a thing,
For we who so long powerless have been,
To raise our standards and thus we will seem
So much the greater, being so small before.

For doubtless, dear sir, an unwritten law
Says that he who his time bides and seems so slow
Reaps far more praise when his power he doth show
And maintains his promise when it is due.
Yes, dear reader, we will make this our way.
No doubt at all, it will bring us our day.

24th   Little Tommy saw his mother and big sister, Lizzie, crying their eyes out in
the kitchen.
'What's the matter, mum?'
'It's nothing to do with you, son; he run-off outside and play.'
'But mum you always say that I should keep on asking questions and you will
answer them if you can - so why not now?.
His mother hesitated and then said, 'we are crying….. because….well,
because Lizzie has lost her innocence…'
There was a moment of silence while Tommy eyed his sister and her
obviously large tummy, which he hadn't really noticed before..'
His 10-year-old eyes widened and he smiled.
'It's OK, mum, don't cry; I think I know where to find it.'

25th *It is fair to say, I think, that 'Mary Had a Little Lamb' is known for it's first verse. Few people have even heard the remainder of the verses. This is a pity as they are gentle and life-afforming, which is not always the case with nursery rhymes, as we have seen. It was written by Sarah Hale and published in America in 1830' It was inspired by an incident that happened in the school where Sarah was teaching.*

Mary had a little lamb,
Its fleece was white as snow.
And everywhere that Mary went,
The lamb was sure to go.
He followed her to school one day,
That was against the rule.
It made the children laugh and play
To see a lamb at school.

And so the teacher turned him out,
But still he lingered near,
And waited patiently about
Till Mary did appear.
And then he ran to her, and laid
His head upon her arm,
As if he said 'I'm not afraid,
You'll keep me from all harm.'

'What makes the lamb love Mary so?'
The eager children smile.
'Oh, Mary loves the lamb, you know,'
The teacher did reply.
'And you each gentle animal
In confidence may bind,
And make them follow at your call,
If you are always kind.'

(Some years later a school student had a different vision of sweet lamb.)
Mary had a little lamb,
With lots of peas and carrots;
It had tomatoes and gravy, too,
Mother called it 'Italian ragu'.

Brother John said, 'No, it's not,
Though it's nearly got the lot,
Just needs beetroot for Lancashire hot-pot.

'Give over,' said Dad,
It's Irish if in it there are peas,
And Moroccan if it's cooked in tagines.'

Aunt Nargis said, 'It's none of those;
It seems to be real spicy nosh,
So it's definitely my favourite Rogan Josh.'

Mary raised her hand to stop them,'
Lifted her head from her recipe book,
'It says her what I always knew;
It's just called quite simply My Lamb Stew'.

26th A *report by Millie Tant to her manager.*
I was walking over new floorboards, which I shouldn't have done.
The temporary floorboard was not screwed down, which it should have been.
A board flipped up and hit me in the face, which it shouldn't have done.
The men on the production line burst out laughing which they shouldn't have done.
I suffered broken nose, which I shouldn't have done.
It will be a pleasure to sue the company when I retire next week, which I shall do.

27th   **Ode to the School Reunion**
In fifty years many students came,
And each made a distinctive mark.
Nostalgia is now the name of the game;
Banter rules, as memories spark.

No talk of Shakespeare or quadratic equations,
Not a mention of an irregular verb.
But lots about teachers who earned admiration,
And the time old Dragon tripped over a curb.

And tales of old Dave and his numerical tricks.
And the smarties we got from old Margaret,

And old Bob's accuracy with deft chalk flics,
Never failing to hit their target.

Remember, Fred, you loved pulling my pigtails;
Of this you used to boast.
Well. my thought of what I would do to you never fails,
When sticking a knife in the roast.

'Jeff, Jenny, and Pat, you haven't changed a bit!
I'd know you anywhere.'
'Actually, I'm Pete, and I'm Bess, and I'm Sid,
And you weren't even in our year.'

.

'O Cliff, you drove us all stark-raving mad,
You'd argue the legs off a donkey.'
'O miss, I haven't changed the least tad;
I'm now a professor of absurdity.'

'Goodness me, Gus , you've come up in the world;
How come, when work you'd avoid all?'
'Sir, it's done with back-handers and upper-lip curled,
And a posh voice, slightly adenoidal.'

You don't fool me, Colin, with your bushy beard?
Those big feet give you away.
Your antics into my memory are seared;
Now, could I have your long-promised essay?

That brings us all to this jolly evening,
Full of laughter and good cheer.
Knowing through others' sadness and grieving,
How lucky we are to be here.

28th   There has always been a curious 'love-hate relationship between teachers
and the taught. Even in the 1st century BCE
It drove the teacher and philosopher Seneca to cry,
*'It is when the gods hate a man with uncommon abhorrence that they drive
him into the profession of a schoolmaster.'*.
He had good cause to be concerned about his position

Remember…. Seneca was poisoned by his former pupil, Nero, Emperor of Rome. He survived and was then forced into committing suicide….. by Nero. I think it can safely be said that standards of pupil behaviour and relationships between teachers and pupils have……. on the whole, improved.

29th *An anthology of humour would be incomplete without something from 'Round the Horne' a radio masterpiece of the 1930s and 60s.*
In one sketch I remember Kenneth Horne was playing Lou King a film agent, a really glamorous job in Hollywood – except that King is in Sidcup.
One day a girl enters his office, with a figure that 'no loom could provide sufficient cloth for'. In her low-cut blouse she leaned over his desk to address him.
'Are you Lou King?' she said.
   'Well, I've really no choice,' answers Horne suavely.

30th

From the virtual pages of the bootable magazine 'fantasy cricket', comes this disturbing prophecy
With the current pace of technology development, the rise and rise of 20/20 cricket and the dominance of the of the extra man at Third Man – Sinister Money, can it be long before Virtual Cricket becomes all the rage? Now that the series has been confirmed we review below the rules and how the series will be fought out:-
Three match Test Series (4 days) played over a four week period, will be known as Amazing Prime Test Series.
The rules are clear:
The captain winning the toss will as usual choose whether to bat or bowl, and also choose the venue from test grounds in either country.
11 "Virtual Players" per side will use equipment provided by EA Sports ensuring no technology gains by anyone.
No bias towards Gender and all players self- isolate for the duration of the Series
Players available for selection are as current rules for "real cricket". This will enable England to continue their tradition of fielding 'South Africans'

Tests will begin at 4pm close of play 11pm or earlier if 90 overs bowled, in line with TV requirements.

Each Virtual Player can choose any Test Player who has represented their country since 2000. They will then assume this identity for the entire series.

No requirement for umpires, appealing or appeals. Technology automatically determines when a batsman is out.

"Whole series passes" will be available prior to the commencement of play on December 26th. Day tickets also available with "Surge Pricing" in operation.

England will be captained by Belinda Stokes, the

popular, fiery red head who was third in the recent European Cricket Tournament. She told reporters, 'it is a real honour to captain England. I look forward to seeing my name on the boards at Lords whenever Covid and successor diseases allow.' Belinda hopes to motivate her team with new strategies not seen since the days of Douglas Jardine. Her biggest concern is the toss which is the only thing outside anyone's control. Belinda confirmed that no one is sure yet how the coin toss will happen.

'I will deal with it as my namesake Old Ben Stokes would,' she added.

Australia will be captained by the most famous "sports gamer" of them all, Seamus Sinclair, identified as the spitting image of that great Aussie batsman and gamer of a past era, who played under the pseudonym Smith.

Seamus said, 'I am really looking forward to the challenge of virtually getting into my opposite number's virtual head.'

He agreed that this carried on the usual strategy of the Aussies in any Ashes series. He later confirmed that he would be taking Belinda out with him to inspect the wicket, the sight-screen, the covers the stumps, the ball and anything else she wanted to inspect.

'Inclusivity is essential,' he added (and got Belinda to check his spelling of 'inclusivity'…. and 'essential'.)

The whole world awaits with bated breath the dawn of this new concept in world sport, and the opportunity to further the attraction of sport and sportsmanship.

SEPTEMBER

"Ouch!"

1st   Before tucking into Miss Fry's traditional Founders Day celebration school lunch the large gathering of former pupils joined in a hearty and nostalgic rendering of *'He who would valiant be'.*

2nd   *In 1871, the Western Australia newspaper, 'The Herald', reported*:
In the days of Women's Rights, and, with precedents afforded by the Mother country, we shall be adjudged guilty of starting no revolutionary principle when we suggest that members of local boards of education need not necessarily be selected exclusively from the ranks of the sterner sex.'

3rd   *And a couple more Aussie 'Ockerisms'*
Too many cooks spoil the barbie.
  and
This little piggy went upmarket!

4th   *It was many years before I learned that this favourite rhyme actually referred to the Oxford Martyrs, Bisgop Hugh Latimer, Bishop Nicholas Ridley and Archbishop Thomas Cranmer, who were beheaded in 1556 for 'blindly' sticking to their protestant faith, instead of turning to Catholicism.*

Three blind mice;
See how they run;
They all run after the farmer's wife,
Who cut off their tails with a carving knife'
Did you ever see such a thing in your life,
As three blind mice.

For a modern cautionary verse I thought it best to keep away from mice and politics!

Three sorry moggies,
See how they prowl;
They wait to pounce on little birds,
Before the songsters their purings have heard;
So I shoo them off before they've stirred,
Those three sorry moggies.

5th   *In 1900 the Western Australia Education Department ruefully noted that objections had been received from parents to their daughters attending Laundry classes, owing to their delicate health.*
The Chief Inspector replied that:

'As these classes became better known they would become as popular as Cookery, but the co-operation of parents is necessary if the classes are to accomplish their object – to prepare girls for their active duties of life.'
But, once again, WA showed a far-sighted view of education and 'life' when the Department sent out a Circular which said:
'Boys who indulge in smoking do not make such good progress as non-smokers.'
It was taking into account research that had been carried out in the USA.

6th   The Deputy Headmistress has told the Science Department that she is currently rather cool about the white heat of technology because when anyone rings the doorbell her radio comes on or goes off
The Head of Science has advised her that this is not strictly a scientific problem…. but helpfully suggested that the most effective solution would be to put a notice on the door asking callers NOT to ring the bell between 7.00pm and 7.15pm when *'The Archers'* is on.

7th   **Rustic Ruminations: Autumn**

Autumn, season of bounteous harvesting;
Joyful cutting, picking and garnering
Long days and nights under the stars,
So a grateful nation can fill its jam jars.

8th

Miss Foskitt Meets Wayne

Miss Foskitt fussed the lesson through,
Clucking her way round the class;
Do this Ted and stop that Fred,
Addressing each lad and lass.

The square on the hypotenuse
Is equal to…. Wayne, what was that?
Whatever it was just bin it,
Or you'll find yourself on the mat.

I'm telling you, Wayne, you really must desist,
Stop pulling little Delilah's hair.
It's quite a vice, and isn't nice,
So, stand up on the naughty stair!

Hannah you are in such a hurry,
With your hat held in your hand,
I know the bell has told the knell,
And going home is grand,

But just wait a little moment,
And let all the seniors dash,
Or take it from me you will never see,
How to avoid a crash.

Yes, I know that Wayne has gone now,
That's typical of little boys;
And, Hannah, I'm really sorry,
He's taken one of your toys.

9th   **From a Laboratory Technician**

My colleague the Senior Lab Technician, Mr.Trick, asked me to retrieve a pipette from a cupboard. When I opened the door a large snake was coiled inside with its head waving to and fro, and seemingly ready to strike. I reeled back and tripped over a stool, thus spraining my ankle. Mr. Trick rang me at home later and said he was ringing 'to apologise on behalf of the snake'. He then said he was grateful to me for finding the snake as he had quite forgotten that he had brought it into work.

10th *There are a number of speculations on the origin of this popular nursery rhyme, first recorded in the 18th century. The tale I like best is that the mouse is based on the cat in Exeter Cathedral, for whom a hole was made in the cathedral's astronomical clock to enable it to leap out on invasive mice!*

Hickory dickory dock.
The mouse ran up the clock.
The clock struck one,
The mouse ran down,
Hickory dickory dock.
/

The original rhyme is rather matter-of-fact about the mouse's fate. I suspect that today there are many who would show more sympathy to the mouse. So this 'modern' version is for them.

Hickory dickory dock,
A mouse just ran up the clock.
The clock struck ten.
The mouse went deaf;
And wished he hadn't chosen Big Ben.

Hickory dickory dock,
We'll treat the mouse for shock.

11th **History Teacher:** How many wives did Henry the Eighth have?
Ollie: Too many…. My dad says one's enough

12th **Jim** (aged 10): Miss, if we can have actors and actresses, and tailors and tailoresses and misters and mistresses, why don't we have doctors and doctoresses? When they were inventing these names what did they call women who cured people?
Teacher: Witches.

13th **Livia** (to a fellow rising-five classmate Emily): Will you be my best friend?
Emily: No.
Livia: Then I do bash you.

14th *Another encounter from the 1950s radio comedy Round the Horne - as far as I remember it!*
Lady approaching Kenneth Horne in his office,
'Hello, I am Blodwyn Blubber from Wales.'

'Ho, ho,' mutters Horne, 'Blubber from Wales'….. the lengths writers will go to, to get a laugh!'

15th *During the 2020/21 Covid 19pandemic lockdowns thousands of teachers and support staff held daily on-line classes, with great dedication, skill….. and infinite cheerfulness. The kids contributed a fair share of good humour, too.*
Teacher (at the end of n on-line virtual lesson to his class of 9 year olds): Last lesson I set homework for the week, so tell me Eunice what you are going to do till we meet this afternoon.
Eunice: Crikey, sir, can you ask me this afternoon. I only woke up two minutes before the lesson began and I'm still in bed in my pyjamas!

16th   **Rustic Ruminations: Cows**

Moo cows have calves,
Moo bulls have horns;
A moo heifer has neither,
And is a heffer not hyifer.

17th Mrs. H was a school cleaner. One evening, having completed her sweeping and cleaning of the science laboratories she surveyed her handiwork and nodded in self-satisfaction; it was a good job done.
Just before she left the lab Mrs. H. stooped to turnoff the fan heater. She slipped on the water she had used on the floor and banged her head on the heater, twisting her ankle as she fell to the floor. Then as she struggled up she banged her head again, this time on a. overhanging bench top.
She reached up to rub her head and knocked a tin of paint off the bench onto her head, which was painful and left a large lump. She lay on the floor and looked up. She saw a large jar of clear liquid swaying on the edge of the bench about to topple over….. At this point her stoicism left her and in the expectation of being flooded with five litres of chemical she let out a piercing scream……. Although the falling bottle gave her a sharp blow in the solar plexus it only contained distilled water, so no direct harm there,,,,, and so when Tom the Head Caretaker rushed in to investigate the scream, he found a reasonably content Mrs H lying on her back on the floor clutching a large glass bottle. She smiled at him from her recumbent position and sighed:
             Oh Tom, I seem to have done it again……'

From Mrs. B. Goode, school governor

On my weekly visit to the school I filled a bowl of water for Samantha Bingham in Year 2 so that she could bathe her little dolly which she was holding. She refused to fill the bowl or to wash the baby so I showed her how to do so by bathing the doll vigorously myself. She refused again and again to follow suit and refused to take back the dolly when washed.

She continued to refuse when urged to do so by the class teacher, Miss Tellwright. On enquiry from Miss Tellwright, Samantha finally admitted she had been forced to wee in the water earlier, and so had her friend Gladys, when they had been unable to reach the toilet in time.

I was quite overcome. I am taking advice on what the long-term effects might be. I thought you would want to know.

19th *This is an anecdote that many school leavers might tell.*

In between leaving school and going o to university I was employed for a month as an ice-cream seller with the biggest ice-cream maker in the country,. From Day 1 – after a one-hour 'training' session, I was off on the road with my personal ice-cream van. I specialised, as I was instructed, in covering local fetes, shows, festivals and fairgrounds and made absolutely no profit whatsoever at my biggest event of the month, Nantwich Show, which was a complete washout! It rained 'cats and dogs'!

I said I '*was employed for a for a month* selling ice-cream. This was a bit of an exaggeration. Actually it turned out to be only three weeks. Walls Ice-cream, my employer, relegated me to the cold-store for my final week after discovering that I had made too much of an inroad into the company profits, by my over-testing of the products! But I had not earned any commission on my sales anyway……. Mainly because I had hardly any sales!

20th *It is one of those amazing truths that fate can sometimes be very, very discerning so that justice is served and seen to be served!*

We had one maths teacher when I was at secondary school who was pompous to the point of arrogance. She prided herself on our accurately she could draw circles, squares and triangles effortlessly freehand. This was fine, but she had the habit of criticising rather cynically those of us who could not.

One day she directed me to draw a circle on the blackboard in front of the whole class. She handed me a piece of squeaky white chalk and I managed a wonky circle that resembled a rugby ball. With a grunt of disdain she wiped the circle of the board, and circumscribed her usual perfect round object and then, as usual, capped the exercise by bashing chalk in the centre of circle - hitting the exact centre. The blackboard retaliated
by leaping off the wall and falling on top of her!
'O Fortuna,' I muttered to myself.

21st   **Serving the Nation**

The concept of 'National Service'….the compulsory requirement to 'serve the nation in a military or quasi-military fashion…. is one that has pretty well faded from the British consciousness, although it had persisted for most of the first sixty years of the 20th century.
It should not be allowed to fade away without recording actual experiences….. for history.
Young men…. and it was men…. were expected to join the armed services and to give their service, for a specified period. The call came when you were 17years old, but you could defer your actual service 'good reason' such as going off to university or learning a skilled trade.
Now, teenagers did not become officially an adult in those days until they reached 21….which meant in effect, you were 'allowed'…. nay 'expected'…. to fight and perhaps die for your country from 17 years old – although, to be fair, you had to be officially 19 to serve abroad and die for your country there! On the other hand, you were not deemed fit enough to vote for the government that sent you to your fate….until you were 21! The feudal system took a long time to die!
You will have already noticed a Tale indicating the significance of my experience as an infantry platoon commander.
        What might also be interesting to record is the experience of the infamous 'Basic Training' that all service-men…of whatever arm of service…and whether a 'regular' professional…. or reluctant conscripted national service soldier…had to undergo on being 'called up'.
Tommies', as the British soldier is called, are traditionally portrayed as people with a terrific sense of humour, to compensate for all the pain and tribulation, I suppose. This was never more evident than in the First World War where trench humour amidst all the horrors was truly amazing.

Seeing the funny side was still a feature of army life during National Service, so I shall concentrate on some of the many amusing, anecdotal incidents that came my way during my service. I am sure you would rather be amused than horrified. But nevertheless, we should not forget the training, discipline, and mental and physical stamina that go with being a soldier. I hope that a sense of these attributes shines through my account.

22nd It was the first day of our 'National Service'. My pal, Gary, and I finished our journey to Catterick Camp, Yorkshire via a one-ton army truck from the garrison station. We were dumped unceremoniously outside the gate of Menin Lines, *'Home of the Training Regiment RAC (The Royal Armoured Corps)'* as the sign said.

Gary had tears in his eyes already, and we had only just arrived.

'Just 104 weeks to push before our demob.' I muttered to Gary, trying to be jocular.

Strangled sobs from Gary. 'These huts,' he whispered. 'They must be pre-war.'

'O yes.' I replied cheerfully…… I was knowledgeable…. I was, after all, a veteran of four school CCF camps……

 'Yes, pre World War 2 but post-First World War -just, you'll be glad to know.' I had no idea whether they were or not, but I knew Menin was a First World War battle and therefore the huts would most likely have been constructed after that. I was just trying to amuse Gary and take his mind off the grimness of what he assumed lay before us.

Wooden huts, with rough brick bases and stubby stove-pipes sticking up through the corrugated iron roofs were indeed a bit forbidding. They were Nissen huts, designed by a Major Nissen in the first world war and in use extensively in the second – and even much later. They were half cylinders of corrugated steel with a coke stove in the middle with a pipe going up through the roof to take the smoke, or some of it anyway.

'Welcome to 'Chez Nissen', our comfortable country retreat.

' I think I was trying to cheer myself up as much as brighten Gary's hour. But he was not to be consoled.

'How many sleep in them?' Gary was focused on the likely loss of home comforts he had been used to.

All I could remember was a week in a similar contraption on a week's school cadet course in Chester. I had fallen ill there with flu but I reckoned that bit of information would not cheer Gary up, so I answered in an off-hand fashion.

'There's room for eight.'

'O that's not too bad, is it?' Gary replied brightening up

'But they'll probably have upwards of twenty four actually.'
I thought Gary was going to faint.

23rd It was when we had reported to the Orderly Room by the main gate that we
first learned that "The Training Regiment RAC' was actually, and for the next
three years, The Royal Scots Greys, a famous old cavalry regiment that had
achieved its finest hour at the Battle of Waterloo when Sergeant Ewart
captured one of Napoleon's standards. The cap badge of the Greys was
Napoleon's imperial eagle...... but we were not going to wear that. Our
badge was to be the Armoured Corps tank surrounded by a wreath.
'Scots! Will we understand a word they say?' I asked Gary. All I got was a
repeat of his strangulated moan.
'Scottish.........?... I've never been north of Chester before now....' Gary's
mouth was ajar. There was nothing that I could say.
Having parked our belongings in our Nissen hut home we went off to the
Mess Hall for tea with half a dozen new 18 year olds..
The cake was rock-hard but filling. The tea itself was a strange purple colour.
It was always rumoured that the army tipped barrels of bromide into soldiers'
tea, to dampen their natural ardour and to induce incipient celibacy.
Our first encounter with it went a long way to confirm the rumour! ...... It
seemed a waste, however, as even the most powerful aphrodisiac and a
platoon of naked nurses could not have aroused us in these surroundings.
By 6 o'clock, the army 18:00 hours, our troop of 21 national service
conscripts had gathered in 'The Hut'. We were a mixture of public school,
grammar school and secondary modern school boys.
        We got on remarkably well for the whole of our basic training. Our
civvy Street social status took second place to our common cause - the
struggle against a common enemy that had to be resisted – the 'system', the
means by which the army turned schoolboys into soldiers.
 It involved obeying orders to the letter and instantly; burning bobbles off
your boots and shining so that you could see your face in them; blanchoing
belts and gaiters until the blanco on them was so thick that it fell off in clouds
of greenish khaki as soon as you stamped a foot; this sand- papering
scratches in brass buckles and shining them until no blemishes were visible
amd you could see your face in them. And folding sheets and blankets every
morning, planting one on top of another and then wrapping one blanket
round them all to form a box; then, 'pulling through' the barrel of your
personal firearm a piece of 4x2 rag to ensure the barrel gleamed like silver;
and most important of all, learning commands and instructions that made no
sense to anyone outside the army or indeed our little bit of it.

It was different from life at home.

24th At 6.30pm came the first 'significant event' of my National Service. We had gathered in the lecture room at 6.00 to meet the Squadron Commander, and our Troop Leader, a National Service second lieutenant, plus our Troop Sergeant.

This was interesting but unmemorable. The officers had been to the same independent schools as many of the public schoolboy 'squaddies' around me and they could all could talk the talk.

'How's the grouse season ging, Mainwaring?'... and so on.

The sergeant, Sergeant 'Paisley', hopped from foot to foot desperate but unable to get at us. He was a tough soldier with wartime experience but he was an avuncular sort, not your war film stereotype. It was all beguilingly comfortable. The memorable encounter came immediately afterwards when we were introduced to our Troop Corporal.

We had returned to our hut in a state of euphoria. The door was suddenly flung open and in strutted an immaculately turned-out corporal, standing feet apart in the doorway, and slapping a polished swagger stick against his left hand in slow rhythmic movements, before advancing down the centre of the hut until he reached the stove, where he suddenly swung round and moved his eyes slowly round, eyeing us standing or sitting rigid in amazement. Well, at least I presumed he was eyeing us all. It was actually impossible to see his eyes. All we could see were a red nose and a jutting chin, underneath a small peak which dropped almost vertically from his khaki cap. A long red neck which he thrust forward and then jerked back, completed the picture of a demented turkey. He was followed by a slighter, less theatrical lance corporal. It was amazingly and intimidatory theatrical.

With sudden violence the corporal struck the stove with his cane, at the same time screaming something in an unintelligible Glaswegian accent. He added menacingly,

'You are an 'orrible lot of nerks, with no manners and no recognition of your betters. Stand up when an NCO or officer enters the room!'

We complied but before we had straightened up he had yelled, 'Sit down!'

The Lance-corporal, acting as a kind of Ernie Wise to the corporal's Eric Morecambe now addressed us in a soft Lowland accent.

'It would be best if you paid close attention to Corporal Glasgow. Believe me, it would be best, definitely, definitely in your best interests.'

Very ominous but not at all clear. What exactly was expected of us? There was a stand-off at this point. I think the corporal was hoping one of us would ask a question so that he would have an object to vent his derision on. None of us were prepared on our first day in the regular army to be self-sacrificial. Corporal Glasgow broke first.

'I expect you all want to know what a 'nerk' is, eh?'

We did actually, but none of us was going to admit it.

'A Nerk is 'an 'erk' and you all know what 'an 'erk' is (We didn't) So what are you? (without pausing) You are useless, pathetic, idle.' Corporal Glasgow paced slowly down the hut.

'Just look at youse.' His eye traversed the room. 'Idle youse are….. Idle, idle, idle. And I will not have idleness in this troop.'

And so it was that we learned that idleness was the worst army sin of all, well beyond mere uselessness and pathos.

So long as we remembered that at all times we would survive Basic Training…..

25ᵗʰ (continued) … ad survive I did, and also tank driving instruction, wireless communication training and gunnery training…. and then passing the War Office Selection Board for officer training…. And I had scarcely been in the army 12 weeks!

One thing above all else I had taken aboard was that I was not physically nor mentally suited to the interior of tanks. I requested, almost pleaded, to be transferred to the infantry, where I could dig my own hidey-hole. Request granted, I then had to wait around in Catterick for a posting to the Infantry Officer Cadet Training School at Eaton Hall, Chester, home of the Dukes of Westminster

All my fellow tankies disappeared to their regiments or to the Armoured Corps Officer Training School in Aldershot….. all except one. Hanging around with me, also waiting for a posting, was a 19 year old lord of the realm, who had been my hut neighbour for the past twelve weeks.

His family owned and ran huge tracts of the United Kingdom and my family ran a corner shop in North Staffordshire, but it mattered not. My lordly friend could get on with anyone…. and in the two weeks while we waited we had a fine old time.

He was full of good humour and wiliness. No-one wanted to be bothered with us as the next intake had taken up residence and were in training. So, we got up late, had a leisurely breakfast, wandered through the camp carrying brushes so that whenever an officer or NCO appeared we could quickly set to and brush up a few leaves.

A lot of the time we just lingered in the NAAFI (the Navy, Army and Air Force Institute) which ran cafes both in camps and out on exercises. Soldiers just referred to it as 'the Naafi'. Naafis were wonderful social places but their tea-brewing (by which all

Naafis could vary, and sometimes their excellent cake and sandwiches left a bit to be desired. His Lordship, although not very voluble, would sometimes come out with a real purler! He would scrutinise a curly sandwich, sigh, and remark, *'Another gastronomic delight'*, or *'It is for this we protect a grateful nation.'* On one occasion he suddenly gobbled his cake, grabbed hold of his yard brush and proclaimed*, 'thus fortified we can go forth and confront the enemy without fear.'* Priceless!

One day he was more than usually bored with this way of life and proposed that we should whitewash all the curbs of the entrance to the camp. He knew the corporal in the stores, he said, and had no difficulty in persuading a pot of white paint from him.

So it was that in two days we had painted every curb we could find in Menin Lines. No-one stopped us; I expect they thought we were on 'jankers', the army name, taken from a Hindu word for menial punishment tasks. But it was our legacy to the Scots Greys.

It is small wonder that regular army officers and soldiers wanted to see the back of us National Servicemen! As it happened there were not many after us. National Service was due to go…..The fact that I served in the Territorial Army for a further fourteen years is another story.

26th   **Admit One**
One of the greatest….and certainly most famous, poetic monologues is Marriott Edgar's 'Albert and The Lion'…… memorably performed by Stanley Holloway. It has inspired many others to 'have a go', so I thought I would, too…….it is not as easy as it might seem! Anyway here are the Fosdyke's vetting a school….

There's a well known academy up north that's famed for learning and such,
The Fosdykes went there with son Tyrone, to see if it was up to very much.
Tyrone did not like the journey and Pa Fosdyke thought the buildings were small.
Not thrilled by first impressions, they met 'Security' in the school's entrance hall.

'Good morning,' said the guard in his helmet, 'there's only one little snag.
I have to pat you down, you gentlemen, while, madam, please open your bag.'
That welcome eventually over, they met Principal lady in her room.
The Principal peered over her glasses with a look that presaged doom.

'Do sit down,' said Ms Ann Throp, waving them to a row of plush chairs,
While she shuffled a mass of papers, placing them neatly in pairs.
The files, Ma could see, were marked 'Fosdyke', and some said 'Confidential', too.
'Pa,' said Ma in a whisper, 'I think we've got summat to do.'

Ma sat down as requested; she was determined to keep her cool.
'I see, Miss, you know about Tyrone; well we want to know about t'school.
'Tyrone,' said Principal in a Principalish voice, 'I'm afraid you will have to leave,
'If you don't take your shoes off the furniture, and stop wiping your nose on your
sleeve.'

Pa did not like the woman's attitude, but did not know what to do next.
He leaned over, nudged Ma and whispered, 'You take over, as I'm feeling rather
vexed.'
So Ma rummaged round in her handbag and brought out a pencil and notebook.
She flicked over pages and pages and at her questions she had a good look.

'Now, do you do sex with relatives?' asked Ma in her stentorian voice.
'Sex and Relationship Studies are compulsory,' replied Ms Throp, 'not a choice.
The students find it instructive and learn lots of things they don't know.'
'You're telling me!' cried Ma excitedly, 'and at some learnin' kids are not slow!

Tyrone, I can tell you, gets some very odd ideas indeed!
He asked me once if we'd 'done it' - in the car and on the back seat.
Tell me, Miss Principal, I ask you, what kind of question is that?
Everyone knows - but perhaps you don't - it's impossible in a little Fiat.'

But Principal's mind had wandered to a night some forty years ago,
And Henry and a sports car, and moonlight…. and her cheeks all red and aglow.
She hadn't heard Ma's last words, so didn't know what she had said.
'Yes, it is a great deal easier,' she had muttered, 'if you 'do it' while you're tucked
up in bed'.

At this father Fosdyke was astonished, and Ma quite taken aback.
But Tyrone winked at the Principal, who quickly changed her tack.
'Now can we discuss Tyrone's behaviour? It's laid out here in his files.
It seems he has been excluded… a lot… for his various nefarious wiles.

'You may have heard of his offences but he's got some good points as well.'

Mother knew how to change direction and which side of her son she could sell.
'It's all there in his probation report, which tells of his high spirits and zeal,
His enterprise and his cunning, all the things which to you should appeal.'

Said Principal Throp to Tyrone, 'I understand you want to come here....do you?'
'es, he does.' said Ma, 'We're investigating.... to see if your school is the one that will do.`
At this the Principal bridled. She could see that the school's reputation was at stake.
'This school is a top academy, you know....the icing on the league table cake.'

'Well,' said Ma, 'we want more than that; you may be good at cooking,
But it's at your teaching of technology and business that we shall be partic'ly looking.
None of them Classics or Politics or Philosophy, and definitely no Sociology.
We can do without your prissy stuff, the things that Prime Ministers study.

And we don't want Tyrone speaking foreign; his English is trouble enough.
His last school said his spelling is 'personal' and grammar he finds rather tough.
But he's not afraid of talking, and his vocabulary is certainly vast;
The school said his use of expletives was, in their experience, unsurpassed.

'Expletives are Latin, Miss Throp,' said Pa, waking up from his apneic doze.
'Our Tyrone will have one foot on the ladder if he becomes an expert in those.
I remember when I used them....' but Ma 'ushed him up with a snort.
'Stop mithering t' Principal, father. You can see she's not one of that sort.'

Principal did not want to take Tyrone; he was one of the worst of her fears;
She shuddered at the thought of his being let loose.... amongst her little dears.
She could see nothing but trouble and strife if she admitted the egregious Tyrone,
She could see he would hit her school like an aggressive, unstoppable cyclone,

But her trustees had firmly warned her she must take pupils with any special need.
So she gritted her teeth and pursed her lips as she contemplated the awful deed.
'I have given this matter a great deal of thought and can take just one extra child.
But as she viewed Tyrone smirking her temper grew progressively wild.

'One extra!' cried Ma, 'Just one!' said Pa, who laughed till his eyes filled with tears.
To come there's Pat, Joan and Debra and then Wayne and Billy and Piers,
After them there's twins Fred and Lilly, and finally little redhead Russ.

You'll be glad to know, 'eadmistress, we've brought all ten of 'em in t'car with us.

But Principal was no longer attending; she stared into space, her mind blank.
Time stood still while she gaped at Fosdykes, and her heart and hopes quietly
sank.
Ma said, 'I know you're astounded, and thinking 'here's a right 'how-d'ye-do'
But you see, Madam Principal, we had no tele…. till I was nearly forty two.'

27th   **Learning the Ropes**

*The late Professor Ted Wragg illustrated and summed up the new teacher's
dilemma in his collection of essays 'The Art and Science of Teaching and
Learning'.*
A chemistry graduate once arrived at his teaching practice school in
January. Before commencing his own teaching he watched a third-year
class's regular chemistry teacher take a double period of practical work.
After a brief exposition, delivered, whilst seated on the front bench, plus one
or two shared jokes and asides, the experienced chemistry teacher signalled
the start of the practical phase with,
'Right 3C, you know what to do, so get the gear out and make a start.'
The class dispersed briskly to hidden cupboards and far recesses for various
pieces of equipment, and an hour of earnest and purposeful experimental
work ensued.
In the following week the chemistry graduate took the class himself and
began by lolling on the front bench in imitation of the apparently effortless
and casual manner he had witnessed only seven days earlier. After a few
minutes of introduction, he delivered an almost identical instruction to the
one given by the experienced man the week before,
'Right 3C, get the gear out and do the experiment.' Within seconds pupils
were elbowing their fellows out of the way, wrestling each other for bunsen
burners, slamming cupboard doors. He spent most of the practical phase
calling for less noise and reprimanding the many pupils who misbehaved.
This true story illustrates the problems faced by student teachers. What they
have not seen is how experienced teachers' first encounters with their
classes in early September at the beginning of the school year establish the
rules and relationships. Crucial stuff!

A teacher told a court that the incident the court was considering began when young Snelling in Year 10 said out aloud that his teaching was useless – or words to that effect - and that he would be better off grooming the heifers on the family farm. He said,
'I'm off out of here.', left his seat and made for the exit.
The teacher continued,
I rugby-tackled him as he reached the door. It was a natural reaction, I think. Anyway Snelling sustained minor head injuries; I on the other hand broke my arm.'
The court deliberated long and hard then finally accepted that the teacher had used 'proportionate force' and had acted 'reasonably' in preventing Hayden from breaching the rule against leaving a classroom without permission. It was important, and still is, that school staff can use reasonable force to prevent harm to themselves and others and to stop a pupil from breaking the law.
Ultimately 'reasonableness' is not what you and I might define. It is ultimately determined by judges, in courts.

29th   **Memo to the Headteacher from a Languages teacher**

Re: Your latest 'Pandemic' round-robin to staff: I note that you are requiring me to keep to a minimum of 2 metres 'social- distancing' when Year 10 returns next week. I would like you to know that I am very happy to distance myself by 20 metres from all members of 10G.

30th **Science Teacher:** Now, class, what steps should you take before doing experiments with chemical compounds?
Brian: Very long ones, I reckon, sir….. I'm furthest from the door.

OCTOBER

A giant came to my front door,
He stood there ten foot two;
I said to him 'O, Giant' I said,
O, Giant, who's scared of YOU?!'
And he hit me.
Colin Sell

2nd **A conference organiser closed the county's Sixth** Form Conference with a 'grand gesture.*
'I shall close the Conference with some choice words on life, death and the nature of the universe, and then tell you when the buses leave.'

3rd The school magazine's Ear met one of the oldest and grandest of Former Pupils – an Old Boy, in fact, as he was now 87 and had been at the school when it was a boys grammar school, with the Girls High School opposite…..
The Ear saw he was peering at the present-day students and shaking his head at the casual dress and the easy conversation going on outside the School Office.
  'A bit different from your day, I imagine, Mr. Winkle, eh?'
He shook his head one more time…..
'I was in the Sixth Form at a time when NOT taking off your school cap on meeting a girl from the girls high school was tantamount to an indecent assault…… we had to troop over to the Girls School andapologise to the headmistress.

4th When tourist Steve got to the till in a Dublin supermarket the cashier told him the price of his goods.
'10.66,' she said.
' Ah, the battle of Hastings, eh?' said clever clogs Steve.
The cashier turned to her supervisor , ' Do we stock bottles of hastings, Mchael?'

There are plenty of glamorous superstars playing top-flight soccer these days but none, it seems to me, are in the same league as Leigh Richmond Roose who was an amateur footballer, a goalkeeper, in the early 1900s. His main job was as a surgeon in a London hospital but he was passionate about his football, and as an amateur he was able to play for any club who wanted him. Amongst others he played for Aston Villa, Sunderland and Stoke city. He was so good that he was capped for Wales on a number of occasions. Even though based in London he thought nothing of travelling up to Sunderland for a game and then back again.

On one memorable occasion he was invited to play in Birmingham on a Saturday afternoon. When he got to Euston station after a night the train had left. Undaunted, Leigh simply hired his own train and travelled to Birmingham all alone. Legend has it that he presented the bill to the club with the first item reading - use of toilets (twice) 2 pence.

What style!

6th   *continuing the story of Leigh Richmond Roose* .... He played nearly 150 times for Stoke city but eventually fell out with the management and subsequently went to keep goal for the rival club in Stoke, Port Vale. As luck, or misfortune, would have it he immediately appeared in goal for Port Vale against Stoke city at Stoke's Victoria ground.. He is reported to have made a wonderful save at one point ensuring that Port Vale prevailed. So incensed were the Stoke city supporters that they surged onto the pitch at full-time picked Lee up and dropped into the River Trent!

7th   To complete the story of Leigh' Richmond Roose …. At the outbreak of the First World War in 1914 Leigh signed on immediately to serve as a medical officer and served in the Gallipoli campaign. A he returned to England in 1916 and for reasons which are uncertain resigned his commission and rejoined the army as a private soldier. He was posted to the Royal Fusiliers and in the battle of the Somme he was awarded the Military Medal for his bravery .

He was promoted to Lance Corporal and killed a couple of weeks later. His body was never found and so his name appears on the memorial to soldiers with no known grave at Thiepval…… an end as enigmatic as his life.

8th

A Little Learning

Ronnie Cold of Year 7 heard his classmate, Bess Weston, tell their tutor that her father and his fellow workers at British Oxygen had gone on strike. In between floods of tears Ronnie asked Miss Take if they were all now going to choke to death. Miss reassured the class that British Oxygen had sufficient reserves to get by for a month or two….. but it might be a good idea if they all kept very quiet for the next four weeks.

9th   Year 7 have been studying the Norman Conquest. The school magazine's Listening Ear's roving reporter, *The Eye*, has learned that exciting new revelations have been noted in Lower School History lessons. Blenkinsop wrote that at the Battle of Hastings King Harold sustained an arrow to his eye which gave him a headache and 'was quite detrimental to his health'.

10th

Rime of the Ancient Adviser

This bouncy aria is based on the Admiral's biographical outpouring in Gilbert and S Sullivan's 'HMS Pinafore'. It started out as a comic reflection on the role of parliamentary lobbyists….. but you try to find umpteen rhymes for 'lobbyist …. so 'the government adviser' is observed at work.

When I was an adviser to Britain's PM,
I worked all day at number ten.
I could sack the secretaries permanent or temp.
I made everyone quake in the government.
The power that I had could stop Big Ben
Because I advised at Number Ten.

I belonged to no party, I didn't hold the whip,
I was not beholden to any partnership.
When the PM humphed and the Chancellor hawed

I made sure Whitehall held its breath and paused.
I then told ministers what to do and when,
Because I was an advisor at Number Ten.

Those that turned out to be unbendable,
I made their position utterly untenable.
The misguided who told me to 'go and boil it',
Were 'spoken to' quietly in the appropriate toilet.
I had oodles of influence over women and men,
Because I was an adviser at Number Ten.

The PM had plans for this and for that,
I coached him till he had 'em off pat.
And if he got it wrong because he felt 'inspired',
I made sure another U turn transpired.
He toed my line and didn't do it again,
Because I was an adviser to Number Ten.

The PM tried once to make a decision
And almost did it with some precision,
It didn't take long to get him befuddled,
To get his plan characteristically muddled.
I filled him with statistics and loads of gen,
Because I am an adviser to Number Ten.

At cooking books I was a genius,
With pounds and pence I couldn't be serious.
To create a stir but avoid a fuss,
I'd just write some figures on the side of a bus.
No-one knew what on earth they meant,
Because I am an adviser to the government.

With Acts and Regs I knew my stuff,
I could move very fast if the going got tough.
And when pesky peers tried to exert their power
I mentioned 'abolition' and pointed to the Tower.
They very soon bent to my intent,
Cos I'm an adviser to the government.
They very soon bent to his intent,

I was the top of the firmament,
Respected by Members of Parliament.
Just occasionally a rule required a wee dent,
Suggested by an adviser to the government.
I would no more consider breaking the rules,
Than think of stealing the realms crown jewels..

The Northern Powerhouse I wanted to champion,
If it hadn't been the pet of Osborne and Cameron.
I didn't want has-beens and never-weres,
I wanted instant solutions and quick answers.
So I sent half the ministries to Burton-on-Trent,
My very best advice to the government..

To get back to the city every chance they seized,,
And did whatever it was I pleased..
They bowed and scraped, and scraped and bowed,
Until I thought them suitably cowered.
Then off to London they'd be sent,
To better serve my government.

And when I'd…. occasionally…. overstep the mark,
I could always find solace in an urban park,
Where common folk wander and do ordinary things,
Who could only marvel at their betters with wings.
Or I picked white roses along with the PM,
Dancing round the garden of Number Ten.

11th At a Lower School Parents Evening Mr Moggs, Head of European Studies, told Mrs. B that her daughter did a lot of yawning in his class. Mrs. B pointed out that her daughter went to bed early and was always wide-awake when she left for school….. 'positively bubbling,' she said…. I can't think what the reason could be for her boredom, she added coyly….

12th At the next table Stanley P's father and mother were mortified to hear from Mr. Greatrex that Stanley was 'very wiggly-waggly'……. 'very up and down….. 'sometimes competent, often disappointing'….. 'He needs to be set in concrete for a year or two.'

Mr. Greatrex paused and raised his hand in front of him, as though about to bless the good parents…. 'He is, shall we say, consistently inconsistent.' That was Mr. G's verdict…….

Mrs. P beamed, 'I am so glad you are so positive about him…..'

13th   The next parent up for Mr. Greatrex's professional verdict announced that he had come about John, his son..

' I am a straight up-and-down sort of person…. I want to hear the truth… and nothing but the truth….'

'Ah ah,' said Mr. Greatrex……John?…. Yes…. I am so glad you came. I have been wanting to meet you for a long time…..to warn you that if your son does not pull his socks up he is not going to do himself justice in the GCSE next summer…. He is not taking adequate note…. not thinking about what he is doing…. makes too many silly mistakes,,, not doing his homework….'

As this litany of failureswas pouring out Father John's face grew darker and darker, his mouth twitched and finally his hands banged down on the table.

'Wait till I get home!' he growled, 'I'll GCSE him….. he has told his ma and me he is doing fine….. high marks and high praise from you….. his favourite subject… that's what he said…. Well, his feet won't touch the ground when I get home…… I can assure you, Mr. Greatrex that he will be a changed boy….. I guarantee it…..'

Mr. G. was pleased to have effected a change….. very satisfactory…… he went home feeling that for once some good had come out of the tedious waltzing round the wardrobe of half-truths that seemed to characterise most parents evenings.

This self-satisfaction took a severe knock before school next moment when timid John Harper, the wise owl of 10A… the most conscientious boy Greatrex had taught for a long time…. approached his desk, red-eyed with tears.

'What did you tell my father last night, sir?….. He gave e the worst dressing-down I have ever had, and when I tried to tell him I was doing well he cuffed my ears and told me not to lie…… why, sir, why……?'

By now Mr. G had gone white….jaw dropped…. knuckles white with tension…. He realised what he had done….. this was JOHN Harper…. And he had been speaking to MR. HARPER about John…… while he thought he had been talking to the egregious David John's father, Mr. John….. who, it now turned out, had not even been at the parents evening….. O Lor'…….

With the aid of the headteacher, the chair of governors, the local authority psychiatrist, a teacher union representative and the school lawyers, a new chapter is being added to the Art of Apology.

14th

The Afternoon Hymn
Afternoon school is over,
The sun is going down;
Now grey shadows lengthen;
The school is now at rest.

The building is shutting its weary eyes,
Nodding its wise old head,
Thinking of you and me,
And putting itself to bed.

Peace and quiet invade the classrooms.
Noise has sunk to its knees;
The only sound that now intrudes,
Is the rattle of the caretaker's keys.

But hark, something new is stirring,
Walls are starting to tap their feet;
Doors are opening in harmony;
Buckets and brushes knock out the beat.

The corridors are alive with music,
The school mice prance around in pairs,
Competing with the rats and bats,
Wild country dancing on the stairs.

The cleaners join in the merriment,
And perform a sprightly can-can;
Caretaker Cuthbert is the conductor;
Waving in the air his brush and pan.

But wait a minute, what is this?
We spot danger lurking nearby;
Witches on jet propelled broomsticks
Zoom in squadrons across the sky.

Boom… boom… crackeroo!
Pow… pow… pow.. pow…pow!..
squidge… squidge… squidgeree do!
Bark…. Bark… Miaow…. Miaow!

They're banking right above our roof,
And dive-bombing the outside loos.
And look! They're being piloted
By pupils from Rival School!

Splosh, plonk, gedonk… gedonk!
Gobletedy, gobbledey gongs!
Jimminy cricket, zeberdee zoo!
Crikey,,,, cripes… and mighty pongs!

Caretaker Cuthbert now took charge,
Shouted, 'Guard the doors and windows!
Mice get ready to do your stuff,
Bugs and spiders and fire your salvos!'

Whizz bang,… yarooh…and blimee!
Weee.. ee…. Brm, brmm….. watch out!
Brmmm…. Brmmm… Yeeow, kow-tow…
Cor'blimmee…yarooh and… ouch!

Soon pens and pencils filled the air;
Piercing each broomstick and bottom.
Cuthbert yelled a loud 'Hooray!
'Well done, kids, we've got 'em!'

Hooray, hooray, hooray, hooray,
Hooray, hooray, hooray, hooray,
The Rival School has slunk away;
Hooray, hooray, hooray, hooray.

No-one is left in the school now;
The playground stands empty and quiet;
There's no more running and jumping,
No laughter nor shouts of delight.

No matter. , O alma mater,
We will always remember you,

15th *This rhyme could be one of a number of children's rhymes that mock personality. Jack Sprat comes from an era renowned for getting rich on the fat of the land.*

Jack Waving Grasses could eat no fat,
His wife could eat no lean.
And so between them both, you see,
They licked the platter clean.

This might be more fitting today.
Jack Sprat could eat no fat,
His wife could eat no lean.
So, Jack's too lean,
And his wife's too fat,
And they are seeing a dietician,
For advice on that.

16th Gulam's response on a request for an essay on 'The Royal Family' contained the following memorable observation:
'The Monarch is above the common herd, but the Prince and Princess of Wales are real human beings.'

17th Foreigners, foreign ways and foreign language are perennial sources of unintentional humour….. and it is not always British children that are saddled with the howler:
(taken from a letter from a French pen-friend):…
'I like very much athletics and often have the runs.'

18th *Overheard in the village pub.*
Old Farmer: I've just been feeding the pigs with my grandchildren.
Young Farmer: O aye…. And did they enjoy it?
Old Farmer: They certainly did…. those porkers are always wanting something different.

19th The vicar gave an impassioned sermon on the evils of 'the blame culture', but taking personal responsibility, failing to encourage team-work, joint endeavour, a sense of community…. and so on. After brief silence when he had rounded off with encouragement to see others' point of view, he announced the next hymn.

Perhaps because he was still reeling from the intoxication of the vicar's rousing words, the organist played one tune while the congregation sang another. The vicar allowed the chaos to reign for longer than he should before calling a halt. He then learned from the organist that he was playing the tune on the service schedule he had been given.

Shaking with rage as he saw his effective the vicar roared don from the pulpit, 'It is all the fault of the curate….. and I only gave him one thing to do!' The audible mirth and visible squirming of the congregation soon grabbed him, and his voice trailed off, and a haunted expression took over….. But he had not become a vicar, responsible for spreading God's word without a talent for retrieving the seemingly irretrievable..

'I apologise for losing my patience and tolerance….from the bottom of my heart…. to the curate, organist and all of you…..

And I let you know here and now that nest Sunday's sermon will be on 'God's Forgiveness of Human Fallibility'.

20th *A report from a teacher on playground duty:*
I put up my hand to stop Warren from falling into a hole and his face inadvertently caught my arm, bruising my wrist and breaking his nose. I immediately sought help from a first-aider who put my arm in a sling. It was too tight and I fainted. I came to in the headmistress's arms.

21st **History Teacher** (to Clarissa): And what did Henry the Eighth do to Ann Boleyn.
Clarissa (after a long pause): Well, miss, the least offensive way I can put it is this…. he put a bun in the oven and then cut the icing off the cake. Will that do?

22nd *Horace Walpole, son of the first British Prime Minister, Sir Robert Walpole, extolled the virtues of schooling.*
'Alexander, the head of the world, never tasted the true pleasure that boys of his own age have enjoyed as the head of a school.' *(Horace Walpole 1736)*

23rd *B.F. Skinner, the 20th century American psychologist, is saying below (in arguing that human actions depend on previous actions) is much the same as Walpole…. i.e. education' is more than the sum of what you learn…… it defines what you are.*
'Education is what survives when what has been learned has been forgotten.'
(B.F. Skinner 1964)

24th *On the other hand the eighteenth century genial Irish poet and playwright, Oliver Goldsmith, seems rather more dismissive about 'schooling'…..*
Let school masters puzzle their brain,
With grammar and nonsense and learning.
Good liquor I stoutly maintain,
Gives genius a better discerning.
(Oliver Goldsmith 1730- 74 – She Stoops to Conquer)

25th *But let's give the summing-up on the effect of education back to American Mark Twain …. it is witty, common-sensical and understandable, as his own education was 'life'…. as a printer and river-boat pilot:*
'Soap and education are not as sudden as a massacre, but they are more deadly in the long run.'

26th *A splendid quiddity from the pen of the former secretary of the Cambridge University Tiddlywinks Club.*

In October 1957 my attention was attracted by a headline in 'The Spectator':

Does Prince Philip cheat at Tiddlywinks?

As I was secretary of the Cambridge University Tiddlywinks Club (CUTwC), I clearly had to react to this so I wrote to Prince Philip suggesting that he might like to prove that he did not cheat at tiddlywinks by coming to play in Cambridge. He replied to say that he could not come in person but would like to appoint some 'champions' to play on his behalf. Could we suggest somebody?
We suggested the Goons as they were very popular at that time. A few days later, to my astonishment, a registered parcel arrived at my room in college. It contained a leather gauntlet and the message:
'Hear ye, varlet, to your sword do take 'pon, the date to be fixed, Sir Spike the Milligan'.

The date was fixed – for Saturday, March 1st, 1958. The four months preceding the match were a swirl of activities, including
--finding sponsors (the Goons signed up with Guinness, so we went for Babycham) an appearance on prime time television in 'Sportsnight with David Coleman' making the practical arrangements for the match (the tickets were sold out in a day and changed hands in the black market for ten times their face value).

Cambridge won the match in the Cambridge Guildhall. In spite of the efforts of Spike Milligan, Peter Sellers and Harry Secombe to intimidate us by their antics.

John Snagge and Chris Brasher were the umpires and the event ended with Harry Secombe singing the 'Tiddlywinks Anthem' to the tune of the March of the Men of Harlech (It was, after all, St. David's Day):

Other nations are before us,
With their Sputniks and Explorers
What can confidence restore us?
Naught but tiddlywinks!
On the fields of Eton, Former foes were beaten,
But today, all patriots play this sport which needs such grit and concentration.
Through this game of skill and power,
England knows her finest hour
And her stronghold, shield and tower, must be
TIDDLYWINKS !

The event raised hundreds of pounds for the National Playing fields Association, chosen by Prince Philip because tiddlywinks is one of the few sporting activities which does not require a playing-field, only a mat and a set of winks.

27th

For three years in the 1960s I played three matches for the Territorial Army rugby team against the Army. The Army team was always well trained and very fit; the TA team was a scratch XV making up for a lack of co-ordination by packing the team with internationals and top club players. It was a case of training and drilling versus know-how and skill.

In the one match the TA won the Army team needed just one try and a conversion to win.

A few minutes before the final whistle Army fly half hoisted a huge up-and-under kick towards the smallest player on our side, and England trialist famed for his side- steps and speed off the mark. The ball hung in the heavens for an age before dropping towards our diminutive winger. He took one look at the descending ball and at the huge forward hurtling towards him, did a s side-step to the left and then wanted the right and was off the field, without the ball but out of harm's way.

The Army forward was so surprised he slid to a halt and stared back at the flying winger.

The ball, bearing no fear nor favour, fell on the big man's head and bounced into touch. It was our throw-in and moments later the game was over...... a rare win for the TA.

Our winger claimed afterwards, and forevermore, but his mood was a deliberate ploy.

'It always works, you know… Never fails.'

I am still inclined to believe him.

28th   *While life goes on so do health and safety incidents, particularly in schools, where teacher anxiety leads to many incidents being reported in dystopian terms.*

'Re: the damage to the school mini-bus: I was driving out of the school gates when the notice-board saying 'Drive Carefully' hit the bumper.'

29th   **Play the Game**

In eighteen twenty three, at Rugby School;
At Rugby School…
William Webb-Ellis did something cool;
Something cool…

He caught a football and started to run;
Started to run…
Crying, 'I've invented rugger; isn't this fun?'

Isn't this fun?..

The sporting world was never again the same;
After Webb-Ellis founded the running game.

Webb-Ellis, Webb-Ellis, the greatness of the man;
Picked up the ball and ran and ran and ran;
Now the whole world has followed this up,
Competing e for the William Webb-Ellis cup.

Association and Union under a separate secretariat,
Separate secretariat …
Became soccer and rugger to the proletariat.
The proletariat….
Soccer stuck with teams of five or eleven;
Rugger, being posher, had fifteen or seven.

But disgruntled Northerners in 1895,
In 1895…
Decided they could on their own survive;
On their own survive…
They met in Huddersfield with much intrigue,
Turned professional and created the Rugby League;

Then women decided they could play the same,
Could play the same…
Proving that rugger is everyone's game.
Everyone's game…

They can swerve and side-step and tackle hard;
Push to save an inch, and shove to gain a yard.

William Webb-Ellis rests in a Riviera cemetery,
A Riviera cemetery…
Cared for by the French in awful symmetry,
Awful symmetry.
Though they'd killed Will's father in the Peninsular War,
Comradeship and respect is Rugby's common law.

Webb-Ellis, Webb-Ellis, the greatness of the man;

Picked up the ball and ran and ran and ran;
And now the whole world has followed this up,
Competing for the William Webb-Ellis cup.

30th *Retirement comes with its satisfactions and disappointments like the rest of life. There are gains and losses – like this one narrated by an old pal in a nostalgic mood.*

How I Lost My Bike

It was a Sunday morning, at least 10 years ago, probably more. I set off on my old bike, as was my wont on Sunday mornings, for Beacon Fell Country Park, a "designated area of outstanding natural beauty" about 6 miles or so from our village. It is the first bit of high ground one reaches if travelling east from the Lancashire coast across the flat Fylde plain, and stands in splendid isolation. Sadly it is only 873 feet high, and, therefore, does not qualify as a Marilyn.

The views from the summit are magnificent – the Lancashire coast to the west, and the Isle of Man on a clear day, the Lakeland fells to the north, the Forest of Bowland to the east and the Welsh hills to the south - with Deepdale, the home of Preston North End, in the foreground.

It is covered with coniferous woodland, criss-crossed by trails, has a one-way circular road around it below the summit, and a little café – an ideal destination for a bike ride.

It derives its name from being one of a chain of exposed hills where fires were once lit to warn of imminent danger. The earliest recorded beacon was in 1002, and beacons were lit there to warn of the Spanish Armada in 1588. They were also lit to warn of those pesky French in 1795 and 1815. The last time a beacon was lit was in 1977 to celebrate the Queen's Silver Jubilee.

My bicycle had an interesting history. It had belonged to the village policeman, and, legend has it, had been handed down over the years to each incumbent. At the time of my story Constable Martin had been our local bobby for some years. He lived with his family in the village police station a couple of doors down from our house, Downing. It is the same name as my Cambridge College, but I must make it clear that our house was not named by me in some daft act of self-aggrandisement. Its origins went back to 1767, some 30 years before the college was established, and it had been known as Downing ever since. Just happenchance that we came to live there.

Today the police station is still there, but sadly no local bobby. He has been replaced by two PCSOs, who are rarely to be seen. Former PC Martin, on the other hand, was always to be seen pedalling his way round the village during the day, and in our local pub in the evenings. All crime times covered.

I have to say, I greatly admired his bike. It was a traditional policeman's bike, possibly a BSA, A sturdy structure with big, heavy wheels and tyres, upright handlebars, mudguards of course, a Sturmey-Archer 3-speed gear, plus a large, soft, comfortable saddle with saddle bag, a front wheel dynamo, a chain cover and a loud bell. Immaculate.

Martin and I retired about the same time. As a consequence he had to relinquish the police house, and left the village. I did not know what had happened to his bicycle. But then, at my next birthday, my wife presented me with the finest present of all – PC Martin's bicycle! A secret deal she had made. Joy of joys. And so began my regular rides to Beacon Fell.

The route took me along quiet, flat country lanes for several miles until the approach to the Fell, when an ever-steepening lane led to the Fell circular road. No problem for me - and my Sturmey- Archer, of course (well, most times, anyway). Then a circular ride round the fell and a stop for a coffee, followed by the easy, downhill cycle home.

Then came the particular day in question. I was about half a mile from home when I was passed by another cyclist. He was wearing a cycling helmet, special cycling shoes which were held to the pedals by fancy clips, and he was clothed from neck to knee in lycra. I assumed he was a MAMIL (you know, a 'middle-aged man in lycra'), or something younger. I noticed that his cycle was in sharp contrast to my bike. It was ultra-light weight, with wheels so thin that they looked as if they might buckle at any minute, with similarly flimsy looking tyres. It had drop handlebars, an extremely thin and painful looking saddle, and a 1920-something derailleur gear. No mudguards, no chain cover, no lights, no saddle bag. What sort of a bike is that?

Then I noticed that he had stopped a hundred yards or so ahead. As I approached, I saw he had removed his helmet, and that he was an elderly man, probably in his eighties, and certainly a good ten years older than me, an EMIL *(an 'elderly man etc…)* rather than a MAMIL.

He was breathing heavily and I wondered whether he needed assistance, especially when he waved me down, but no, he was fine. He soon got his breath back as I pulled up alongside him.

Then came the bombshell.

"Sorry to stop you", he said, "but I just wanted to tell you that, in all my years of cycling, you are the first rider I have ever overtaken".

With that, he unsteadily mounted his cycle and accelerated smoothly through his twenty-something gears into the distance. Then I pedalled slowly the short distance home, deeply distressed.

I was not to be consoled. I left my bike in the garage and hung up my bicycle trouser clips. The following day my bicycle was collected by a local charity. My cycling days were over.

31st

During the coded pandemic years *The Oxford English dictionary* added a number of new words, like Covid 19 and lockdown. Inexplicably the list did not include the excuse of the year- 'unprecedented', which was the final refuge of politicians and many others with responsibilities who needed to explain away this agreeable facts.

Never Been A Rhyme Like It
Hooray for the new expression that's entered the lexicon,
A lifeline for common folk, like me, to fetch upon.
A positive product of the Covid pandemic,
A welcome addition to the life semantic,

Instead of the excuses you've pinched or invented,
All you say now is, 'It was
UNPRECEDENTED.'

By adopting such a beautiful concept,
Politicians have cleverly side-stepped
Inevitable criticisms of policy and precept.
When voters protested, wrung hands and then wept.

They banked on smelling rather more sweet-scented,
If they insisted, 'The times were
UNPRECEDENTED'.

So we, Joe public, with zeal can use it,
Every misdemeanour we can deftly excuse it,
Taking care that we do not abuse it,
As others, behind, may want to choose it.

We can show we are every bit as talented
At proving our mistakes were
UNPRECEDENTED.

So, on a night out a bloke takes one over the eight,
And drives his car home, at a very slow rate,
There's always someone unreasonably irate,
When he removes the paint from his neighbour's gate.

Your dignity will be, indubitably, augmented,
When your cry, 'Your Honour, it was
UNPRECEDENTED.'

When your partner checks the results of your shopping,
And asks, why no sugar, nor steak for chopping,
Why the chips are soggy and the carrots are flopping,
Why the chicken is so small and the turkey so whopping,

And why are six soup tins badly dented?
Don't grovel, just mumble, 'It was
UNPRECEDENTED.

And when the Maker who saw fit to put us here,
Surveys his creation over a pandemic year,
He will tip off a blind and ancient seer,
To predict the next world will be raised up a gear.

Because this project he'd never before attempted;
Not bad for a first that was,
UNPRECEDENTED

NOVEMBER

Lament of the Newly Qualified Teacher

Testing is all we have to do,
Right through stages one and two.
We will know what they can do,
But will they know what we're up to?

So whether or not I really hate it,
If it moves, I'll evaluate it.
I shan't think twice, it's rather nice.
To grade the little blighters.

We won't bother with tedious preaching.
We can leave all that classroom screeching
To computers, games and internet teaching.
Assessment rules, OK!

Rustic Ruminations: Pigs

A pig is a pig - it's not a ham nor pork;
(unless, I suppose, the ham's from York);
A pig's not bacon, rasher or streaky;
It's just a little piggie, a grunter or squeaky.

Except for boars and runts and greedy suckers,
Barrows and growers, and other muddy muckers;
Shoaters, and hogs, gilts and them little weaners,
And shoats and mishers and other has-beeners;

Half the pigs are sows, but all are swine,
So remember this now, and then for all time,
A pig, is a pig, however old or big;
A pig is a pig, is a pig.

I'm Sorry I Haven't A Clue

I said to my father the other day.
'I'm feeling unhappy, distinctly blue;'
Dad replied knowingly, as fathers do,
'You need your spirits lifting.

what will surely enliven you;
Is a dose of
I'm Sorry I haven't A Clue.'

It's a radio show,
A piece of medicinal insanity
Under the care of old Dr. Garden
Aided by a team of the same healing bent,
In a theatre where insanity is sane,
Just like the show that gave it Caesarean birth,
I'm Sorry I'll Read That Again.

4th

Loyal Party Men

We are loyal party men.
We don't make decisions; we don't ask for gen.
Knowing the facts is not our forte,
Asking questions would be quite naughty.

We are loyal party men,
We are consulted – now and again.
Once our opinion was often sought;
But we are low on original thought.

We are loyal party men.
We lift our hands if they tell us when.
Up down, up down, whatever they ask.
We are loyal party men.

5th   During the final rehearsal for the concert in the town hall, the Choir Secretary gave out her final instructions. 'At the end of the evening I expect the choir to leave the stage in the normal reverse order. The last thing I need is a mass evacuation by the basses.'

6th   **Maths Teacher:** If you are adding 756895 to 487294 and have added the 4 and 5 what do you do next?
Dirk: Give up.

The Chain of Life

Have you noticed how life goes on,
And on, and on, and on.

Everything depends on everything else;
But nothing is ever quite the same.
Everything dances and twirls together,
Life is a ball but also a chain;
And so life goes on and on.

The sun gives life to the grass and the trees;
Cows eat the grass and deer eat leaves,
We eat both the cows and the deers;
And so life goes on and on.

Tiny plankton live on light and algae,
Fish eat the algae in the deep ble sea,
We eat the fish for a scrumptious tea.;
And so life goes on and on.

Birds drop seeds which grow into flowers and trees,
The flowers yield nectar for worker bees,
We pick the fruit and collect the sweet honey,
And so life goes on and on.

Everything depends on everything else;
But nothing is ever quite the same.
Everything dances and twirls together,
Life is a ball but also a chain;
And so life goes on and on.

8th   *A mother told me that during a third Covid lockdown her daughter had written the following letter addressed to her headteacher. '*
Dear Miss, I am fed up with having to do all my work on a computer. Please send a teacher, by first-class post. And tell them to hurry up.'

9th

Sign of the Times

Time to get up,
Time to get ready for school.
The weather is fine,
The traffic is light,
You will enjoy a morning stroll.

I'm not going today,
But thanks for waking me like this.
I can do all the things I like to do,
And stay in bed much longer, too,
O what blissful bliss!

Don't be so silly,
Just get yourself ready, please do.
The bus will be arriving,

Your friend, Jim, will be driving,
And loads of others will be, expecting you.

I'm definitely not going,
I'm better off staying at home.
The teachers don't like me,
The kids only slightly,
The work makes me shudder and groan.

That is as maybe,
But think carefully of your street cred.
Don't be infuriatingly slow,
Just get up now and go;
You are after all, the Head.

Good Morning

Andrew, told me that he and his wife had walked along the south coast of Crete to Khora Sfakion, a delightful small fishing village.
'We found a room on the first floor by the harbour and woke the next morning to the sun shining over the waterside. I wandered out to see the fishermen tending their boats and mending nets. I had no Greek, but the odd word had stuck and I ambled round greeting them happily with my "Good morning", using a terribly upbeat voice. They nodded curiously back to m… simple folk, I thought, who met very few tourists in this off-beat place. They muttered cheerily to each other as I passed, and smiled to each other. What delightful people they were!
I returned to our room and happily repeated my greeting to my wife.'
'Kalamari',' I said.
She sighed. 'Squid to you too!... 'Good morning is' 'Kalameerah'. You'll have people thinking you're barmy".

I glanced out of the window and a large, smiling group of fishermen waved back.
A cock-up …. or did I add another chapter to international relations.

11th   This day was Armistice Day in 1918 when The Great War, the 'war to end wars' came to a shaky end. The nearest Sunday is now 'Remembrance Day' in the UK, when the nation remembers the sacrifices made in all wars.

For me there is a particular memory of meeting my father properly for the first time, in November 1944. It was on Platform 2 of Stoke-on-Trent station.

He had gone away to war when I was four and was returning from the war in Burma via hospitals in India and England. I was now seven and mum stood with us on Platform 2 amid a throng of servicemen and families and watched a thin, gaunt figure in RAF blue approach us.

Mum, unbeknown to us, had visited Dad in hospital some days before so there was no great show of emotion from her. She pointed to Dad and said, 'This is your dad.'

I did not know what to do, but I was well brought up, so thrust out my hand and said, 'Pleased to meet you.'
Dad ignored the hand and took me I his arms.

My sister, Elizabeth, however, was still too shy to greet this strange man and hid behind her mother. It was some days before she would leap into his arms.

And so, while the nation remembers with the customary dignity, I shall have my own personal world of remembrance, my memory of what war means to individuals and families and will wonder why 'the war to end wars' has done no such thing.

12th

Different Hills

She said the hills
Were alive with music.
But the only music we hear
In the hills near here,
Come from baas and *moos* and mobiles,.
Plus a Peregrine falcon spitting a screech
Before it dives from near 500 feet,

At 200kph, to grab some meat.

But I prefer the silence,
When you can hear yourself speak
But don't want to;
And watch the sun go down,
But can't do,
Because it's getting dark
And they'll shut the car park,
And then what on earth shall I do?

13th School Assemblies, acts of collective worship – compulsory in all state schools in the UK. – used to end with 'Notices' read out by the Head teacher from the stage, addressed, in secondary schools, to a mass audience of less than attentive teenagers…. . seething with worries, hormones and spots……
Not volunteers …. It was a captive audience.
Nowadays such 'Notices' can be delivered by electronic means, more efficient, but unlikely to generate the propensity for hilarity that were the bane of Head Teachers' lives.
One colleague remembers up to this day his first head teacher delivering one morning an apoplectic harangue about traffic jams on the staircases. 'He got completely carried away……. 'You know the school rule,' he shouted, scarlet in the face. *You go up the stairs on the left, and you come down the stairs on the right!'* Two hours of traffic chaos followed.

14th *(continued)* My colleague also recalls ruefully that a real killer was the notice thrust into your hands just before going onto the stage.

'One day, he said, a note was thrust into my hand by the deputy headmistress with a whispered request.' *Would you mind reading this notice?'*

Preoccupied with my last-minute planning of the assembly content, I would tuck the paper behind my notes and stride to my elevated position on the platform. Story, hymn or prayer over, I would proceed with the notices. Room changes, Saturday's sports results, tonight's meeting of the PTA and then, as I retrieve her unread note, 'Finally, a notice from Miss Wallace . . .

'Boys are still playing with their balls in the enclosed playground. This must stop….'

I folded the paper and bounded down the stage steps pronto.

15th   This same colleague vowed to be more vigilant at checking Assembly Notices, but was still caught out three weeks later.

'To be fair,' he said, 'This time it was a more complicated notice. It occupied two pages. At the bottom of the first page I got to, *The Medical Room is being redecorated: girls who feel unwell are to report instead to the secretary's office'*- I turn over the page and carried on - *'If possible, between periods.'*

Another quick bound off the stage was required.

16th   *It does not have to be a senior member of staff to cause embarrassment to a Head. My colleague's recollections included one occasion when tit was - the Prime Minister.*

He remembers 1973….. telling the governor that we had a choir that could sing in harmony. Therefore, we should hold a proper carol service in the town's Abbey Church. But Edward Heath, during a period of industrial and political chaos, had decreed the national three-day working week. and for long periods the electricity was liable to be cut off at any moment.

At two o'clock on the day we learned that the Abbey Church was to be plunged in darkness from 5.00 pm till 10.00, and foolishly I said that we would move the whole thing to the big school hall. We worked desperately to set it up - none harder than the event manager.

I wanted spotlights on the choir, I told her, and spotlights on the lectern for the readers. It was six-thirty before I was ready to drive the nine miles home to change, and parents and governors would be arriving in thirty minutes time.

When I got home, Prime Minister Heath had struck again. The whole village was in darkness.

An anxious wife met me at the door with a sandwich…. and a candle. 'I've put candles upstairs,' she said, 'and your interview suit is hanging on the wardrobe door.' By the skin of our teeth we made it back to school, and I stood in the concourse to greet the Mayor and the governors. At twenty nine minutes past seven I walked into the Hall, crossing in front of the assembled staff to take my seat.

As I did so, with a modicum of self-satisfaction, the young art teacher leaned forward and said, quietly but quite distinctly,

'I see you've started smoking again, Headmaster.' I must have looked confused at this, for she gestured towards my feet. I glanced down - and my heart stopped. From my collar to my waist I was impeccably dressed. … but from my waist to my shoes I was wearing, unmistakably, my painting trousers!

The nearest sanctuary was the boys' toilets. So, ignoring two surprised fifth formers and a strong smell of tobacco, I desperately scratched at the multi-coloured paint marks. No improvement. Back in the concourse I met an anxious event manager. No time for explanations

"I want all the spotlights out!' I told her.

'But Headmaster . . .' she tried to say.

'Out!!' I cried . . . and in semi-darkness and with murder in my heart, sat down beside my somewhat mystified wife.

'Do you know what you've done?' I hissed and gestured at my knees. There was a little yelp of horror. 'You'll have to make an announcement,' she said.

I didn't, of course, and somehow, the choir and the readers and I got through the evening. The staff and the governors found the whole thing hilarious . .and so, once my injured pride had healed, did I.

17th My colleague completed his account of his Assembly Days with a tale about an Assembly where his headmasterly reflections were based on his memory of an inscription on a column erected by Emperor Trajan, which was found during his National Service in Jordan in the 1950s. 'It was exquisitely carved,' he told me, ' and I remembered the term the Romans used to describe true workmanship. They would say it was *sine cera* – literally 'without the beeswax' – a substance that a dishonest mason would use, mixed with granite dust, to hide a false chisel cut. It's the origin of our word 'sincere'.

So there, in outline, was my next assembly: a story, a phrase of Latin, a theme. Perfect.

I demanded and got, with difficulty, a blackboard and chalk. So wrapped up was I in how to lead into my talk that I paid no attention to the thumbs-down sign by my colleague who had produced the backboard….. not even when he mouthed, ' a bit dodgy'.

The next few moments were pure West End comic extravaganza. I explained that I was going to tell them a story about the Romans in 12AD…. And I am going to start by writing two short Latin words.. With a flourish I wielded my piece of chalk and with a firm hand I began to write SINCER……

Halfway through the down stroke of the R, the right hand easel peg (it proved to be a much-chewed HB pencil) parted company with the easel. The blackboard crashed on to my foot, toppled over the edge of the platform and with a sickening crack landed squarely on the heads of three attentive 12 year olds in the front row. There was a stunned silence in the hall.

With commendable disregard for what felt like a broken toe, I leapt lightly down to minister to the wounded pupils. In my haste I landed on the blackboard itself, feet at an angle, black gown flowing from my shoulders, and together, blackboard and I sped across the parquet floor, crashed into the piano, and came to rest beneath it.

For a long moment the silence held, then there was a storm of rapturous laughter, mingled with appreciative applause.

I looked up into the not wholly sympathetic face of the head of music, and asked him feebly to announce the hymn.

It was *Bright the vision that delighted,* but few of those present were in any state to sing it.

18th   **The Cock-up Chant**

The chant of HM' Loyal Opposition in Parliament

Recessions, Repressions,
Intercessions, Depressions,
Aggressions, Transgressions.
Debacles two a penny,
Calamities come and go.

Progressions, Regressions,
Processions, Successions,
Compressions, Suppressions.
You wouldn't believe it,
If I didn't tell you so.

Inflations, Deflations,
Stagnations, Indignations,
Sensations, Agitations.
Murder and massacre,
Makes our anger grow.

In fact --
It's – just – one- big – laborious,
Never-ending –– nauseous,
Long-standing --- glutinous,
On-going --- calamitous,
Foot-stamping – spurious

Teeth-grinding -- ,contrarious
Just an old-fashioned -- tear-jerking -- glorious – almighty
….. COCK-UP!

19th *A friend told me this touching story recently.*

For some years our next-door neighbour was a pleasant, but somewhat batty lady….. plus her miserable dog, a mongrel trying to be an Irish wolf hound
One day the lady made a tray of jam tarts. She removed them from the oven and set them down to cool. For some reason she was distracted and went to open the front door. Returning to the kitchen she found that the jam tarts had vanished but 'dog; was still visible.
'You wicked dog!' she screamed, raising her arm like a prize-winning boxer. The dog took one look and then was off….. vanishing into thin air. ….
through the front door, down the street and out of sight round the corner. It had its tail between its legs According to other neighbours said dog had looked even more miserable than usual …. with a look that suggested he had given up on being a mighty wolfhound!
The lady banged the front door shut and returned to the kitchen where she discovered her jam tarts, intact, exactly where she had left them.
We heard her shouting and wailing on her doorstep,
'Come back! I didn't mean it.'

20th **A Past Pupil's Paean of Praise**

Praise to the lord, my dear headteacher,
Highest oracle and wit that I know.
Professor, mentor, inspiring preacher,
Magnetic, galvanised, all get up and go.

Praise to the employers who thought to appoint them,
Wise and cunning they must have been.
On blackboard shrines we should anoint them,
Chalk successes where they're sure to be seen.

Praise to the subservient acolytes,
The teachers, whether tottering or bold,
Content to be the classroom Hittites,
Having to do whatever they're told.

That is how things should be ordered,

Bosses, chiefs and then all the rest.
The lowly workers must be lauded,
Or they'll never ever give of their best.

I hope that history will repeat itself,
And the status quo will forever be.
I need such a boost to my mental health,
Because now that headteacher is me.

Quis Didit? Quis Dedit?

Caesar ad sum iam forte;
Dum Brutus aderat.

iam forte?
O Yea, O Yea.

Unde Gloria?

Gloria forte et possum curre,
Plus extra totarum.

Forte? Ahweh!!
O yea! O yea!
Craequay!
O Yea., O Yea.

Tellus more…. tellus feste… tellus lauda.

Gloria, mundi, sic in transit;
Caesar sic in omnibus.
Sed Brutus, sic indicat.

Indicat!
O Haec… O Hac!
O Hoc… O Hic!
Tellus more… tellus more… tellus feste.

Apollo sed
'Super Caesar cadaver bonus;

Sed dum Brutus iusta agrunt.'
Apollo sed, ''
Gloria, putabit ergo interim!'
Gloria seder woad .

Seder woad! Seder woad!
Gloria seder woad?

O Hanc, O Hinc! O flippin' His!
Quid effectus?Quid finis?
O Hi! O Hae! O bloomin' Ha''
Quid fecit gloriosa Gloria?

Gloria iusta didit… Brutus fixit…. Caesar dedit….
Historia nunc est finis…
Gloria iusta didit… Brutus fixit… Caesar dedit…
Historia nunc est finis…

O Mi… O Mae… O Ma!
Dedit est, O Caesar!

O Hic , O Haec! O Fortuna!
Finis nunc sed historia!

22nd   *Notice on church noticeboard.*

WHAT IS HELL?
Come and listen to the sermon on Sunday

23rd   **The School Brochure**

An error in the new School Brochure has been brought to the Listening Ear's eager attention:
'
The school's intake depends on parental performance. Great weight and importance is attached to this criterion, which may be tested by the governors…. in their own time, and at their own discretion.'
The Ear presumes the phrase should be 'parental preference'…. But you never know these days. We look forward to the Principal's explanation.

Rustic Ruminations: The Farmyard

The cows are a-mooing, the sheep are a-baaing,
A porker is chasing a black and white sow;
While the hens are a-clucking;
The sheep dog's a-barking;
How do you sleep with such a row?

25th

A Scheming Boss

(with more apologies to Messrs Gilbert and Sullivan)
As some day it may happen that a teacher must be found,
To do an extra duty on the open-air playground,
Then I've got a little list, yes, I've got a little list
Of victims who are innocently wandering around,
Who are hoping to be missed, by good Fortune to be kissed.

There's the pestilential nuisance who rings up after prayers
To tell me they'll be absent through sundry personal cares.
And the school trip leaders, who are far too bloomin' keen,
Who know where they are going, but don't know where they have been.
I've got them on the list; they'll none of them be missed.

And teachers who invigilate but seldom with good grace,
Who grumble, snort, prevaricate, and pull a childish face,
And those who question why I'm always free,
And say I am not working when I leave the school at 3,
I'll have them on my list; they certainly won't be missed.

In fact, all those who on criticising me insist.
None of them will be missed; all of them are on my list.

26th *'Little Jack Horner' is also an 18th century children's rhyme, with once again a likely reference to a real person., but who cares about that! It has always been a favourite with parents introducing words and actions to small children.*

Little Jack Horner
Sat in the corner,
Eating his Christmas pie;
He put in his thumb,
And pulled out a plum,
And said, "What a good boy am I!"

It doesn't really need to be amended to appeal to children today, but I am going to give it a little twist.

Little Annie Mabel
Sat at the table,
Eating a meal from the deli.
She plonked in her fork,
Pulled out a piece of pork,
And said what a great biryani'.

27th   There are many ways of celebrating retirements, but one ritual has now gone forever. That was the attendance, before a proper retirement dinner, at the afternoon performance at the famous London Windmill Theatre, famous until its closure as a theatre in 1964 for its scantily clad 'Windmill Girls'. It was the only theatre allowed by the Lord Chamberlain to have semi-nude girls on stage – but under severe restrictions!

The girls had to have some sort of covering when dancing – usually large feathers expertly flicked and controlled. When standing or sitting still they had to be facing to stage right so that there was no chance of even accidental full-frontal nudity.

My informant, Paul, , tells me that when he was taken there for his retirement 'do' with a strictly male group of office colleagues it was pointed out to him that the most sought-after seat in the house was front row extreme left. After that came anywhere to the left of centre front. I only appreciated all this when I got into the theatre and understood why I had been unceremoniously pushed out of the way immediately the box office opened.

'By the time I staggered into the auditorium,' said Adam, 'all the front row and second row seats were occupied and then the first seat both left and right of every other row behind the first row. There was absolutely no-one in the centre seats at all - except me. I decided that it might be fun - and politic - to remain about ten rows back and watch what happened. It did not take long to work out the tactics.

The programme ran continuously through from 2.00pm to late at night. Men (and it was, it seemed, all men in the afternoon) would leave at various times and if a front row seat was vacated one of the men on the left or right would quickly move forward. One would fall into the front row seat; the others would all move one row down.

Now, one of my colleagues was Roger who claimed to be a de-frocked priest, although none of us were sure whether this was true or not. It meant, however, that he was known as Rev at work.

I watched my saintly colleague, 'Rev, making his way by calculated steps down the left-hand side clutching his briefcase. I also noticed a large man in a brown mac keeping pace down the right.

Eventually they were level two rows back. A seat became available near the middle of the front row and our currently frocked 'Rev' set off at speed.

His opponent was faster but hampered by the fact that the person vacating the seat in the middle front was moving out in his direction. It meant thaty Rev and Brown Mac were neck and neck pushing their way along the front row between the orchestra pit and the front row feet.

Meanwhile, the sparse audience was in two minds as to which to keep an eye on......stage or auditorium I feel sure that bets would have been laid…..but events were moving swiftly to a climax…. the girls on-stage were high-kicking above them….fans were flouncing……other things were bouncing…. and Brown Mac and the Rev were near to pouncing. The world seem to stop…..The horses were running neck and neck.

Brown Mac, stronger, faster…..and probably more experienced…… might just have won by a short head…..but at the crucial moment, our Rev….confident perhaps of his spiritual superiority…. had halted and was swinging his bag to and fro and gazing intently at the vacant seat ahead of him. The orchestra just below the front row played even louder….the girls above them kicked even higher…..

As the brown job got to within one seat of the winning tape the Rev completed his swing and lobbed his bag…. with speed and precision…..straight into the vacant seat from six feet away. They both stared at one another and at the briefcase…..

A moment's pause and then the Rev was heard to say above the crescendo of the 'Can-Can',

'Mine, I think.'

And so it was….

The conductor slashed a final beat of his baton across his chest....the cymbals and timpani let out a resounding crash...... the girls leaped in the sir and came down in a single row of straddles......feathered fans deftly covered all indelicacies.

Winner took all! And that was 'Rev'.

I speculated on whether this kind of briefcase-lobbing' was the origin of the phrase 'to bag' something! But nice as this explanation might be, I suspect that 'bagging' something comes from hunting, shooting and slaughtering .....though come to think of it, that suits this occasion perfectly.

28th *A short extract from a radio interview*
interviewer: I understand your childhood was quite difficult.
Interviewee: Yes, I lived with my parents in a two-up two-down terraced house. There were 15 of us children. Dad worked down the coalmine.
Interviewer: Not often, it appears.

29th *The stand-off between the West and the 'Eastern Block' in the second half of the 20th century,, known as The Cold War, brought to the surface once again the British affection for good humour in the face of adversity.... This prevailing mood was echoed in the writings of teenagers in school magazines. Here is one set of entries from my collection:*

Important Announcement by the Editor

In view of the deterioration in relations between 'The West' and 'The East'.... somewhere or other.... notices will shortly be posted in all work areas – except the staff toilets - with instructions to be followed in the event of a sudden nuclear attack.. These must be learned and followed.... in addition to fire drill.

The danger will be signalled by three short rings on the automatic bell – which is a distant high-pitched whining, not unlike the sound that emanates from Lower School Assembly hymn-singing each morning....or if that does not work, the Headmaster will ring the school hand-bell with noticeable rhythmic vigour.

On the ringing of the alarm the following will hppen:

The School Office will be closed, except for emergencies.
All books must be returned to the Library IMMEDIATELY.

ALL LOWER SCHOOL PUPILS MUST GET INTO THEIR PAPER SACKS AND HIDE UNDER THEIR DESKS BEFORE THE FIRST BOMB DROPS.

This is essential. Any Lower School pupil caught outside a bag will be put into Headmaster's detention…. which will take place at the earliest opportunity…. When an appropriate bag is available.

If you are ordered to crawl under desks to avoid blast you MUST take care not to bump your head, as it is likely that the school nurse will be out of action under her own desk.

The Senior school will assemble in the School Hall where the orchestra will play *'Abide with me, fast falls the eventide.'* The Choir will sing their new descant.

The Upper Sixth physicists will stand by to observe the Doppler effect.

  All suspected fatalities will be marked in the School Register with a cross in PENCIL (in case of error).

All near-fatalities must bring excuse notes to the office WITHIN THREE DAYS.

The Head Boy and Head Girl wishes to emphasise that they intend to go down with the school.

30th   **Lateral thinking**

Question: How do you get an elephant into a fridge?
Answer: Easy…. You just open the door and put it in.
Question: so, how do you get a kangaroo in?
Answer: You can't….. There's already an elephant in there.

DECEMBER

Rustic Ruminations: Winter

Winter kicks in with promises a-plenty,
Toboggans, cheery faces, mulled wine for the gentry.
This, I'm afraid, is largely balderdash;
Most of us in winter are strapped for cash.

But lest you think I'm a craven cynic,
I now aver to all, in public,
Country living, I am sure, is really idyllic.

Santa's Grotto

It was probably the most exciting day in Charlie Short's life, so far. It was one year after the end of the second world war and The city's largest department store had announced that for the first time in six years Santa would be appearing, exclusively, in the store's Christmas grotto. Gifts were available for children on the day of the visit and orders for Christmas presents could be whispered into Santa's ear.

' At last!' thought Charlie, 'a chance to find out if Christmas is what mum has been describing to us for six years!

'Will we really get something different from the yellow rubber duck …. the same-looking one each year, that Santa had been able to deliver throughout the war?'

He knew what he wanted, and after all his deprivations during the war he reckoned he deserved it.

Santa's grotto was easy to find. Music, lights, tinsel and cut-outs of scantily dressed fairies and scary pink and green gremlins marked the route. But what was strange was that many families were coming in the opposite direction, leaving the grotto. Only a few were joining the queue. In fact, there was only one family outside the grotto entrance when they got there, - a mum with a small boy and older girl.

'What's going on?' asked Mrs. Short.

'We've been told to wait,' said the lady. 'No reason given.

I'm thinking of leaving. 'It's not good enough.'

Charles, ever inquisitive, sidled towards the closed grotto curtains. Just as he got there the curtains were thrown open and a lanky-legged, tinsel-laden fairy carrying a lethal-looking wand confronted him.

'What d'yer want, lad?.... The grotto's closed. Can't yer see?' growled the fairy in a broad North Staffordshire accent.

'Perhaps people from Lapland speak many languages,' he mused. After all, they do get about a bit. And he was getting more than sceptical about the proliferation of Santas in the world. There were at least three Santas advertised in the city's shops that same day, he had noted. It was understandable that Santa would need a fair number of 'deputy Santas' these days when there were more people in the world….. but three in one place…..well…. I mean…..This smacks of commercial exploitation of the real Lapland Santa Claus…..It needed investigating.

'Just wondering when you were going to open,' he said….in his 'innocent-sounding voice. 'Have you lost Santa then?'

Charles was feeling a little mischievous. The fairy's face hardened…. And darkened.

'You just watch it, lad. Or you'll get this wand round yer jacksie,' she hissed.

Then she stepped back, contrived a smile, which despite her best efforts looked more like a lop-sided grin, and assumed a fairy-like pose in front of the entrance. Then suddenly some loud music blared out from the depths of the grotto and Fairy Jane started hopping in a non-ballet-like fashion from foot to foot, very nearly in time with Jingle Bells that had started to chime out of a crackly sound system.

She smiled sweetly at the two families and the others beginning to join the queue.

'Santa will be with us soon, boys and girls,' she said with what Charlie considered a leer, but was meant to be a welcoming smile. 'She needs more practice,' he thought.

The fairy hopped and skipped down the growing queue, leaving Charles the chance to edge towards the curtain that was now blowing about in a draught from behind. He was just in time to see a large red dressing gown being pulled off a jacketless man in braces and large white beard half hanging from his chin. He was lying prone on the floor, surrounded by two blokes in brown overalls and a dapper man in a grey suit..

'Get him out of here, Walker, as quick as you can,' cried Grey Suit through gritted teeth. 'And the bottles, too,' he added.

'And you, Fred, get that outfit on double quick, or we'll lose all the customers. Jane is out there strutting her stuff and telling the punters we will soon be ready for them.'

Fairy Jane had, in fact, moved back to the front of the queue to encourage Mrs. Short and the others to remain where they were. She offered to up her entertainment but got no encouragement.

She was just gathering herself to make a gigantic, eye-catching leap when She caught sight of Charles bending down at the entrance.

'You again!' she hissed even more menacingly.

'Are all fairies like you?' asked Charles giving her his sweetest sile yet.

Fairy Jane had had enough…. She let out an animal-like growl, started to aim a kick at Charlie's backside, but stopped in mid-air when she saw customers turning to look for the source of the commotion. And with an extraordinary and dextrous twist of her thigh turned the kick into a wobbly arabesque, while at the same time peering down at Charles and whispering.

'Get back in the queue, yer little so-and-so!'

Before she could add any further threat Charles pointed into the grotto and said as nonchalantly as he could muster for a ten-year-going-eleven year old,

'I see you've found another Santa, then. How many have you got?'

'Don't be so bloomin' insolent, yer smardie little beggar….. Get back in the queue, NOW!' The fairy' agitation was showing….as well as her khaki knickers, now popping out of her too small tu-tu..

'My mother says we must never swear,' said Charles as angelically as he could. 'It's not nice.'

Fairy Jane did not answer. The crowd was now eying the entrance in anticipation. The little girl at the front of the queue was close to the flapping curtains. She suddenly turned to her mum with wide open eyes.

'Mum. That's not Santa! He's not got a Santa beard. Heh, it's… it's… Fred Adams from down our road!'

'No, it's not, little girl. You are mistaken,' squeaked the fairy hastily. 'Our manager is just getting Santa's new clothes ready for his arrival. Didn't you see Santa in his sledge at the weekend driving through the centre of the city – with all his reindeer and sacks of presents, eh?'

'Yes, I did,' admitted the little girl. 'But that wasn't Fred Adams. It was the real Santa!'

Fairy Jane once again stopped hopping as she got the signal from the grotto.

'Well, I am sure that Santa has got here now. So in you go. Tickets first, please. Thank you. Put your names on this sticky label and then you are ready to meet Santa Claus. They entitle you to one Santa present each today, and the chance to sit next to Santa'and tell him what you want for Christmas. Where are you from children?' She addressed the leading family group.

'Longton.'

'I'm sure Santa will know that you come from… Longton,' she said raising her voice. 'Longton, eh. That's nice. In you go, young Longton.'

Charles and Ian stood together outside waiting for the reappearance of the Longton family. The curtains opened almost immediately. No time wasted. The Longton family swept out, the little girl protesting. 'It WAS Frank Adams, ma. You could see him behind the beard.'

Ma had had enough. 'I bring you here and all you do is cause trouble. You've got your presents. Let's go.'

The last Charles and his mum heard was the lady from Longton muttering,

'Yer dad always says that Christmases do more harm than good.' Then they were gone and Charles and Ian were in the grotto, alone with Santa.

Charles had told the fairy that they were from Middle Wallop under Needwood, which he reckoned would be far too long for Santa to pick up in the grotto, hampered as he was by an unfamiliar covering of his ears by white cotton wool.

To Charles's chagrin Santa did not bother to repeat where they came from.

'Come and sit next to me and whisper in my ear,' said Santa, with a beaming smile and shower of cotton wool

'No, thanks, Santa,' replied Charles briskly. 'I've just come to tell you I want a Hornby train set. That's all.'

'I'll sit next to you,' cried Ian, putting his hand up as though he were at school. Ian did not want to hedge his bets. For ten Dinky cars and a model garage he was happy to risk bristles of Santa's beard.

Santa turned away from Charles and smiled at Ian. This time he swept the cotton wool away from his mouth.

'Come on, then, little boy….. I think this is going to be a bumper Christmas for a nice boy like you.'

While Ian was leaping to Santa's side with enthusiasm, Santa gave Charles a disapproving glance.

'Some boys don't deserve presents but kind little boys might get everything they ask for…. 'Now whisper in my ear what you want. You can give me two choices if you like.'

Charles duly obliged, and when Santa drew back, said,

'Don't you want to know where to deliver it, Santa?'

Charles waited, expectant,

'That'll teach you,' he thought.

But Santa was ahead of the game. He had stood in before as Santa's deputy.

'Oh, Oh, Oh,' he chortled in true Santa fashion, 'I know where you live, …er, Ian. Don't you worry about anything. Santa and his little helpers know EVERYTHING. Now pick a present from my sack over there quickly, and off you go.'

'Oh, clever,' thought Charles admiringly, grabbing the top parcel. Ian did likewise.

'I hope it's not another yellow rubber bath duck like last year,' Charles said to his mum when they re-joined her. 'Not worth a penny let alone sixpence.'

'Please don't be ungrateful, Charles. Whatever it is, it's a present and we should be grateful that after a war we have any presents at all.'

'Yes, I suppose so, mum. Can we go to the café and have tea and cake and open the parcels?'

'No. We have to get back to dad. He's on his own minding the shop. You can open them on the bus.' She knew there was no point in trying to get the boys to keep the presents till Christmas day. She did not want the inevitable pestering.

The bus back home was just as crowded and Ian had to perch on mother's knee. Charles stood holding on to the back of a seat. He started to open the parcel as they left the bus station but did not get it open till Hartshill. Ian got the paper off first.

'It's a pistol,' he cried out much to the amusement of the returning shoppers. 'Look, Charles. It's a water pistol. Wow. Just wait till we get home.'

'How nice,' said mum without much enthusiasm.

'It's all right,' said Charles. 'I'll show you how to shoot it.'

'No you won't, our Charles. I know you. You'll pinch it.' Ian tucked it protectively under his armpit.

Charles shrugged his shoulders. was not bothered. He had got to the last piece of ripping off, and then the plain box. He peered in. He lifted his head to the heavens.

'I can't believe it!' he muttered. 'It's not a yellow rubber duck. It's a ruddy blue one!'

He lifted it in the air, wishing he could lob it through the window. 'Who could possibly want two rubber ducks?' He looked around, 'Does anyone want a blue duck,

……sixpence …. very rare?'

3rd   Mother and father sat daughter Sandra down and told her in
       high excitement that they had booked a summer holiday to Turkey.
       'Aaaarrgh,' cried Sandra in ear-splitting volume…..

'I've told you before…. I HATE turkey!…. we have it at school and it's disgusting. o you can stuff your turkey!'

4th   *And another turkey tale.*
Two primary school pupils chatting in the playground:
Sian: My dad went to China today via Turkey.
Catrin: Well, my dad went to Australia by aeroplane.

5th   *And a final Turkish delight:*
Religious Education teacher: How would you define 'eternity' Peter?
Peter (without a pause for thought): A Christmas turkey, miss.

6th
The Bubble of Birmingham

William Butler Yeats was a towering genius with words, but also a practical man of hid time, a Fleet Street journalist, co-founder of The Abbey Theatre, Dublin, a Senator in the first days of the Irish Free State and a Nobel prize-winner.
*   ' The Lake Isle of Innisfree' is a dreamy poem…. an expression of his longing to get away from London and disappear to the isolate lake isle of Innisfree where his parents used to take him in his youth.*
I wondered in my own idle moment during the strange 2020 pandemic lockdown periods what a young worker in London might write at this time, when solitariness had been forced on so many by the Covid crisis.

I cannot arise now and go to Innisfree,
No small cabin can I build there with clay and wattles made.
I am locked down in Birmingham with my friend and his family,
A babbling bubble, like a bee-loud glade.

Only six people have gathered here, the number that's been decreed,
Drowsiness catches us nightly from the wine, the gin and the beer;
The aroma rises from the alley where late drinkers have stopped and pee'd,

Masks will keep my air fresh and clear.
I wash my hands as instructed, though no-one has mentioned my face,
Keeping two metres apart from my neighbour, doing nothing in excess,

I know I am doing my duty as I wait for a test or a trace,

Saving the country's hard-pressed NHS.
(for my many foreign friends – the NHS is the National Health Service, which like so many other medical and nursing services around the world performed major and minor miracles on a daily basis during the Covid19 period)

7th   Mr Bagshot was a handsome entertainer, renowned for entertaining senior citizens at Christmas time. One year, the British sherry had flowed freely in the factory canteen and Mr B in the guise of Santa Claus pranced jauntily onto the canteen stage. He hailed the merry pensioners and swung his bag round and round. Overcome by Christmas cheer he twirled his sack once too often and too fast and flung himself into the air. His flailing body crashed down somewhat ungracefully onto the front row of admiring oldies, who thought it was all part of the Bagshot act.
Mr. Bagshot commented from his hospital bed,
'Although I fractured my right hand (my writing hand). I must commend the concern shown for my welfare by one of the ladies who, quite unnecessarily, attempted to give me the kiss of life. 'She showed surprising persistence for a 8- year old.'

8th   *An ICT Exam Question*
Question: What is a 'stand-alone computer system?
Agatha: One that comes without a chair.

9th   *Another ICT Question*
Teacher: What are the advantages of video-conferencing?
Alistair: (1) You cannot smell the other people at the meeting.
(2) You can go and get a cup of tea without being noticed.
(3) You can laugh at the others without being seen.

10th Demure and infuriatingly clever 12 year old Ruth put her hand up in an English grammar lesson just before Christmas, and asked Mr. Shelley 'Are Santa's little helpers subordinate clauses.'
She was immediately invited to join the school magazine team.

11th

A Grieving Couple

Gordon' King-Wenceslas looked out
From his study in St Stephen,
While the snow was lying about,
Deep and crisp and even.

He saw a person across the field,
Staggering through frost so cruel,
With his scarf his face did shield,
Gathering winter fuel.

'Heather Page, come quick,' said he,
And his deputy came running.
'Know'st thou who yon thief might be,
Anti-social, disruptive, cunning?'

'A. Porman, who was a pupil here,
And was always cadging goodies,
At cheating Porman had no peer,
At uni he did Media Studies.'

'Where dwells he now, in this snow?'
'Sir, he lives 'neath the mountain
In a modest bungalow
By St Aggy's School fountain,

A Restraining Order do I advise,
Plus a simple prosecution
He's taken twigs of varying size,
He is not worth our absolution.'

'But St Stephens is a community school,'
Thought Gord, and very caring.
'Take to him logs and gooseberry fool,
And meat and veg unsparing.'

'Oh no!' quoth she,' for goodness sake,
'Tis beyond my obligations.
No unfair directions can you make,
It offends the regulations.

'Twill freeze my blood, attack my bones
So against Gord I have a grievance.
O, mighty judges, hear my moans,
Reward my perseverance.'

'She wore my heated boots,' said Gord
She lacketh basic charity.'
The judges, though clearly bored,
Spoke with crystal clarity.

'Through rude winter's wild lamenting
Page and Wenceslas must struggle,
To take food and logs a 'plenty.
And give poor folks a cuddle.'

So be assured you teachers all
Rank or power possessing
Do what's right what 'ere may fall,
You'll get the judges' blessing.

12th   It is well known that parents can be easily aggrieved and even litigious when schools seem to err. But a new feature was evident recently at Much Knowing Primary School where its precocious pupils have become aware of the endless and profitable possibilities of litigation. They found fertile ground in the annual nativity play.

    The first sign of impending trouble came after the Head's announcement at morning assembly that Simeon would not be continuing with the part of the Archangel Gabriel because extorting sweets from Year 3 pupils for unspecified angelic favours was unseasonably naughty.

    Simeon waited just one day before delivering his solicitor parents' brief letter suggesting that either Simeon was reinstated, or the question of substantial damages for defamation might have to be explored.

    At this point the Head took sick leave. The music teacher was left in sole charge of the production. At the next rehearsal Delilah (aged nine) broke into uncontrollable tears when told that she could certainly not play one of the three Kings, as these were boys' parts. In between sobs she managed to indicate her intricate knowledge of the scope of Part 6 of the *Equality Act 2010.* Her suggestion that the dressing gowns worn by the kings could equally well be worn by girls was considered highly plausible.

    So, Shane now became ex-King Balthasar and was consigned to the back row of the choir of angels, where he demonstrated his disgruntlement by flicking stardust all over the front-of-stage flock of sheep and the attendant shepherds. In this he was aided by shepherd Wayne, who considered the role to be 'cissy'. He had purloined the make-up box – 'for added interest', he pleaded – and had already been prevented from branding the Year 2 sheep with red and black stars.

However, Wayne and Shane's dastardly act was spotted from the back of the hall by the Head who had now been restored to health by a large slug of yellowish liquid kept for medicinal purposes in his desk drawer. He rushed forward, grabbed hold of both boys, and cuffed them about ears. 'Only gently,' he claimed at his subsequent disciplinary hearing, following complaints by Wayne who was the most aggrieved of the two.

Shane considered he had a better chance of success and financial reward under the *Abolition of Corporal Punishment Act 1997* which made corporal punishment a criminal offence, with the enticement of potential civil litigation on the back of it. The case is pending but the Head is relying on the defence that his actions prevented a greater hurt. He is not hopeful.

The calm that descended at this point was shattered by a dreadful scream from the front end of the donkey. Eponymous Joseph, feeling bored with the inactivity at his end of the stable, had shoved a candle from the crib up the backside of the animal. Rear-end Darren leapt in the air causing front-end Erasmus to fall off the stage, dragging the rear end with him. Both suffered cuts and bruises.

The writ when it arrived mentioned the *Health and Safety at Work Etc Act 1974,* the *Occupiers Liability Act 1984*, and 'in loco parentis', citing the school for negligence in not taking into account the propensities of small boys to do unmentionable things with attractive lethal objects.

The Head returned to sick leave.

13th At the age of 90 my mother was taking yet another course at the University of Keele studying Renaissance art. At the end of the year the lecturer got together a party to travel to Florence to see some of the art they had been studying. My mother on the principle of *'see Florence and die….'* promptly put her name down and off she went. She was determined to record as much of the adventure she could and so wrote down the name of each station the train passed through from Pisa airport to Florence. She did this assiduously for an hour until an Italian lady opposite, with a huge smile on her face, mum said, lent forward and whispered, 'excuse me, you have just written 'USCITA' four times; it means 'EXIT'!
'Well, Chris, I learnt something, didn't I?'

In Stubbs Walks

In Stubbs Walks there is a big beech tree,
Up in its branches the whole world you can see;
Right over the Trent Valley to the distant sea;
Or maybe it's Trentham Lake; it's all the same to me.

Below I see Gary being chased by my brother;
He's after his ball …. or perhaps his scooter;
Maisie and Hattie are in a bit of a bother;
Maisie cries, 'Stop it, or I'll tell my mother'!

Allo! Here comes trouble, big Bomber Brian,
And behind slouch his gang all in a line,
Safety in numbers, 'cos they've got no spine;
But the little kids have scarpered; they saw the sign.

Bomber stands dejected in the middle of the ground,
Looking to see if some fun's to be found,
Chasing cats around and around,
Or grinding some noses into the ground,

I think I am better off up in my tree,
High up above all that I can see;
Looking after number One -that's me.
wouldn't you?

Different Hills

She said the hills
Were alive with music.
But the only music we hear
In the hills near here,
Comes from baas and moos and mobiles,.
Plus the lone Peregrine falcon emitting a screech
Before it dives from 500 feet,
At 200kph, to grab some meat.

But I prefer the silence,
When you can hear yourself speak

But don't want to;
And watch the sun go down,
But can't do.
Because it's getting dark
And they'll shut the car park ,
And then what on earth shall I do?

16th   **Much Knowing Primary School's Christmas Concert**

Wishing to keep in the forefront of primary school technological innovation Much Knowing Primary School decided to take its Christmas concert to mew technological, digital and televisual heights. The Head decided that classes would be technologically linked and the subsequent Christmas concert would be broadcast throughout the school via CCTV. He was also a staunch democrat and believed in getting the views of staff and pupils ..... and then deciding himself.

But, as Mr. Cleverly was about to find out, all new technology has its teething problems and not everyone understood what it was all about, or how they had come to agree to it.

In addition, Ms. Hannah Hope's Class Three already had its fair share of problems. However, Hannah's philosophy was 'to give anything a go'.

'Now children, it has been decided that this Christmas

the school will put on a school concert, with each class contributing an item which will then be seen by the rest of the school via our closed-circuit television.

No, Arthur that was not Mr Clerver Clogs... I mean Mr. Cleverly's... decision.... He is the headmaster and could have decided himself..... but it was a democratic decision.... No, not a DEMON CRITIC decision, Arthur, 'democratic'..... well, it might be what your grandad calls democracy..... yes, I know he was a trade union official and ought to know..... but take it from me, the word is 'democratic' and it means doing what the majority of the people want....

Yes I know Maisy, you may not have wanted it, but most pupils did..... and the staff did; Mr. Cleverly told us so ....and, yes, you are right.... you did not get a vote this year, Maisy.... it was decided by the top juniors..... and the senior staff ...But you will get a vote in the future.....

No, Cedric, I do not think I am being hypocritical.....

That's not correct, Maddie, your daddy did not take the hypocritical oath……. it was the 'Hippocratic oath'…. It's when doctors swear to uphold high standards….

No, Arthur, that's not the same as your dad's swearing. I'm quite sure when your dad swears he is not upholding high standards……but there are different ways to swear, you see…..

ARTHUR! I do not want examples of all the ways you can swear……ARTHUR, please!

We will now see what you have remembered from our previous rehearsals, shall we…. everyone stand and turn to your left, all right?….,

Why did you turn to your RIGHT, Arthur?… I see, because I said 'all right'…. my mistake, but you are the only one who did not understand, Arthur…. OK! You are the only one who got it right!.... I'm not arguing any more….. everyone turn round….NOT YOU, Arthur…. You are already facing right!

Good…. Now we can do the *Marching Tune*….. you first, Arthur….get your imaginary drum ready…......It is not on your head, Arthur…. It is in front of you… it does NOT go *bang, crash, wallop*….. it is not a big bass drum…. It is an imaginary small side drum…. fastened round your neck and played at your front…. And it goes *tickety, tickety tick*……. a quiet drum roll….. that's it…. excellent, you are really good at it…. and now the bugles…. Those very clever toilet rolls glued together…. good, well done, bugles!…..and now all you flutes….. a really imaginative use of pencils….. keep going….

Join in now trumpets…. Blow hard down your rolled-up paper….. yes, Maisy…. I can see yours is drooping…. don't' be silly, Maddie, it's not like your little brother's 'Billy'…. and it's not a 'billy', it's a….. oh never mind, just keep blowing….and marching round…

That's it…. . Good…..not too loud….

That's better…..phew…… sit down and take a rest …..

Now everybody, watch the screen and you will see Mister Carr's class about to perform…. The Class Captain, Goran Czerniawski will introduce 3C's item…. There he is….. on the screen…. welcome to Goran……

There is no need to whistle, Freddie……just clap….. politely…. Goran has not sprouted wings, Arthur…. They are his ears….please do not be disrespectful…. It is very bad manners….

3C do not look like a zoo, Evie…. They are very nicely lined up….now, everyone, listen to the 3C choir….

Yes, Mr. Carr we can hear you and see them…… CHILDREN!…there's really no need for all of you to shout *'they're behind you!'*…. we can see they are…

Do you hear what Goran is saying… 3C has updated a carol to fit the modern age….. *'We Three Kings'* is it, Mr. Carr?….that's interesting, isn't it, children? I wonder how they have modernised it….Here they go….'

We the kids of 3C are;
We're the tops; we are the star
Off to yonder canteen we go,
Following Mister Carr.

(Silence)

'Is that it, Mr. Carr?…. Oh it is…. I see…. they are still working on the refrain…. Right…. I am not sure what direction it is going in, Mr. Carr….. no, Arthur, that is not the direction it is going in…not necessarily….
Thank you, Mr. Carr and 3C….. I think we have proved the technology works……. Oh!... they've disappeared….. perhaps I accidentally switched them off….That's a shame, isn't it?'

17th   **Rustic Ruminations: Organisation**

To understand how society is best organised,
You don't have to be Mystic Meg;
Just watch how chickens go about it.
The cock does the crowing,
But the hen lays the egg

18th   Glenda reported to er boss that she was off work because she had suffered cuts to the face and a bruise on her head. She thought the office window was down, but it was up, as she found out when she put her head through it.

19th   It is not often you have to use a foreign language dictionary to read a piece of English prose…. But, of course, our Aussie friends manage it! We may know 'cobblers' and 'bushwacker' and 'G'day cobber', but how many of these did you know…. Or could work out?

Ankle Biter	a small child
Aussie Salute	brush fly from your face
Bar fly	pub front bar regular
Bloody	silly person
Bonzer	great/very good
Bugalugs	term of endearment/mate

Drop kick	useless person
Fred Nerk	imaginary person
Grouse galah	great/very good
Hard yakka	hard work/difficult job
Hooroo	Good bye
Pack of Galahs	group of disliked people
Rubberdy dub	pub/hotel
Woop woop	somewhere a long way away.

20th *Renowned crooner, Bing Crosby, Had one of the greatest Christmas hits of all time with his singing of Irving Berlin's 1942 s song 'White Christmas. How might he have handled 2020's Covid lockdown Christmas?*

Lockdown Christmas
I'm dreaming of a lockdown Christmas,
Unlike the ones we used to know;
Where the grandkids are missing,
And can't catch us kissing
Under artificial mistletoe.

I'm dreaming of a lockdown Christmas,
With every mince-pie that I munch,
Where we can finish off a turkey,
Though that's not likely,
And sprouts come with a healthy crunch.

I'm dreaming of a lockdown Christmas,
Not giving traders a Christmas box,
Not sending 'thank yee's'
For unwanted hankies
And avoiding more pairs of surgical socks.

21st I am told that on one occasion a government officer manning a desk in a local VAT office became so agitated and exasperated by a constant stream of complainants that he resigned one lunchtime, closed his desk window and stuck a notice on it, which read:
'PLEASE NOTE. I was a civil servant and Your Obedient Servant until five minutes ago. I am no longer civil, obedient or a servant….. and I'm loving it.'
It did not stay up long.is

22nd *One of the best-known nursery rhymes in the English language is 'Humpty Dumpty'. One supposes that Humpty is an egg but the rhyme does not actually say so. It may also be one of the rhymes ridiculing a known personality, a king or politician, but it is all speculation. What it definitely is, is a jolly, bouncing rhyme to recite to a small child..*

Humpty Dumpty sat on a wall;
Humpty Dumpty had a great fall.
All the king's horses and all the king's men
Couldn't put Humpty together again.

I thought a parliamentarian touch might be appropriate, since so many politicians seem to have 'fallen down' in the 21st century.

Humpty Dumpty was an MP,
He sat on a bright green bench;
One day Humpty fell down a deep trench.
All the king's ministers, and newspapermen,
Couldn't get Humpty on the bench again.

23rd **Question:** What is black and steaming , and comes out of cows ?
Answer: The Isle of White Ferry.

24th **All In Good   Time**

CHORUS
Tonight, tonight
The Stave is alive tonight,
The bars are noisy, the lights are bright,
It's party time on The Stave
Tonight. tonight, tonight, tonight,;

TRIO
Granpa Breve is puffing on his flute
Granma Semi is strumming her lute,
Then come the Minims and the Family Crotchet,
Some White, some Black, some really quite dotty;
Finally eight Quavers with twinkle-toes Semi
Skipping along with sparky son Demi.

CHORUS
Raucous leaping and prancing,
Breves and Semibreves all line-dancing,
Quavers and crotchets swirl and twirl,
Semiquavers polish off a cream whirl.
Minims eat in excess –
Yes, the party's a great success!

SEMIBREVES
Semibreves plodding slowly,
Four-beat semibreves.

MINIMS
Minims, minims, dancing daintily,
Dancing quaintly too.
Minims know just what to do…

CROTCHETS
Crotchets can be fast or slow,
Thought you'd like to know;
1, 2, 3, 4 in a row,
Thought you'd like to know.
Get a bunch of crotchets and you go!

QUAVERS
Quavers tripping, quavers flipping,
Nipping, slipping,
Ticka ticka-tee!
Quavers sprightly, daily nightly,
Ticka ticka ticka ticka ticka-tee!

ALL
Semibreves, minims, crotchets, quavers –
Having themselves a party today!

25th *While billions are celebrating the central Christmas event, the birth of Jesus Christ, I am taking a moment to reflect on whatever happened to the Christmas Supporting Cast, the Shepherds, the Innkeeper, the Magi and even the animals in the manger.*

Away From The Manger
The Mystery of the Christmas Supporting Cast

The air is chill; the sky is clear;
Silent men, on donkeys draw ever near.

Who are they?? We wish we knew.
Where do they come from? What do they do?
Wish we knew, wish we knew.

A speckle of stars lights up their way;
we cannot hear what they say;
The riders are radiant; they look elated ;
Their asses are tired; they plod on deflated;

Who are you?? We wish we knew.
Where do you come from? What do you do?
Wish we knew, wish we knew.

26th **Away From The Manger** (cont)
The Shepherds Story

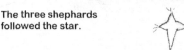

The three shephards
followed the star.

SHEPHERDS
Well, we are the shepherds who watched our flocks by night,
When suddenly we were bathed in a dazzling light;
This chap appeared, as the Gospel tells you,
With golden wings; and a bright yellow halo.

SHEPHERD 1: I thought I saw two.
SHEPHERD 2: I saw them too.
SHEPHERD 3: No, I am sure it was four;
SHEPHERD 4: Or perhaps even more.

ALL THE SHEPHERDS:
Yes …. it was a host of angels, for sure… for sure,
A host of angels for sure.
We saw them in the dazzling light,
Of the star that shone so bright.
A host of angels for sure,
A host of angels for sure.

CHORUS
They were sore afraid;
Called God to their aid;
A star hovered over;
They huddled even closer'
A strange figure appeared
They were even more afeared.

One star in the heavens shone clear and bright;
The angel's wings glowed in its light.
Hope flitted across the shepherd's brows,
Awe and wonder framed wide-open mouths;
Awe and wonder; wonder and awe…
Awe and wonder framed wide-open mouth.

27th   **The Shepherds Continue Their Story**

SHEPHERDS
'Don't be frit,' said this golden Gabriel bloke,
'Go seek Christ the King, as it's bespoke.
In a manger in Bethlehem, I kid ye not,
Christ Your Saviour, you'll find, in a cot.'

CHORUS
And so they did;
As they were bid.

A baby they found;
Sleeping safe and sound;
In a lowly manger,
Was anything ever stranger?
Jesus was his name;
Soon wide was his fame.

They marvelled that they were the ones chosen,
First footers at this miraculous showdown.
Why was it shepherds who had been so honoured?
On the way there they wondered and pondered.
On the way home they pondered and wondered.

SHEPHERD 1:
What was our Lord doing in a manger?
Could anything have been any stranger?
SHEPHERD 2.
And a bale of straw, for a king so proud;;
That's not right; shouldn't be allowed.
SHEPHERD 3.
What about all the dazzling light?
You wouldn't see that on our hill at night.
SHEPHERD 4.
Let's face it, it's a miracle, beyond our ken;
We are only ordinary mortal me.

SHEPHERDS TOGETHER:
Of course, the answer is blazingly clear;
He's the Lamb of God, held so dear,
And we're the shepherds who know what's what;
We've got what it takes; we've got the lot.
We watch over him with love, not the rod;
And we'll be saved by the Lord our God.

Hosanna in the Highest…… Glory shines around;
Praise to the Highest…. Let Love abound.
Now we're back in our pastures, gleaming with glory,
But we've only got sheep to spread our cheerful story.

CHORUS

No help was nigh;
They could only sigh;
Wish air and light,
Could spread this sight;
Could carry the message,
To every new age.

CHORUS AND SHEPHERDS
But lo and behold it happened at last;
People twigged that the die was cast;
Jesus had been born in Bethlehem;
Ready to save all women and men.

CHORUS
And so it came to pass that the Word was hurled;
Across land and sea, across the whole world,
That God cares for the rich, the poor, those in need,
Regardless of age, or of race or of creed.
Jesus had been born in Bethlehem;
Ready to save all women and men.

(A woman enters, dressed in expensive gear. She turns out to be the owner of the Inn at Bethlehem, now Hotel Paradiso.)

28th **Mrs Innkeeper**

CHORUS and SHEPHERDS
Who are you?? We wish we knew.
Where do you come from? What do you do?
Wish we knew, wish we knew.

What's she doing; dressed up to the nines?
With a shammy shimmy…..
And gormless grinny,
A bit of 'a show-off, it's got all the signs.

INN KEEPER
I am the inn-keeper in Bethlehem town;
Hotel Paradiso, with rosette and a crown.
A restaurant in the Good Food Guide,
The leisure centre's our joy and pride.
Come and stay when you are able;
There's special rates for the de luxe stable;

SHEPHERDS.
We know the inn; we know the inn;
The inn's the inn in which we were in!
Beds in a stable;
Feet under the table'
Baby in a manger;
Nothing could be stranger.
We came there from afar,
Following a single bright star.

INN KEEPER
A single star? A single star?
Piddlin' stuff is a single star.
It's got five stars now and a rosette, too.

We've come a long way since we put up with you.
What with the folk who came to the census,
And the tourist trade and those on adventures;
And those who religion seek to find;
Jews, Moslems and Christian kind.
We are overflowsering every night;
Dripping with gold, flying high as a kite.

It's a tale you all ought to go and tell.
It's all go at the Paradiso Hotel .

(Beasts and Birds enter)

CHORUS
What's this we see….. are our eyes deceiving us?
A whole menagerie is descending upon us.

29th   **Lament Of The Beasts And Birds**

BEASTS AND BIRDS
You've forgotten us! forgotten us;
You've forgotten us, you rotters;
Forgotten we are; forgotten we are,
Unfair, but typical …. simply quite rotten.

Remember us; remember us, if you are able;
We, too, remember, were in the stable.
Beasts of burden, birds of a feather;
All united, all gathered together.
Now replaced by reindeer, and gobbly turkey;
Pies and pudding, food really quite quirky;
Deer with antlers; turkeys with stuffing;
Millions of cooks huffing and puffing;
All eyes open at the groaning table;
You've forgotten us, forgotten us,
We , too, remember, were in the stable.

You've forgotten us! forgotten us;
You've forgotten us, you rotters;
Unfair, but typical …. simply quite rotten.

SHEPHERDS
Goodness! There are more of them!
Who are you?? We wish we knew.
Where do you come from? What do you do?
Wish we knew, wish we knew.
Looking so guilty, even embarrassed,
A wee bit wan and just a tad harassed;

Wise Men versus Kings

WISE MEN *(pompous, patronising)*
We're the wise men,
Who predicted Christ's arrival on this earth;
Got there a bit late; we're afraid,
Months after his birth;
While priests and scribes, or so it seems,
Boasted to the king and spilled the beans.
So, giving the baby our prezzies with a great big smile,
We left in a hurry before Herod in his guile,
Unleashed murder, and massacre, in all Judea;
Mayhem that soon all the world would hear.

CHORUS
Yes, they dropped off their prezzies at the manger,
Then quickly disappeared, out of all danger.

Let this be a lesson to all of you;
Listen to what wise men say,
But watch carefully what they do.

SHEPHERDS
Goodness! Even more!
This lot look up for it, that's for sure!

Who are you?? We wish we knew.
Where do you come from? What do you do?
Wish we knew, wish we knew.
Looking so haughty,
With manner so jaunty;
Who are you?

THREE KINGS
We three kings from the orient are;
Casper, Moloch and Balthazar;
We're in the Bible, disguised as you wise men,
State secrecy, and our safety, clearly the reason,
But look at the great paintings in all the galleries,
See men with gold, chaps with high salaries;
Carrying bags of frankincense, magnums of myrrh;
Do we look like scribes, or priests, no sir!
So we rest our case; we're the true followers;

You doddery old men, must now give way to us!
Because we three kings from orient are;
Casper, Moloch and Balthazar;

WISE MEN
Imposters, fakes, fraudsters and rascals!
You are NOT in the Bible; NOT in the Gospels;
Nothing but con-men, mutton dressed up as lamb!
We know what you're up to, can see through your scam!
Get gone! Get gone! Climb back in your frames;
We want no more of your naff fun and games.

We're the true actors in the Christmas pageant;
We're the stars in the Nativity Play!

SHEPHERD 1:
And what was that talk about Frank Incest and mirth?

Doesn't seem proper at an infant's birth.
SHEPHERD 2:
You've got that wrong, ignorant sir!
It was actually frankincense and myrrh.
SHEPHERD 3
And what about that gold, all over the floor;
It belongs to the rich, not us poor.
SHEPHERD 4
Why were we first, before the rich men?
Why did we come before other brethren?)

31st **Love and Light**

CHORUS OF ANGELS
Stop ! Stop! Stop this unseemly row;
Stop your bickering; stop right now.
Hope is abroad; Peace the goal;
Friendship assured; Love lights up the soul.

Christ is the Shepherd; Christ is the King;
God is the Wise Man, so the angels sing.
The Holy Spirit draws us all near;
When Love is everywhere; there is nothing to fear.
Nothing to fear; nothing to fear;
When Love is everywhere, there is nothing to fear.
EVERYONE
Peace and harmony reign at this Christmas-tide
Now is the time to be on one side.

Christ is the Shepherd; Christ is the King;
God is the Wise Man, so the angels sing.
The Holy Spirit draws us all near;
When Love is everywhere; there is nothing to fear.
Nothing to fear; nothing to fear;
When Love is everywhere, there is nothing to fear.

ACKNOWLEDGEMENTS AND REFLECTIONS
With yet more Quips and Quiddities

A book such as this requires more than just an acknowledgement of contributors, because so much is owed to so many who have kept me laughing and smiling over the past 80 odd years - from my primary school mates in the 1940s to my neighbours around us today. They remind one of the best things in life usually involve the life-affirming good nature of others.

I inherit my sense of the 'comedie humaine', a sense of the absurdity that surrounds human activity, from my parents, Betty and Harry. Like most people of their era they left school at 14, but they retained a desire to learn for the rest of their lives. While raising three children, keeping a corner shop in an area gradually being demolished around them, and with no gas or electricity in the home they nevertheless continued their education at university adult education courses. Despite all the hardships, and there were many, they remained cheerful and conveyed their love of life and learning to their children.

In her nineties mum rang me and told me that Keele University had congratulated her on gaining more points towards a degree.

'I shall be a BA by the time I am 132! Isn't that good news?'

I did not know my dad properly till I was 7 years old when he returned from the war in Burma in1944. He died too early at 57 years old carrying latent diseases from the war, but his good nature and optimism were an inspiration. And every time I pick up a packet of cheese I shake my head, remembering how dad had taught me how slice please should be properly wrapped.

My family's predisposition to the philosophy of a 'cup half full' is shared by my sisters, Elizabeth (known as Ban because at the age of two I could not pronounce Elizabeth Ann), their families and all aunts, uncles, cousins and their families. and especially cousins Kay and Tony Maguire and Michael and Dorothy Haynes who in recent years have added so much to our lives.

My father-in-law, Francis Travers was an artist who graduated from terrace houses of Newcastle-under-Lyme and the Royal College of Art in London during the First World War. His paintings and ceramic sculptures around our house give us daily enjoyment.

Mary's mother, Eva, was a true wife and mother of the early 20th century, giving her married life to running home and family. After Francis died in 1965 she, too, satisfied, a thirst for knowledge and experiences. For the next twenty-five years she helped look after our two boys, learned to drive in her sixties, attended a variety of adult evening classes, took up learning French again and went abroad for the first time in her life.

As one of the first post-war pupils to pass the 11+ in 1946. I joined a classful of grammar schoolboys all trying to find out who they were and what they were doing there. It meant many hours of tearful but many more hours of cheerful discovery. So, despite the war and its aftermath, my childhood friends were full of hope and good humour. Most of them have now passed on but my dear old friend sculptor Gordon Baddeley, a fellow Stokie, supporter of Stoke city F.C. and the other Potteries club, Port Vale (which is enough for a smile on its own) is still around to remember 'those good old days', shared with cheerful chappies like Derek Wilshaw, Alan Bell and David Barnes.

Conferences with other schools, particularly the local girls grammar schools, brought different perspectives and outlooks that were manna from heaven in the difficult years after World War 2. New worlds were opening up for us and even more so when I moved into the next phase of my life, National Service in the army and subsequently 14 more years in the Territorial Army.

Such military service brought me into contact with a group of witty, gritty comrades in arms, like the late Don Cameron and Steve Johnson; and Derek Borman (now Sir Derek), Graham Bannister, Alan Sherratt, Jim Blood, Peter Goodwin, Brian Lewis, Hugh Willmore, Lawrence Chell and Terry Collins and the late Paul Gallagher in the North Staffords, all of whom are in the debt of Lev and Janice Wood for their painstaking research into regimental history.

Then, when serving in the Royal Leicesters I added to my list of bons viveurs the late Bill Wallace, Bill Dawson and John Ward in the Royal Leicesters and at the end of my TA career the officers and men of 4 Company 5 Royal Anglian, which I had the honour of commanding.

This book also owes a lot to the unfailing wit of my 'old' and dear pals who formed a close-knit but diverse little group at university, Known as The Blackbirds - Dai Roberts and his late wife, Sheila, , Roy and Bridget Farmer, Michael Lynch and his late wife Sally, Richard and Smuggles Culver, Andrew and Pauline MacTavish, Richard and Anne Morgan, Nicholas and Carien Smith, Mike Swift and his wife, Anne-Marie, John Temperley and his late wife Greta, the late Tom Venables and his wife Marlene and the late Dave and Liz Swift, Dave Miller, Tim Bailey and Brian Cole who passed away so young

During my teaching career it was a delight to have spent many good-humoured days and evenings with friends and colleagues in the Royal Opera House, Covent Garden.

Because I insisted that students at Prince William School should have the opportunity to experience operas and musicals as well as plays I became known to the Education Department of the Royal Opera House – or perhaps I just 'infiltrated' it as I rang the Opera Education Officer, Pauline Tambling, one Friday afternoon, having read about her appointment in the *Times Educational Supplement*. I asked her if she had anyone advising her on school opera. She told me she had some willing teachers in London and I let out a loud, 'Typical!! It's always London!' She invited me to join in on the spot . I eventually became the Chair of the Education Council and then, to my astonishment, a member of the Board of the Royal Opera and the Board of the Royal Opera House, where I sat amongst a host of memorable operatic stars and their supporters.

Whenever I was with Pauline and her colleagues - Caroline Maxwell, Darryl Jaffray, who was the Ballet Education Officer, the late, great tenor and educator, John Dobson, and the brilliant mezzo-soprano Elizabeth Sikora, who made an enormous impact on and contribution to staff and students in the 1980s and early 1990s, along with mezzo-soprano Marian Bryfdir and accompanist the late Nina Walker, I knew I would be treated to a fund of hilarious stories about…. well, everything.

It was a strange world for up-country students to fully comprehend. But, my goodness, they not only came to appreciate the rigour and joy of opera they added a few new dimensions to opera-making!

John Dobson loved to tell the tale of walking onto the school stage in the smugglers scene in our 'Carmen' and finding two nuns in the middle of the smugglers. 'What are you two doing here?' whispered John. 'You were in the Seville scene in the First Act.'

'Well,' said one, 'My friend is on stage, so I am.'

'There's no answer to that.' said John. 'It's an utterly rational explanation... and I have often wished for a distraction like that in some of the other desultory versions of 'Carmen' round the world.'

As President of the European School Heads Association for four years in the 1990s I was privileged to be supported by a truly 'European' General Secretary, Sabin Schoofs, with whom I spent many hours on flight's and in hotels exchanging anecdotes. We had the privilege of inaugurating the first Headteachers association in Ukraine alongside our late and truly far-sighted colleague, Oksana Kondratuik. The ceremony and celebrations in Lviv University were magnificent. She was a great loss to the Ukrainian people when she was killed in the streets of Lviv. I still wear with pride the beautiful fur hat I received from the then Minister of Education with Oksana and Sabin in attendance.

I was also privileged to visit and encourage the school principals of Lithuania, even before they had finally broken free from the USSR yoke. One of the experiences of my life was to be isolated along with John Sutton in the Parliament building in Vilnius alongside members of the government, parliamentarians and a few Lithuanian soldiers, surrounded by a regiment of Soviet tanks and infantry pointing their guns at us– trying as hard as I could to broadcast a message out of Vilnius to the citizens of Lithuania and the rest of the world about the reality of what was going on, while the regiment of the Red Army outside was putting out a quite different slant on things. Not a funny story, but one to smile over.... when I got home.

The courage of the people of those former vassal states is known to every free citizen in the world. I will choose my friends Aurimas Juozaitis and Romantas Zelvys to represent all those who have striven to bring lasting peace, freedom and joy to their people..

I pay my respects to my successor as president, Eeva Penttila from Finland, and my processor, Anton van Rooijen from the Netherlands. I am delighted to still be corresponding with Anton and also Fernand Faber in Luxembourg and Carmelo Ruggieri in Italy, as well as Jack Delaney and Rob McConachie former Presidents of the International Confederation of Principals. I also remain in contact with Anil and Renu Malhotra and radiant colleagues M.V. Prasad and Gupta and Mrs Mahalakshmi, in India and remember fondly the light-hearted hospitality they offered in schools and homes.

Since so much of ESHA's work was done via conferences, before the Zooming days, I am eternally grateful for the energy and experience of Arthur Jones and his late wife, Janet and to Nargis Rashid for their support and enthusiasm in organising international conferences.

Other international friends I have much to give thanks to are Ursula Schnell and Wolfgang, in Germany, while in France we have had the good fortune to share so many happy hours with Annette and Roland Berra; and yet more joyful times with Alan and Chantal Austin, Jim and Gill Pearce, Eddy and Marian Hurst and all our other friends in the fellowship of St. Michael's Church of the Gard, our lovely friends Herve and Genevieve and Elisabeth Begot, David in the Fons outre Gardon village store, who gets hold of fine local fruit and veg as often as he can, and the life-enhancing team at the boulangerie, led by Alysson, whose bread and patisserie are one of the world's hidden secrets.

But, of course, the bulk of my eternal gratitude is reserved for the staff I served with and he students we served, at the four schools I taught at during my teaching career -Trinity School of John Whitgift in Croydon, the City of Leicester School, Wyggeston Boys School, Leicester and Prince William School, Oundle, where I was headteacher for nigh on 29 years. These schools, like all others, I expect, are a never-ending source of funny stories and smiley characters.

I remember with affection colleagues like Frank Drewett, who has remained a friend since the first day we met at Trinity School, my first post, and our colleague Ian Waters. He enjoyed pointing to the unfortunate juxtaposition of his given names' initials and d surname – Ian Peter Waters!....

I also had the privilege of teaching Colin Sell there….. aged 12, and now the renowned pianist for 50 years in the BBC radio panel game *'I'm Sorry I Haven't A Clue'*. Sixty years after our first classroom confrontation he and I are composing comic cantatas and oratorios together. Colin has kindly contributed some of his wit to *'Carry On Smiling'*. Both of us take our hats off to our publisher of the scores, Vincent Davy, one-time colleague at PWS and now Director of Thrapston Plaza Opera.

All three of us are grateful to the support for school and youth music-making offered by the *First Note Music Trust* under the management of Juliet Ranger and her team and with the earnest encouragement of the trustees and advice of Keith Arrowsmith.

At 'City Boys', Leicester I was fortunate to share jocular times with irrepressible Simon Tong, a man of much wit, matched, I hasten to add, by his wife', Rosemary's own quick eye for the ridiculous. Our holidays together are punctuated by bursts of laughter and smiles.

I also have so much of our friend John Gates's rich sense of humour to be thankful for. While co-editing our book in 1964, *Selections from the English Novelists*, we needed every inch of it! We remember with affection the happy times we spent with them and the late Michael Palmer and wife Margaret.

While at City Boys in summer 1966, I led a truly eye-opening school trip to Moscow and the then Leningrad with Niall Kearney and Mike Haddon. We had the distinction of being invited to play volleyball in the Moscow Dynamo stadium, against the Under 19 Ladies team, who appeared to all come from Georgia. We were truly thrashed, rarely seeing the ball as it whistled past us... a different game from any I had seen previously. Our hosts then insisted we played one of the Dynamo youth soccer teams. We protested that we had no kit, but to no avail. They wore full kit and boots, while City Boys played in long trousers and shoes. They allowed us to include two adults, which saved us, as Mike was a former Cambridge soccer Blue and City Boys was a successful soccer-playing grammar school. To our astonishment and their chagrin we won by the odd goal. Sadly, it was never added to the school's Honours Board.

I also have happy memories of teaching at 'Wyggie'. Antiquarian and TV presenter, Lars Tharp, remains a friend to this day, and Professor Michael Mangan, has unknowingly contributed his early 16-year-old wit, since I have pinched his contribution from an old school magazine!

It will surprise no-one that many, many quips and quiddities come from my 29 years at Prince William School, ….. from my colleagues and a myriad of students.

I owe an enormous debt to Deputy Head and long-standing friend, the late Val Heppell , who had a firmness of resolve that rubbed off on us all; and Deputy John Melhuish and his wife, Margaret, with whom we shared so many hilarious New Year's Eve parties along with Trevor and Sue Hold and our dear friend Christine Styles - playing, with a ferocity that would have amazed our colleagues, a particularly devious version of Animal Grab. I have a couple of scars still!

It was a privilege, too, to share so many good times with Deputy Heads Tom Hutchinson and his wife, Eileen, and Mike Jakeways and his late wife Nicky, and Sara and Chris Davey, all of whom had an amused view of humanity's goings-on.

I salute my 'very old' colleague John Rhodes, who served with me for three years at Wyggie and then moved to Northamptonshire with me and retired on the same day. Everyone who met John can testify to his wit and erudition.

Magnificent support, along with a vast repertoire of anecdotes was provided by my second Chair of the Governing Body, Lovel Garrett, and Chairmen who followed him, Alan Styles, Chris Hart and Glyn James.

Lovel's stories mainly focused on his wartime experiences as a prisoner-of-war for five years, having been captured during the 1940 Dunkirk evacuation Lovel's fighting ended when he was blown up by a grenade near St. Valery. He came to in a ditch and swears he heard the immortal words from his captor, 'For you, Englishman, the war is over…..' The young officer wielding the pistol aimed at his head spoke perfect English and turned out to have been a contemporary of Lovel's at Oxford about five years previously. Such is the daftness of war.

The Chairmen and I were blessed with a stream of governors who wanted to enjoy and not just endure governor meetings. Schools have much to thank volunteer governors for. I consider myself more than a touch lucky…. and some of their tales have found their way into these pages

I have received magnificent encouragement over the past three years of book-writing from Jenny and David Blount, who have been pillars of the 'Old Staff and Student' network, along with parent, Pat Rutterford, who with her late husband set up The James Rutterford Trust in memory of their son and have raised thousands of pounds for student needs. Their service to the school is second to none.

I have good memories, too, of the late, great Welshman Haydn Adams, a senior colleague and co-founder of the Oundle RUFC which has done so much good for ex-students of the school and the town in general. He and I used to confer with fellow union reps - Derek Jones and Steve Dalzell; we shared many a laugh as well as an argument, while performing our union representative duties - me representing a membership of one; they representing dozens. Some of Steve's and my union talk was conducted on the boundary fielding for the staff cricket team. It is a very good place to avoid strife!

I shall never cease to thank my good fortune at serving with the two hundred other teaching and support staff who passed through the school during my headship. They are all special, but I will mention as their representatives some long-standing members of staff.

John Hadman, was one of the first to join the new Upper School. He ran the school's archaeology courses and quickly covered local fields with first-world war trench systems while unearthing a load of ancient treasures, including a 4th century font and the skeleton of a Roman soldier. This latter discovery initiated years of discussion about what ceremony should be used in a reburial. Everyone seemed to care, except a soldier.

One day a local building Inspector saw the diggings and plonked a Restraining Order on 'further' work. The note read that all further house-building infrastructure should cease until the owner had obtained building permission. John took delight in informing the Council that the owner would have been pleased to oblige but had been dead for 1,600 years!

I also pay tribute to the long and good-humoured service of the late George Blackman and Pauline Turner , and likewise to David Colson, Chris Ellard, Christine Marsters, Arlene Peterson, Barbara Rafer, Rod Brattel, Angela Bullock, Karen Collings, John Whitcombe, the late Liz Chamberlin, Richard Hamilton, Steve and Karen Davis, Noel Bailey, Mary and Peter Wiles, Nick Watkins, and the late Commander Harry Stern, who came to teach Maths after retiring from a distinguished Royal Naval career which resulted in the award of an MBE. He once kept a Maths inspector spellbound while teaching a Year 10 group about calculating distances, speed and angles, by using examples of ships shelling other ship as and angles of 'aim-off' to hit a moving ship, or to calculate the speed of a submarine's crash-dive. They do not appear in any Maths books as far as I know, but I do know that they are still remembered 25 years later by ex-students.

None of us who served at the school will forget the ebullience of the first caretaker Tom Johnson, a seasoned Chief Petty Officer who brought both hilarity and anxiety to the senior staff as he 'ran the ship', ably assisted by Betty Belcher, whose good cheer made light of all problems. His successor, Derek Harrison, also had the knack of making us feel safe without fuss. They have influenced some of the tales in the book. And at those times when I got above myself and let it be known that it was me that was Head of the school, I would be reminded that it was the caretaker who held the keys, not me, and could close the school…. whether I liked it, or not! It pays to be kind to the keyholder!

It is fair to say that none of the teaching staff could have done such a good job but for the calm, skilled and superb way the support staff gave their service,….. and with such cheerfulness and grace. I do not know what I would have done without the Daphnes, Cynthias, Pats, Julies, Lizzie's and Sarahs, and all the others in the administrative staff. Their contribution to the mental well-being of myself, in particular, is immeasurable! And so was the dedication of the departmental support staff, the cleaning and grounds staff.

All our daily work went on while in the school canteen the cheerful and chatty kitchen staff set about cooking and serving up to 1,000 meals every school day. That's worth a smile….

Bless 'em all!

No-one who was ever on the PWS staff will mind if I single out two colleagues for a special mention, because this book is entitled 'Carry On Smiling' and both did so in abundance. I am personally indebted to colleague Graham Snelling. Who spent all his 41 years of teaching career at Prince William School, with unfailing good humour that rubbed off on all around him, even when he was not himself feeling particularly good humoured, and who continued to offer his service to the town and school after retiring. … and finally to Councillor Reg Sutton MBE, the first Chair of the Governing Body of the new school which opened in 1971, whose tireless efforts over two decades resulted in the new secondary school in Oundle being funded and founded….. Reg kept us all smiling and guffawing at his tales of the political goings-on. A small man in stature, but a great-hearted man of the people.

And then there were the students, the kids. This book would be the poorer but for the fund of stories by, from and about the wonderful students who kept me smiling.,

I can only choose a handful to illustrate the variety of talent – talent that every secondary school possesses and should shout about as loud as possible.

From the early days, I remember artists like Mary and Rachel Sumner, who have made careers out of their brilliant skills, and Paul Crick a distinguished editor of books himself, and then students who are making their way in the entertainment world like Katherine Jakeways - now finding rightful praise for her radio and TV playwriting; whose comedic talent was honed on the school stage, to the delight of all; and like Nev Fountain, TV dramatist and radio's Dead Ringers lead script-writer and staffer on Private Eye, and like musicians Rachel Helliwell, a solo flautist, Katie Fenn and Lisa MacDonald, singers, I remember, too, sporting students like Stephen Walters, a gifted player on the field and gifted musician in the orchestra; Ann Cox, athlete, Beverley Roberts, circus entertainer, Sam Eden and Nina Houssain, gymnasts , and cricketers Colin Keal and Denis Compton, and rugby players William Bowley and Ben Russell and Troy Thacker. In a different world altogether is Sarah Champion, Member of Parliament, which certainly merits a smile from all who wish her well as a representative of the people.

Sam Northwood, now a headteacher is remembered for being principal singer in the school's specially commissioned opera The Button Moulder composed by Edward Lambert. The co-star from those operatic days, Michelle King, is now the Reverend Michelle Lepine and bringing her charm and communication skills to very lucky parishioners;

What a pleasure and privilege it was to have met you and the other 8,000 or so students who graced the school in the 29 years that I was there.

I have received wonderful tales and yarns from a host of friends - Michael Duffy, David and Barbara Tee, Brian Lewis, Colin Keal, Andy Willis, Alan Sherratt, Jim Blood, , Stewart Francis, Amanda Flint, Eugene Blackmore, Diana and Andrew Hart, Peter Downes, Brian Lightman, Roger and Jo Neal, Gwyneth Barnwell, old colleagues and friends John and Ruth Broadbent and Martin and Penny Cain, and many more quiddities from my dear friends and colleagues from my time as President of the Secondary Heads Association (now the Association of School and Collee Leaders) Russell Clarke, Mike Howells, Bob Hargreaves Richard Bird, Mike Pugh, Rod Wilson, Angie and John Hulme, Ann Williamson and Maureen Cruikshank - not forgetting the great raconteurs John Sutton and Max Hill, now sadly passed away.. They, along with are my Aussie pals, Ken Fraser, Duncan Stalker, have lightened many a day both in person and on-line. I must also thank the local middle school headteachers Graham Bate and Tom Lowe who shared many hours of both professional dialogue and light-hearted banter, which kept us all sane!re on the way back from France

I put my hands up and confess that many of their contributions have been lost, twisted and turned in the editorial process, as hope and intention met the barrier of space availability…. and the number of days in a year.

During my search for contributions, I have come across real gems by sheer chance. For example, while in Western Australia as a visiting professor I came across Tullio Rubinich's book, *"Teachers And Students And Schools'*. It is an anthology of extracts from school and government records over the past 200 years. Painstakingly researched, it is a delightful testament to human comedy characterising the difference in law, policy and attitude, between then and now. The extracts in this book will certainly bring a smile to your face.

We can all be grateful, too, to another Aussie, Phillip Adams, whose collection of 'Ockerisms' in *'The Jumbuck Stops Here'* is legendary

I thank, too, friend and poet Jill Rhodes for sending me two of her fine, humorous poems… You will be delighted to get to them.

Illustrations
The front cover illustration is by the talented Abigail Terry (*www. Sustainability exposed.com*).

Abigail's numerous illustrations come with lines from the Blackbird song, sung repeatedly by the Cambridge Blackbirds – in their own version of the song about a wurzel tree made famous by the 1950s group, The Wurzels. The BBs have continued to give rendering of it at least once per year for the past sixty years – with much appreciation…. usually. (they were asked to leave one snooty restaurant for doing so.)

Other illustrations come from Chris Ellard, Steve Lancaster, Jonathan Lowe, Andrew MacTavish, Michael Swift and the Metzler family: Gemma, Leo and Chloe; Matt and Matilda Dixon (with their galaxy of traditional Welsh ladies).

Mary and I are so lucky to have the help and support of our neighbours and friends Adele and David, staunch Baggies supporters and Linda and Mike Eades, Wolves supporters.

I acknowledge the continuing support I get from The Royal National Institute of Blind People (RNIB) and Blind Veterans UK and the Shropshire County Council' staff who have always given me practical advice and support.

And finally….
Nothing could have been achieved without the love and support of my family while I was writing and compiling the anthology- and at the same time coping with increasing blindness. It enabled me to get it done. I will just say a heartfelt'Ta' to my wife Mary and our sons, Simon and Jonathan, and Kath and Elena, and our wider family of cousins and nephews a and nieces, who over the years have filled life with their good humour. Without their fund of stories this book would never have seen the light of day.

A special thanks to our granddaughter, Evie, a UK champion skipper, or jump-roper if you prefer the modern term; she is been the bringer of many smiles to grandad and grandma from Year Dot to now, 20 years later.

My apologies to anyone who feels left out. There comes a time in the affairs of mankind when allowances have to be made for the blind, the deaf, the halting, and the forgetful….. and I am all of them…

Cheswardine 2023

Printed in Great Britain
by Amazon

28807727R00139